2 Poppins Lane

2 Poppins Lane

Patricia Striar Rohner

Bridge House

British Library Cataloguing in Publication Data
A Record of this Publication is available from the British
Library

ISBN 978-1-917854-01-6

This edition published 2025 by Bridge House Publishing
Manchester, England

Contents

PROLOGUE - 1953

Susan clenched her fists and dreamt of lunging at Larry. He entered her room in his pajamas, wearing his horn-rimmed glasses like a nerd, and when he took off his spectacles, he put them on her night table and climbed on top of her. Larry was tall and sinewy, with long legs and hair the color of an apple. His body was soft because he never did anything athletic. Spreading his long legs on either side of Susan's ten-year-old body and bending down like a jockey, Larry started rocking back and forth, resembling a hobby horse. She pretended to be sleeping, but he got harder and harder. Susan felt him pressing into her. The bed began to rattle and shake. Her crayons fell to the floor. She hoped they didn't break. A new box with assorted colors, berry red, mustard yellow, deep indigo, copper, honey, gray, jet black, baby blue, and pink, had been at the end of her bed.

She took her hands and tightened her fingers around his neck. She wanted to give him a chokehold and compress his neck, but he tried to break free. Then she let go and struck his head with her left fist, her best hand. She flew at him, her fingers like claws, punching and kicking, pulling his hair, scratching his face. She wanted to strangle him to death, to slap his face and quickly closed her grip back around his neck. Not confident that she could complete this task, she removed the weapon from under her pillow and plunged a large, shiny butcher blade into his doughy side. Larry groaned in pain. Sticky blood covered both his hands and the blanket.

Susan broke her grip on Larry's body and pushed him off of her. She didn't care if he was dead because she wanted justice. Larry won't take away her life. Her eyes misted up, and relief flooded her core. And then Susan woke up.

PART ONE

Chapter One

Susan Stern's house on 2 Poppins Lane was large, pink, and important looking. It sat across from the local high school and off Main Street in the northeast coastal town of Massachusetts named Georgeport. The whole family lived in this Victorian house on the corner, one of the few remaining in this town. They loved all the little cupboards and decorations, the sliding pocket doors, the cupola, and the gingerbread. The home had round angles, a tower, a bay window, stained glass, and a steep gabled roof. Susan's favorite part of the home was the front porch that wrapped around the outside.

The other residences along Poppins Lane and the side street, Johnson Street, were primarily small capes in different colors with beige shingled roofs and white trim. They had pie-shaped backyards with picket fences and views of the high school football field. There were a few larger homes with front screened-in porches and bigger yards, one brick colonial and one with an attached barn. However, it was the homes along Main Street that were special. They were Federalists, Greek Revivals, antique colonials with graduated clapboards and wooden shutters, bubble glass, and wide pine floors. They were the dwellings that people admired, along with the Victorian on the corner of Poppins Lane and Main Street. These were the houses that had third-floor suites, like the one that was known as the Eaton House. A converted bed and breakfast once served ale to the colonists in Georgeport, Massachusetts, population of 25,000.

The high school stood tall and vital looking, and the coeds spilled out at two-thirty p.m. They walked with firm legs, tight asses, and perky tits. It was 1953, and they dressed in pleated or straight skirts with headbands on their pageboy haircuts. The boys had crew cuts or duck's asses, depending on which group they belonged to. They wore stadium jackets with a letter on the back. Susan and Ellen, her Irish twin, were enthralled and couldn't wait to be old enough to go there.

The Sterns were a sizeable family: with four siblings, a maid named Odell, their Aunt Flo, her son Larry, and assorted helpers. Aunt Flo and Larry moved into the spare bedroom on the third floor next to their father's billiard room. The mother and son shared a bathroom and had their private suite. Aunt Flo's husband had dropped dead ten years earlier of a heart attack at the age of forty-four; they lived in their old home in Virginia until life got too overwhelming, and now, they resided with the Sterns. Flo was a short, chubby lady with dark red hair. She moved quickly and was a take-charge person. Even though she was one of their mother's older siblings, she possessed the energy of a younger woman. Nothing daunted her. She had given birth to Larry late in life after ten years of marriage and finally had a son. Larry was a slim, slightly effeminate sixteen-year-old and an aspiring writer. He and Susan's brother Jeffrey didn't have much in common, so Larry stayed upstairs and cloistered himself while he wrote his great American novel. Larry was reclusive and ate sparingly. Occasionally, when he first arrived six months ago, he took Ellen and Susan out to Taffy's luncheonette for strawberry ice cream sodas, which they slurped until there was nothing left.

Susan's mother liked her posse and never was without her helpers. She didn't enjoy driving, so Ike, the black man who played her lottery tickets every day and ran errands, or her sister Flo, chauffeured her around in her Buick to the bank, the shops, the butcher, and the doctor appointments. Dad worked as a general surgeon at the local hospital and loved his car, a red Cadillac Eldorado convertible, which cost at the high end of seven thousand dollars. He chose general surgery because it covered a lot of areas. Dad performed lifesaving procedures daily: appendectomies, splenectomies, and curative cancer surgeries. Susan was a relatively happy camper in the home, but some things went on that were not kosher, as they say. The family never talked about it because there were rules.

The house on Poppins Lane was formidable. The third floor had a game room with a pool table where Dad could get away. He loved it up there, and he invited his buddies to his billiard room and spent hours shooting pool and sipping brandy. It was his pleasure, as they say. He was allowed free reign in his kingdom.

Since Dr. Stern was the breadwinner of this large brood, he could do whatever he wanted. Mama, who was named Lily, never complained because she and Aunt Flo were busy with their own lives and could get their hair done every week at Eleanor's, have manicures, and read *Vogue*, so she never said a peep. Susan, the middle child, liked to visit her at Eleanor's and watch her mother under the dryer while Lily scrutinized the fashion magazine, got her toes polished in Fire and Ice Revlon nail polish, and ate her jelly beans. Sometimes, Susan would get her hair washed and trimmed if one of the technicians was free and could do it. She loved having her hair done and feeling pampered. It was a treat. Her sisters, Ellen and Ronnie, were jealous if she got special treatment, but it seemed like a gift, and she wouldn't complain.

Her sister, Ellen, and she were twelve months apart by less than three days, Susan being the older one. They were chubby, unattractive girls, much to Mama's chagrin. Their noses were Semitic like Dad's, not chiseled like Ronnie's and their mother's; their hair was straight and delicate, so they wore it like Buster Brown in Dutch cuts. In addition, they were short-waisted, so they looked chubbier than they were. They were also petite, not tall and beautiful like their neighbor Bernice, who was up the street and looked like a princess in her baby blue strapless gown when she got picked up by her handsome date for the senior prom. Ellen and Susan stood on the sidewalk on their Schwinn bikes and watched Bernice float into Prince Charming's arms while they stood mesmerized in shorts with skinned knees. They were wannabes and liked watching Miss America contests and imagining perfection in their one-piece swimsuits. Would they play the flute or do a scene from the *Glass Menagerie* in the talent contest, and could they be witty and forceful, answering the question about which person they most admire?

Sometimes, they had lunch with Mama at the local luncheonette, sitting in the red crinkly booths and deciding which sandwich to choose. Next, they would get ice cream cones with chocolate chips and jimmies on top and feel like life was as good as possible.

Susan waited for the forsythia bushes to bloom and line the street on Poppins Lane. In the spring, they would pop out and burst with bright yellow magic, and then she knew it was a brand new season. The lemon color made her skip on the sidewalk, smile, and breathe in the warmer air. Those sunshine bushes welcomed her home, and she was a happy girl because this was her home, where she had a bed and a dresser full of clothes and a tasty meal for supper.

She didn't know about poor people because few were around, except down on Little Street where the homes were run-down. She didn't understand the caste system or the racial prejudices that existed. She didn't know about pain, backaches, foot aches, migraines, danger, poor dental care, bullets, sexual abuse, and instability. These were all subjects that she would learn about in years to come, like the signing into law of Medicare in 1965, which would help

11

seniors over sixty-five. She read first and second-grade books about Mary Jane. She was going to learn about some of these awful things.

Susan's father sometimes spanked her with a belt. She was not afraid of him, and when he spanked her, she turned her backside to his waiting hand or belt. She would cry when he struck, but soon afterward, she'd be off to her next bit of mischief. Once, when she said "shit", he spanked her. Another time, she stomped her foot in front of relatives because she refused to go to bed, so he took her upstairs, brought her into her room, sat on her bed, put her over his knee, pulled down her underpants, took off his belt, and strapped her. She turned her head to him and screamed, "It doesn't even hurt," as the tears fell down her cheeks. That was the last time he took out his belt.

Her mother Lily used to kick Susan under the table if she said something Lily didn't like. Susan would happily eat her dinner, and then perhaps she would say, "I wonder if we will ever talk to the new neighbors down the street." They were a white-collar black family with a dog and a few kids. They may have been one of the few black families in Georgeport. Suddenly, Susan would get a kick at her ankles with the edge of her mother's high heel. Maybe Aunt Flo was dining with them that evening, and her mother didn't want Flo to think of them as racist. Susan never knew when she would get the kick, and often, she didn't know why.

Susan didn't pay much attention to Larry, but Flo was always around, giving her two cents. Flo was like the matchmaker: the busybody, obnoxious and overbearing. She had no sense of boundaries.

When Larry started visiting her bedroom at night, Susan's life changed. He would silently enter and get on top of her. She pretended to be asleep because she was so frightened. She didn't say one word as he mounted her and rocked back and forth, simulating intercourse. She moaned a little and turned her head right and left as if she was waking up, but she never uttered a peep. Larry would get excited and come all over her blanket, and later on she had to wipe off his wetness so the maid wouldn't see it in the morning.

Susan played possum while her horny cousin released himself, and her fancy parents slept down the hall in a double bed with a quilted headboard. Larry wet the sheets and the covers, but she said nothing, and Dad slept, even though he was a light sleeper.

From observing her mother and sisters, Susan learned they came from a generation of women who dusted themselves off and moved on. Feeling as if she had little recourse to address this vast injustice and illegal activity, she tried to ignore her predatory cousin. She tucked away these infringements because she would become a feminist Hemingway.

However, after the sexual abuse went on for about two months, Susan opened her eyes.

Her brother, Jeffrey, was a baseball player, playing in Little League for the Glovers on second base from nine to twelve, graduating to a more advanced team at thirteen. He collected baseball cards, cheering whenever he could catch a game on TV, and daydreamed of becoming a major league player. Jeffrey sat in front of the TV with a bag of Wise potato chips and followed every pitch, each catch, and all the stolen bases from inning one to the end, his round face beaming at home runs and errors by the opposing team.

Jeffrey was pudgy, curly-haired, and addicted to the sound of Mel Allen's voice announcing the Yankee games. He created a double persona and entertained his friends by copying the cadence of Allen's voice. Susan would sit in his bedroom and listen to Jeffrey and his buddies' baseball chatter. They played stickball, touch football, punchball, and whiffle ball, all variations of a sport with a round object.

Susan liked Jeffrey well enough. He was easy to get along with, and they were three years apart in age – three years and eight days, to be exact. She remembered when his friend Scooter, real name Michael, told Jeffrey's friends about his first time having sex with a girl. Susan was in Jeffrey's bedroom, sitting in a corner, staying silent and listening while Scooter was reclining on Jeffrey's bed.

"It was like dunking donuts," Scooter said. The boys, some leaning against Jeffrey's cherry dresser, listened with interest. Scooter stretched his extended legs on the rug and became the guru of sex. He had bedded Harriet Feinberg, a comely brunette, and was reporting back to the guys. Susan learned about intercourse as he described this milestone event.

Sometimes, Susan would see Jeffrey play second base. In Jeffrey's Little League years, she would go with her sisters, all wearing green baseball hats with Glover's printed on the caps, and sit in the bleachers to cheer Jeff on. Jeff was quick and fast, was good at fielding ground balls, and could bunt. He and his shortstop, Barry, were a gritty duet who worked well on the field. After the game, the sisters would surround Jeff and compliment him. One day, Barry said, "Wow, I didn't know you had so many sisters, Jeff." They smiled at him in unison and Susan said, "Hope you like girls."

"Big family. I bet it's crowded around your dinner table," Barry said.

Susan liked Barry immediately and said, "You should come over and join us. I'm sure my Mama could make room for you at the table."

"Thanks, maybe I will," Barry said as he tipped his hat.

Chapter Two

Two nights later Barry came for dinner, and was impressed by the large Victorian house on Poppins Lane. Beforehand, their father asked about this new fellow. "He's a baseball player and wants to go to college," Jeffrey explained. "I think he wants to be a baseball announcer and study communications," he said. "You know, Dad, I thought maybe I would become an announcer too. What do you think?"

"Well, I never thought of that as a profession, but if that's what you like, maybe. Do you know what they pay and if you could live on that amount, Jeff?" Dad said.

"I don't know, but I'll check it out and get back to you, Pop."

"That's my boy."

When Barry came in the house, Dad called him "Son." Susan could tell he liked Jeff's new friend. Barry made himself right at home and kept looking at all the nooks and crannies of the big Victorian.

"Quite a place you have here," he said. "I've never been inside a house this large and interesting."

Barry lived on the one street in town, Little Street, that had shabby houses. Susan biked to his house with Ellen the next day to check out his home. His house was beige with cranberry shutters and had an open porch with stick furniture. It wasn't bad, but she could tell it was neglected. The detached garage was open and filled with disorganized stuff, and an old junker with bald tires was in the driveway. A small front yard had crabgrass and needed mowing. Susan felt bad for Barry, who lived on this street with kids looking dirty and underfed. She felt her heart go out to him because he struggled. Ellen and Susan biked back home, maybe ten minutes away, and when they returned, she could see the difference between how they lived and Barry.

Barry was the oldest, and he hustled. He had a paper route, so he got up at five in the morning and biked all over town, throwing the local newspaper into people's driveways. He worked hard, saying, "I'm not going to be poor when I grow up. Enough of that." He sometimes substituted as the catcher on the baseball team when the regular player, Brian, was unavailable. Barry had muscular thighs from squatting and a good throwing arm. He was small like catchers often are, but he was strong, and Susan grew fonder of him as she got to know him. Her face would pinken when she saw him, despite herself. Barry was not used to being admired by a girl, but after a while, he knew she liked him, and he would grin and say, "Hi there, firecracker."

One night, at the age of ten and a half, Susan was in her bed. She opened her eyes, and there was her cousin, Larry, on top of her, staring at her without his horn-rimmed glasses and blinking in recognition.

"Ah, you're awake, my sweet one," he said quietly.

"Yes, I am."

"Good, I wanted to talk to you."

"Why?"

"Because I wanted to tell you; you were my special one."

"Your special one?"

"Yes, I love you so much. That is why I can't keep away from you."

He caressed Susan's face and said, "You've got to promise me you won't tell anyone. It's our secret. If you tell, your parents will get mad. They'll think you like me more than them. They'll make me move away, and it will be all your fault. You'll cause so much trouble if you tell."

She was confused. Wasn't it wrong for her cousin to love her that way? But it did make her happy to know Larry

16

thought she was beautiful with pretty eyes, and he had chosen her as his special one, so she agreed not to tell. When they had sex for the first time, Susan bled on her sheets.

Afterwards, he stayed and sang to her before leaving. She went to the kitchen and took out the roast chicken, the coconut cream pie, and a quart of milk. First, she ate a chicken leg and some cranberry sauce, and then some white meat. Next, she devoured a big piece of pie and washed it all down with a cold glass of milk. Her stomach became so full that she had to unbutton her pants. Every time Larry came into her room and had sex with her, she went to the kitchen later and stuffed her face. Larry wore a condom and took it with him in a tissue so no one would see it. He kept telling her she was special, and she believed him. She liked that he chose her, but didn't like that they were cousins.

Another night, as they walked to their separate bedrooms, her sister, Ellen, said, "I've got a secret, but if I tell you, you've got to promise you won't tell anyone else. Larry comes into my room at night."

"What?"

"I said Larry comes into my room and has sex with me."

"No, he can't," Susan stuttered. "He comes into my room too."

"He says I'm his special one," Ellen said.

"No, he can't. That's what he says to me."

Ellen smiled and then went into her room and shut the door.

Susan was so angry at Larry for tricking her that she stormed to the third floor and banged on his bedroom door. "What the fuck," he yelled and opened the door. "What do you want?" he asked.

"You've been sleeping with Ellen and telling her the same stuff. How could you do that, you liar?" She stood there turning red and feeling flustered. She wanted to pounce on him and punch him.

"Stop this. Don't be a baby," he said, smiling like he had fooled them both and got away with it.

She went at him, pushed his face, spat at him. "You dog, you low life, you slime."

Falling backward, he stumbled and caught himself on the night table. "Hey, get out of here, you fatty."

"You sick, dirty bum."

"Don't be a baby," he repeated.

Susan went down to the kitchen and opened the refrigerator. She took out the cold cuts, cheese, potato salad, and coleslaw. It had mixed pickles and a lot of mayonnaise, and Susan loved it. She found the rye bread sliced thin and sprinkled with seeds. Then she got the Russian dressing and made a huge sloppy Joe. She ate the whole thing, and then she made a second one. She didn't care if she blew up and exploded. She wanted to take the butcher knife out of the wooden knife holder, and wished she could stab her cousin Larry in the heart, but she didn't want to go to jail for murder and have to pee in a toilet in front of people. She hated him with all her heart and wasn't too fond of her sister Ellen either.

Chapter Three

Susan couldn't look in the mirror after the incident with cousin Larry and her sister Ellen. She didn't know that person staring back at her. She didn't know who she was. She thought she couldn't trust anyone. She was exhausted from life, and knew she had to calm down. She didn't talk to people and was afraid to reveal herself.

One day, when no others were around, Susan asked Mama, "Why do Larry and Flo have to live with us? I wish we were living here with just our family." She stared at her mother and was unable to tell her the truth.

"Flo is my sister, and I can't turn her away." Mama looked at Susan as if she were crazy. How could she not understand her allegiance to her sister?

"What about me? Every time I come into the room, Flo is there. I can't say anything without her being in the room and listening. I hate it." She wanted to tell her about the creep, Larry. She tried to tell her, but her mouth wouldn't open. She considered telling her father but dismissed the notion. Susan just stared at Mama.

Later, Susan thought about running away and thought about telling Jeffrey. Finally, she went to the kitchen, made a peanut butter and jelly sandwich, and ate it in two bites. She couldn't look in the mirror. What the hell. She was a big fat slob. She had read about how many calories she'd use by running. She wanted to be of average weight, not a blob. She went outside and ran down the block. At the end of the street, she had to stop. It was all she could do. Then she returned to her house on Poppins Lane and said, "Tomorrow, I'll run to the next street. One street at a time. That's how I will do it. One street at a time."

So, it went. Every morning, Susan ran one more street. Slow, but sure, she kept it up. She stopped pigging out and ran every day. She asked Aunt Flo to measure how far she'd run with the car. Sitting in the car beside Flo, Susan watched the mileage go up to four miles. Running, she learned all the streets in town so she could guess when she reached five miles. Then, she turned around and ran five miles back to the Victorian home on the street where she lived. Ten miles and fifteen pounds lighter, it was a start.

Each morning, Susan ran one more street. Slowly but surely, she kept it up. She liked the feeling of being free, the wind in her face, the quiet. She stopped gorging her face, wanting to be healthier, and ran daily. If she only went an extra quarter of a mile, then so be it. She did the best she could. She learned about the landmarks in town, the flower beds, the different trees, the traffic patterns, and the fire hydrants. Every morning she stepped on the scale and weighed herself. Wanting to be a regular weight, she watched what she ate. Little by little, the dial went down, and her new routine made her feel better about herself.

When Susan ran, she thought about what she wanted to do with her life, but when she slept at night, she had terrible dreams and woke up hating Larry. He deserved to be punished and she couldn't look at him when she saw him in her home. He stayed away from both her and Ellen, who refused to discuss the whole sexual abuse issue, saying she would deal with it in her own way. Fine, thought Susan, but she was having flashbacks and feeling vengeful.

Susan started a dream journal because she was suffering from a lack of a peaceful night's sleep. Anxiety and fear coursed through her mind. Her heart beat rapidly when she woke up from a nightmare. Sleeplessness kept claiming her nights, so she read. She loved Agatha Christie's mysteries and Mark Harris's baseball book, *The Southpaw*. Sometimes, she left early in the morning when there was no school, took a bus, went to Boston, and walked around. Up and down Newbury

Street, Charles Street, Harvard Square, and Brattleboro Street, over to the Boston Public Library, the Museum of Fine Arts. She enjoyed discovering bookstores and shops in alleyways and corners or bath boutiques with smells of lotions and soaps of different shapes. When she was back home, she poured oil into a hot bath and relaxed, hoping she would sleep better that night.

She prayed in the dark before she fell asleep. Would God help her? Would He answer her prayers? Was it fruitless? Could she make a deal with God? I'll be nice to Aunt Flo if you give me the courage to speak. Quiet fell over her as she whispered, "Please, dear God, help me make my nightmares stop. He is a sick person. Help me be normal."

Finally, she decided to tell her friend and neighbor, the retired teacher Mrs. Norby. Mrs. Norby lived down the street; sometimes, Susan would go over to see her and show her English compositions. Mrs. Norby encouraged Susan and complimented her writing.

Mrs. Norby was a large woman who always wore black dresses. She had attended the state university and graduated with a double major in French and English. Susan liked her a lot and felt safe with her. Mrs. Norby's office was a cozy room with a fireplace and a brass box stocked with wood. Over the mantel was Susan's oil painting of an old house that Mrs. Norby had framed and hung, saying, "You are a Star." There were books of all types on the shelves and a desk in cherry wood. Mrs. Norby sat at her desk and wore her frame-less spectacles down on the edge of her nose.

"Mrs. Norby, I need to tell you something, but I want it to be just between us, okay?"

She looked at Susan seriously and said, "Susan, if you want to share this secret with me, I agree just between us."

So, Susan told her the whole story about Larry, starting with the first time she pretended to be asleep, how it progressed and when she opened her eyes, how Larry called her special, what Ellen shared, and then how Susan ate later on until she started running.

Mrs. Norby stared at her wide-eyed and shook her head back and forth, disapproving of the entire abuse. She held Susan's hand and rubbed it, trying to comfort her.

"I have the worst nightmares, and I hate that they live in our home, even though he leaves both of us alone now. I don't know what to do, and I'm too embarrassed to tell my parents."

Mrs. Norby asked Susan if she wanted a cup of cocoa, and she said that would be nice. Mrs. Norby was a fine cook and sometimes baked her homemade bread. When they'd settled back down with their cocoa, Mrs. Norby looked at Susan somberly and said, "Susan, what Larry did is against the law. He could go to prison for twenty years in the Commonwealth of Massachusetts for incest. He should be punished." Then she took out a book, opened it up, and said, "Here, let me read this; 'As a juvenile, he should at least be sent to a home for delinquent boys. If a minor 14 years of age or older sexually abuses a child under 14, the juvenile offender can face felony charges, provided that the alleged juvenile offender does not have a serious arrest record, the matter may stay in the juvenile courts.' "

Then she closed the book. "But because Larry is your cousin and your family probably doesn't want to go to the police, we need to focus on getting him out of the house. I suggest you and I have a private meeting with your mother to explain what transpired. I am sure she'll want to move Aunt Flo and him out of your home – your mother is a smart lady."

Susan considered her words and said, "I don't want my father in the room when we tell her. I can't do that. It's too embarrassing."

"I understand. Leave this to me, and I'll call your mother and set it up. I'll arrange a time when we, the three of us, can talk in private. Leave it to me, okay?"

"Thank you so much. I'll try to get Ellen to come. I feel better already."

"I love you, Star."

She didn't know what to say when Mrs. Norby said that.

When Susan left the house, she only thought about twenty years in prison. No one she'd ever known had ever done anything so awful to deserve to be in jail for twenty years. Who was Larry, and how had he become so sick? When Susan returned to Poppins Lane, she saw Ellen alone in the empty hallway by her bedroom and said, "Ellen, I'm going over to Mrs. Norby's house with Mama to discuss the Larry situation. We will figure out how to get him and his mother out of our house. Do you want to come?"

"You mean telling Mama?" she asked. Ellen was now a tad overweight, had straight black fanned-out bangs, and carried herself with a strong presence.

"Yeah, that's right," Susan said.

Ellen shook her head back and forth. "I'm not sure, let me think about it. He's a prick, and I hate him. Maybe I should tell. Two daughters. Can you believe the little bugger was doing us both?" Her eyes lit up, and her cheeks got red.

"Come with me, Ellen," Susan said.

"Yeah, I'm coming. It'll be like old times. You and me, thick as thieves. God, I want to do it. Let me know when Sue."

On Saturday morning, her mother said, "Mrs. Norby wants the two of us to come over to her house and talk to us. She said to come today at 2 p.m. Okay?"

"I'll be ready. Ellen is coming too."

Her mother looked as if she wanted to say more but stopped herself. She didn't ask Susan anything about this, so she knew Mrs. Norby had told her not to discuss it until they came over. Susan and Ellen dressed in blue shorts and white tee shirts, not wanting to bring attention to their appearance. Mama and the two sisters walked over to Mrs. Norby's house, down the street to one of the small capes on Johnson Avenue. She greeted them at the front door and looked formidable in her black dress and large body. "Lily, it's nice to see you. Please come in." They gathered in Mrs. Norby's house in her private office.

Her mother smiled and looked stylish in her straight skirt and matching blouse. She often dressed in outfits.

"How are you, Susan?" Mrs. Norby said.

She was nervous but said, "Fine, just fine."

"Ellen, I'm so glad you decided to join us," Mrs. Norby added.

They settled into the office, which was roomy with two leather chairs. Mama and Susan sat in the leather chairs; Ellen sat in the extra chair set up nearby, even though when Susan came by herself, she sat in the chair by the desk. Mrs. Norby served Mama tea and the girls cool drinks, on the round table between the leather chairs. There was also a small plate of brown sugar cookies. They liked those cookies but didn't feel much like eating.

Mrs. Norby settled herself behind the desk. "Lily, I asked you to come over because something has come up." She hesitated and cleared her throat, clearly uncomfortable with the task. "It seems as if your nephew, Larry, has been going into Susan's room at night and molesting her."

Susan's mother let out a loud yelp, pulled a tissue from her handbag, and covered her mouth. She looked at Susan with shock.

"Yes, and he also has been going into Ellen's room."

24

Mama stared at Ellen.

"He is behaving terribly, and I wanted to let you know. I know this is upsetting news, but we must do something."

Mama looked at both her daughters and back at Mrs. Norby. "I don't believe this. How long has this been going on?" She reached into her pocketbook and took out a pack of Chesterfield cigarettes. "Do you mind if I smoke?"

Mrs. Norby handed her an ashtray, looked at Susan, and nodded.

Susan said, "It started a few months ago, and I didn't say anything because I didn't know how to talk to you about it." Susan looked down, raised her head, and continued. "He came into my room and got on top of me, Mama, and rocked back and forth. I pretended I was sleeping, but I knew what Larry was doing. Sometimes, he got so excited he released himself all over the blankets. It was awful."

Mama looked at her daughter and then put her hand over her mouth. Then she reached into her bag and took out a vial of pills. She placed a small tablet in her mouth and sipped her tea.

Then Ellen said, "He was coming into my room too. He told both of us we were his special girls, but we had no idea he was visiting us both."

"When I finally couldn't take it anymore, I opened my eyes, and then it got worse because he made me have real sex with him. Mama, I hate him with all my heart," Susan said. Their mother's face turned the color of ripe strawberries and her forehead scrunched together.

"Lily, this is a terrible thing, and I know you are as shocked as I am," Mrs. Norby said.

"I don't believe this, but I can't argue with what my daughters are telling me. Where is Ellen in all of this? Tell me, sweetie."

"At first, I said I would deal with things in my own way,"

Ellen said, "but now I am furious and want him punished and thrown out of our house."

"Lily, you must get Flo and her son to leave your home. What this adolescent was doing is against the law. As I told Susan, he could get incarcerated in Massachusetts for twenty years for incest and rape. It is unacceptable," Mrs. Norby looked at the girls' mother with serious eyes. Their mother hung her head in shame. She excused herself and went to the bathroom. The three of them sat in the room and stared at one another. Mrs. Norby told them they were doing fine and to be patient.

Then Mama returned and asked Mrs. Norby, "What shall I say to my sister?"

Mrs. Norby, always the teacher, said, "Explain to her that Larry is being inappropriate with your two young daughters and that she and Larry have to get their own apartment because you can't have him being intimate with your children; simple and straight. It is against the law and unacceptable. Larry needs therapy."

"Oh, my goodness. I have to tell your father."

"He will be furious," Susan added.

"That's for sure," Ellen added.

"The sooner, the better is my advice, Lily," Mrs. Norby added.

There was some discussion about why Larry was so perverse and how he got that way, but no one had any clear theory. Whatever the reasons, Larry was a sick puppy and couldn't stay. They thanked Mrs. Norby for her intervention and left.

Mama told Dad privately, so the girls hardly heard anything about how shocked and upset he had become. However, Susan listened at the door and heard Dad yell, "How dare Larry touch my daughters?"

Mama said, "Quiet your voice," but Dad was adamant

that they leave, so he agreed to finance the move and was more than willing to pay the rent on an apartment.

Later, Dad tried to discuss the abuse with Susan and Ellen by saying, "Sweethearts, how are you doing?"

The sisters bowed and murmured, "Not so grand, Daddy." Then Dad stroked their shoulders and kissed them on top of their heads. Susan felt tears in her eyes and squeezed Ellen's hand, but Dad couldn't say more. As he walked away, Susan wondered why it was so hard for him to help.

Mama couldn't seem to bring herself to have an honest conversation about sex with the girls. She called her sister-in-law, Connie, and cried over the telephone, and Susan heard her say, "My daughters have been damaged."

Within a week, Flo and Larry were gone. During the week, Flo stayed silent, and Larry never left his room. No one said one word of this to anyone in the house. By the end of the week, Flo and Larry were out of the third-floor bedrooms, sheets stripped, the bathroom cleared out, and not one speck of clothing left. They settled about two miles from Susan and her family's house. It was a garden apartment not far from the new shopping center that had recently opened, a small collection of stores with a large Sears and Roebucks in the center, called a cluster mall. Aunt Flo got a job selling clothes at one of the ladies' boutiques, and sometimes Ronnie would drive Mama and the sisters over, and they'd drop in and see her. Mama always managed to buy something while she was there, and the sisters sat on the velvet loveseat and browsed through the magazines.

Flo's apartment looked new, with red bricks and individual steps to different units. It was a two-bedroom unit on Sagamore Way with a kitchen and one bath. Larry went to the community college now; no one ever saw him because he didn't come to 2 Poppins Lane anymore. Mama would go shopping with Flo when she came by in her new car, probably bought by their dad, but otherwise, no one spoke of Larry and what was going on with him. If he was going to therapy, this information was all a secret. Her parents were content as long as he was staying away from the family. Ellen said it was good that Mrs. Norby spoke up, otherwise Flo and Larry would never have left. Susan agreed, saying, "At least we don't have that creep attacking us anymore."

Later on, Susan learned Larry was going to a shrink, but she didn't put much stock in that. Maybe he tried it and went twice. Gratefully, he wasn't working at a kids' summer camp or for the Cub Scouts. She had visions of bumping into him and not knowing what to say. She figured he was a damaged puppy who better not have his own kids. Maybe he would just become a recluse and write that great American novel he always wanted to do. A lot of writers were weird, so he'd fit the mold. Thank God for Mrs. Norby.

Chapter Four

Max Stern, Susan's father, was not a dumb man. Being a Jew in a small New England city in the 1950s did not make him popular. He kept a low profile. He didn't go out of his way to draw attention except for his red Cadillac Eldorado. He was a steady member of the Georgeport Chamber of Commerce and on the board of the local hospital, Georgeport Regional, but didn't socialize much. He heard Puritan whispers about Jews, the aftermath of Hitler, and the way the private clubs and universities limited the Jewish population and memberships.

Then, one day, the local newspaper *Georgeport Daily News* published a front-page article. Ellen saw it first, ran into Susan's room with the paper, and said, "You won't believe this. This is awful."

There on the front page, below the story about Martin Luther King, it said, "Eighteen-year-old arrested for sexually molesting his neighbor." The article went on to describe how Larry Fink had been discovered in the teenage girl's bedroom, rocking on top of her. When the girl's father found him, he threw Larry off his daughter and assaulted him. Now Larry was in the local hospital with a broken jaw and concussion. The family wanted to have him arrested for child molestation since the girl was only thirteen years old. Larry Fink was the nephew of Dr. Max Stern, a surgeon at Georgeport Regional Hospital and a city resident living on 2 Poppins Lane.

"Holy moly," Susan said. "Fucking A," she went on, rolling onto her bed and covering her face.

"What are we going to do?" Ellen asked.

"Oh, Dad is going to be pissed. He should have moved the kid to another state. Bad move, bad decision," Susan said.

A lot of the people in the city started avoiding the family – Dad and Mama especially. Dad's pals no longer came over to shoot pool. Dad was asked to leave the board of the hospital. People made jokes about his red car and how showy it was. Mama was too ashamed to be seen with Flo after Larry was arrested and his trial set for much later in the year. All their kids were ridiculed and teased at the schools, to the point that Jeffrey resigned from the baseball team and only Barry remained his friend. Ronnie, who worked part-time, got fired from Monique's because Lydia, the owner, said it was bad for the shop's image and the customers disapproved of her waiting on them.

People bowed out of programs, canceled last-minute lunch dates with Mama, sent notices of meetings rescheduled, and folks claimed to be sick or were unable to get together. The masseuse Dad used no longer was allowed to come to the Stern's home for his weekly rub down. Fellow physicians at the hospital were not interested in lunching at Dad's table, and other individuals were vanishing. Mama found it harder to leave the house on Poppins Lane. Pedestrians stared, vendors scowled, neighbors smirked, and passersby glared. Mrs. Norby called and asked, "What happened?"

"I should have moved them further away. What was I thinking?" Lily exclaimed.

"Larry needs psychiatric help," Mrs. Norby said.

Dad did some research and tried to get Larry into one of the few psychiatric hospitals in Massachusetts. There was a small one down on Cape Cod, one in a rural area out west, one on the Northshore, and a large one outside of Boston. Pearson's in Brookline, the preferred place, was a private hospital originally opened in 1829 by John Tufts Medical School. It was the first mental hospital in Massachusetts, and in 1879, bought ten acres in Brookline and renamed it Pearson's, changing its name from Insane Hospital. Dad wanted to learn about youths who committed sexual offenses and understood that juveniles were about one-third of the population who committed them against minors. On top of that, they usually reoffended. He had to do something with his nephew. He couldn't let him stay this way.

After spending two weeks in the hospital and two surgeries, Larry was recovering from his injuries. The newspapers ran a few more articles. Flo couldn't handle the pain and the embarrassment of Larry's behavior. Despite her loud, take-charge attitude, she was a timid, diminished woman and was unable to escort her son to the mental hospital. Dad and his lawyer had gotten the justice department to let Larry go to the mental hospital until the time of the trial, which was about a year away. Heartbroken, Flo hid inside her Sagamore Way Garden Apartment.

It was Dad who took care of Larry's preparations. Dad looked into every aspect of Pearson's, especially the doctors' credentials and clinical treatment. He hoped the press would leave Larry alone, and Dad worked hard to ensure he received the best care possible. Cognitive behavior therapy helped patients rethink their deviant behavior. Repeat behavior was addressed, and situations that could lead to relapse were discussed. The hospital suggested Flo and Larry have family therapy, and Max said he would talk to Larry's mother. They also required group therapy.

When Dr. Meisner, a thin Harvard psychiatrist, requested that he be allowed to speak to the family, Dad agreed, pointing out how much he wanted to help his nephew and keep the young man from ruining his life. Dad reported all this to the family around the dining room table. He said, when talking to the doctor that his heartbeat slowed to a murmur in his chest, and he had to keep himself from weeping as he explained, "Dr. Meisner, this is my nephew, and he is very ill. There's something broken inside of him, damaged. Is there any way to fix him?"

The doctor thought for a moment before he said, "Most teenage boys have sexual activity with younger children that they know and spend time with. This includes younger siblings, cousins, children of a neighbor, or children that they babysit. It is unusual for an adolescent boy to have illegal sexual behavior with a child he doesn't know. We will do our best to help your nephew, but there is no guarantee. Let's wait and see how his treatment proceeds."

Dad said no more and whispered, "Thank you."

Later when Dad visited Larry at Pearson's, the young man was pale.

"I'm finished," Larry said morosely as he sat with his legs up and his head on a pillow.

Dad shook his head and left.

Susan wondered why Dad had put so much effort into fixing Larry and so little worrying about her and Ellen. Her heart was broken because her parents didn't seem to care about how awful their daughters felt.

Larry had a difficult time adjusting to Pearson's. He couldn't do what he wanted and spent an excessive amount of time in the men's room jerking off. While he had free time, he roamed the halls and met several other residents. Patients who were inside for overdosing on pills walked around with huge bags under their eyes. They were put in seclusion and were deprived of belts. There were catatonic patients, folks who shuffled around, complex types who were angry or depressed. Some of the patients played scrabble or chess. An anorexic girl had wire-like limbs. Larry wondered if these people were dangerous to society, but he never thought of himself that way. Susan wondered why Dad shared all these reports at the dinner table. He filled the family in on what was happening with Larry.

The hospital grounds were filled with patients who muttered, snarled, and cried. Scissors, nail files, safety razors, and penknives weren't allowed. People acted out. One of the patients was a tall, blond fellow who was inside for accidentally shooting his sister when he was in a fit of rage. Dom was nineteen years old and came from a reasonably wealthy family. He was the favored child of a two-child marriage and had spent his high school years taking long naps in the school's basement. His passion was guns; he collected them and read the National Rifle Association magazine, *American Rifleman*. Dom bought guns and rifles using his parents' money: job earnings he had from a discount store, and from his sister, Barbie, when he could con her into giving him some cash. During an argument with his sister, when she resisted giving him any more money, he shot Barbie. She recovered with minor wounds but was in treatment for panic attacks. The doctor had put her on Valium and taught her breathing exercises. Dom pleaded temporary insanity and was sent to the mental hospital for treatment. When he met Larry, he found someone he could talk to and proceeded to explain his anger at the country, at welfare recipients, at blacks who sat on their steps and did nothing, and his dislike of his father, who was a self-made millionaire after only going as far as the eighth grade. His father, Timothy, was not impressed with Dom's lack of ambition.

"This country is going to hell," Dom said as he sat across from Larry in the rec room. "Too many handouts, too many liberals marching, too many long hair nuts. Look what's going on with the blacks and whites in school."

"I don't know, Dom. There is a lot of poverty out there,

and our country can't let people starve. We are the USA, the land of the free," Larry said.

They read the *National Review*, a conservative magazine, and worried about the government taking their guns. At the same time, Dom complained that the country's businesses were giving the best jobs to blacks and women.

"What are you in here for?" Dom asked.

"I'd rather not say," he answered, hanging his head.

"Aw, come on now. I told you about me. Shoot."

"I'm not too proud of it. I'll tell you when I'm ready, and when I do, you'll have to keep it between the two of us, okay?"

"Sure, sure, no problem. When you're ready, Bud."

Both Larry and Dom grew up in the middle class. They had never been poor. They had this in common. Dom's father was stoic and hardworking, selling encyclopedias at thirteen. He was an only child and supported his mother, whom his father had abandoned. Dom was spoiled because his mother, Clara, indulged him. The parents disagreed on how to bring up their kids. The father remained strict, while the mother was a pushover. Dom hated his father and disliked his domineering personality.

Larry was bitter over losing his father and jealous of the boys who had a dad to discuss things with. He was sick of his mother's voice. As the two Pearson patients got to know each other, Dom swayed Larry's thinking, and he became a right-wing extremist. Dom told Larry about the Ku Klux Klan and the John Birch Society. They grew close and were both afraid of gun control. Dom said, "No one has the right to tell me I can't have a gun." Larry needed something besides his upcoming trial to think about, so he latched on.

Larry finally told Dom how he had sexually abused his cousins and the girl in the apartment next door. He said, "I couldn't stop going into their rooms when I lived in their home and fucked up because I did both sisters."

"Were they hot?"

"Not particularly, just available."

"You crossed the line. I once screwed my cousin, but she was older than me, and it was consensual."

"No, they were kids; one acted like she was sleeping for a while. I told them they were special and hooked them. I flattered the shit out of them. They were chubby girls, not too pretty, and ate it up. I was a prick. I admit it. I did some reading on it and learned that sibling abuse is the most common type of sexual abuse in families. Researchers estimate it occurs between three to four times more often than father-to-daughter sexual abuse. They weren't my siblings, but they were my cousins. The problem is I got moved out and then did it to the girl next door, but her father beat me up, and I got arrested. It's a bloody mess now. I gotta go to court."

"You could go to jail. That sucks," Dom said.

"Don't I know."

Word got out in the hospital because of group therapy, and Larry tried to compensate for the unsavory diagnosis of sexual predator by taking extra care with his appearance. He spent time in front of the mirror checking his hair and skin, brushed his teeth three times a day, wore freshly washed clothes, tucked in his shirt at all times, and used the best table manners. He hated that people looked down on him and held his sickness in the lowest esteem. Dom helped him to take his mind off it by teaching him how to disassemble and assemble weapons, which they did in secret. Larry learned how to do this without looking, which gave him a thrill. Dom hid his stash of weapons in his room.

Neither had much to say to the few black patients at Pearson's. Even though Larry was more inclined to see the liberal side of politics, he began to copy Dom and call the blacks by the "n" word. His views against women went

35

along with his abuse. He was appalled with the feminist movement. In his therapy sessions, he discussed his anger and his need to dominate. He revealed his dislike of his mother, Flo, and her overbearing nature. "She thinks she can run the show. I won't let her."

Larry disliked the long days inside the hospital and his lack of freedom. He tried to write the novel he had started, but his mind was not focused. Larry was anxious and depressed and couldn't keep his mind on the trial preparations. He objected to the food and the required meetings. Dad came to visit with the doctor. He brought Flo for a family conference, and she said, "Larry is the disgrace of my life." Larry admitted that he was lonely, horny, and bored. If Larry continued to defend his actions and show little remorse, Dad feared that the trial would not go well. Maybe Larry felt inadequate with females, said the doctor in charge of Larry's case, and expressed his rage by sexually molesting them. Dom said women were like Nazis, and Larry laughed.

Dom was asked to leave Pearson's because the authorities found his guns and live bullets in his room. So, they packed him up and returned him to his suburban home in Rhode Island. Larry became further depressed and discouraged.

Chapter Five

Wearing her paint-splattered overalls, Susan spent her weekends working on her art after a brisk run and a fruit and cottage cheese breakfast. Susan felt better now that the whole story was out and wasn't entirely shocked at Larry's repeat performance on Sagamore Way. Susan wondered if she would ever forget this incident with her cousin and decided it was part of the mosaic of her life. She would have to absorb it into her voyage and try to make it a positive influence, if possible. She had read somewhere that a healthy person picked the best traits from someone they admired and made them her own. The sexual abuse was not a trait; it was an unfortunate event. She wanted to discuss this with Ellen, when she came banging on Susan's door at 5 p.m., looking to take their daily vigorous walk. When the two sisters walked, they talked loudly to one another and didn't care if they were overheard.

"Elvis Presley is going to be on TV tonight," Susan said.

"We have to watch the Ed Sullivan Show," Ellen replied.

"Dad said Larry wasn't even sorry. He's such a prick."

"Maybe they'll castrate him."

When the case was initially assigned the Georgeport court, the defense requested a change of venue for the trial to avoid too much prejudice and unfair press. Perhaps Salem made more sense since it was larger and had a wider jury pool. People in Salem didn't have a visceral connection to the case, and they could use *voir dire* to rule out prospective jurors with undue bias.

The jury selection, which consisted of six women and six men, eight whites, three African Americans, and one Hispanic, took two weeks. Even though the trial was held in Salem, the Georgeport citizens were keenly aware of the ongoing trial.

The new judge, Judge Fuller, was a fine choice to preside. He looked like a New England Yankee with his lean frame and reserve. He had two grown children, attended church every Sunday, and had a quiet demeanor. Earlier in his career, he had presided over fraud and rape cases. He was known to have a good heart, which gave Dad hope.

The Salem Superior Court building was past its prime and a busy place. Law offices surrounded it. Flo dressed in a conservative suit and had a new hairdo from Eleanor's. She sat solemnly in the first row behind the defense table. The place was packed with people of all ages and reporters from newspapers. Dad was extremely nervous, and Mama had to take two tranquilizers.

The bailiff said, "All rise! The Honorable Judge Fuller presiding."

When the judge entered the courtroom, Larry's attorney, Durenberger, stood up.

The judge said, "Be seated. This trial will begin with the opening statements. This is not a testimony of evidence. It is an outline of what the lawyers will present during the case. The lawyers are here to provide an overview of what the actual evidence will be. Will the prosecution please begin?"

Miss Linda Rubin, an attractive thirty-three-year-old, began. "Larry Fink, aged eighteen, has been accused of molesting a thirteen-year-old girl, Sally Howard. He went into the apartment next door to where he was living. It was the apartment of Bertram Howard. His daughter, Sally Howard, was sleeping in her bedroom. Larry Fink entered at midnight. Her father found him fornicating with her, pulled Larry off Sally's bed, and punched him breaking his jaw and causing him to suffer a concussion. Sally was traumatized and examined by the medical team at Georgeport Regional

Hospital, and they found bleeding in the genitals and the rectum. Lawrence Fink has been accused of oral sex, fondling genitals, buttocks, chest area, and sodomy."

Rubin took a breath and continued. "Those are the facts. They are not in dispute in this case. They were reported in the police report and confirmed. This court case is not about those facts. This court case is about the age of the child who was raped. Larry Fink was raping a girl, underage and without her consent. The police report said that the father punched Larry Fink and broke his jaw. Massachusetts law does not address the anger of the father, but does address the age of the girl and what Larry Fink did to her."

She continued, "Throughout this trial, we will call witnesses who will show this information in more detail. You'll hear from the father, Bertram Howard, and from the mother, Mrs. Deborah Howard."

Child abuse cases have always been the most difficult to prosecute and one of the most underreported of all crimes. Some people live their entire lives without admitting what happened to them. Both Ellen and Susan were prepared for the trial if the news came out and they were called upon to speak, but the thirteen-year-old child, Sally Howard, was the only victim in this case. The prosecutor had a clean, preserved sample of Larry's sperm to present to the court. It would conclusively prove that Larry was guilty, so the burden of proof would be met.

Linda Rubin took another breath and continued, "Once we arrive at the end of the case, once you've heard all the evidence, there will be no doubt that Mr. Fink sexually abused, molested and is guilty of the rape of the child, Sally Howard. As jurors, you're tasked with an important responsibility. You must evaluate the evidence presented to you and make a decision based on the rule of law."

After the prosecutor spoke, Defense Attorney Anthony

Durenberger began. He knew his team had coached Larry to act remorsefully. "Ladies and gentlemen of the jury, the prosecutor summarized the evidence. The prosecutor charged Lawrence Fink with sexual abuse of a minor. This is not a laughing matter." He paused and looked at the jury. "However, there are extenuating circumstances to this behavior. We have a child who grew up fatherless since the age of six. Because of the loneliness of a boy who stayed in his room and a mother who dominated his life, he became an adolescent needing direction. This young boy acted out as I will show you in this trial. You will see and understand why this young boy went off the skids."

His team had lined up two physicians from Pearson's to testify in support of Larry's recovery, but they refused to promise that Larry would not relapse. It was the best they could do.

In his new suit, Larry was brought from his holding cell to the counsel table, and Durenberger got to his feet each time as a gesture of respect to his client. His standing up made the prosecutor, Linda Rubin, look petty for failing to do the same. He offered the jury a fake smile. Durenberger said, "This case is plain and simple. Lawrence Fink has an emotional problem. He has been evaluated by two physicians from Pearson's Hospital for the mentally unwell. He was not mentally fit on the night in question. Over the coming weeks, we will provide witnesses who will prove that Larry Fink did not behave in a responsible way due to severe emotional impairments. He has no responsibility for this rape. Thank you for your time."

Durenberger had written a book on courtroom drama and dynamics and believed in the value of gamesmanship. Now he appeared to consult with the client to show that Larry was building a life and was not a reckless sexual predator. Durenberger developed these themes and emphasized Larry's clean record, his father's death when the young man was only six years old, and that Larry had never been inside of a police station because he had never done anything wrong. The fact that Larry lied repeatedly, took advantage of a thirteen-year-old girl, and used a key to the apartment were all bits of information Durenberger tried to bury.

Was he going to say that Larry was mentally disabled and get a psychiatrist from the hospital who would say Larry was extremely narcissistic and self-centered? There had been a lack of love in Larry's life. The chance of success of an insanity defense was fifty-fifty. Durenberger blames Larry's behavior on family dysfunction because Flo is overprotective, and there is no male figure since his uncle always works. As far as the defense knew, no one ever sexually abused Larry, but Flo was often gone with Lily, and Flo was overly dramatic and intrusive with most other people. Larry was reluctant to blame his family for his bad behavior.

Durenberger told Larry not to speak to anyone. The attorney knew that the boy deserved to be punished and was not remorseful for his horrid behavior. However, the abuser needed a lawyer so he wouldn't spend the next twenty years incarcerated.

During a recess, Dad told Larry's attorney, "Larry needs another chance, and the problem with jail… he could get killed, and the father is out for blood."

"We need to find a way to get Larry medical and psychiatric guidance and to continue his treatment in Pearson's," Durenberger said.

When the prosecutor, Linda Rubin, got up after the trial resumed, she said, "He assaulted her; she resisted. He damaged this virginal child. He didn't care about her at all. He is a letch and must be punished. He assaulted this thirteen-year-old child, and he didn't stop despite her pleas. There can only be one verdict."

Dom drove towards Salem, MA, to attend Larry's trial,

41

stopping on the way at a knife and gun show in Pembroke, MA. He put his firearms under the seat when he arrived at the courthouse. He saw the crowd. The gallery was shoulder to shoulder every day. Members of the public filled the rows of the courtroom. The bailiffs stood at the front of the room, scanning the crowd. Media was on the side of the room. The atmosphere was tense.

Larry behaved coldly and unsympathetically despite the lawyer's advice to become more likable. His demeanor was icy. Plus, he was a Jew, and the North Shore was prejudiced. Sitting in the gallery and watching the entire procedure, Dom knew Larry's conviction was unavoidable. He wanted to take Larry aside and give him advice, but he wasn't sure how he'd get to him, so he wrote a note and gave it to his lawyer, Durenberger.

> *Dear Larry,*
> *I am here at the trial. Is there any way we can talk? I don't think you're being remorseful enough. How do you think this will play out to the jury? Buddy, think smart.*
> *Your friend,*
> *Dom*

Durenberger showed the note to his client, and they somehow arranged for Dom to meet Larry in the courthouse for half an hour before they went inside. They looked at one another like old friends in the conference room with a dark wood table and surrounding chairs.

Dom sat down and said, "Larry, how're you doing?"

Larry looked down at his hands. "I'm not doing very well, Dom. This could be the worst moment of my life."

"Yeah, I know it sucks. But you gotta give it your best shot. I don't think you're projecting enough guilt or remorse. You kind of look like a man with no conscience, too icy.

Warm it up, buddy. If I were in there, I'd be trying to get those suckers to like me, pity me, something. Seduce the suckers, or you'll be sorry. Now!" Dom punched the large conference table for emphasis.

Larry smiled at his friend's enthusiasm. "You know, Dom, you're a good friend. I appreciate your advice. It's just that I'm not feeling it, and I know I should. I've gone into a place that is somewhere else. A hell. An away game. I am so fucked over by what's happened to me I can't connect."

"Well, you sure don't want to go to jail, do you? You'd better warm it up and look like a better person, or they'll be fucking you up the ass. That's all I gotta say."

With that, Dom stood up and left the room. He had said his piece, and if Larry was dumb enough not to take his advice, he deserved what he got. He'd laid it on thick, and if Larry was a jerk, he'd be sorry. Then fuck the kid, so be it. Durenberger overheard the chat and reported it to Susan's father.

When the trial resumed, Bertram Howard, the thirteen-year-old victim's father, came to the stand dressed in a tie and jacket and had his hair combed back with Brylcreem. Bertram was a working-class man with a high school education who was thirty-eight years old and had a job in construction. He had not hired a lawyer because he did not need to. The prosecuting attorney then asked the witness to describe the events of the night of the incident. He said, "I heard noise, groaning, moaning, like you hear when people are having sex." Linda Rubin was going to prove that the girl, Sally Howard, had been emotionally damaged because she had a child's developing brain.

"Continue, please – what else did you hear or see?" Linda Rubin asked.

"I went inside Sally's bedroom and saw the man having

sex with my child, my little girl. He kept rocking back and forth, grunting and ignoring her screams to stop. I became so infuriated that I grabbed him by the shoulder and punched him in the jaw. He fell to the ground and hit his head. That's all I can remember," Bertram said, "but I can't get the image of Larry Fink on top of my little girl out of my mind."

When they called the child's mother, Deborah Howard, to the stand, she stood up and swore on the Bible, then sat down.

"Tell me about your daughter, please," Rubin said.

"Sally was a happy girl who loved holidays, art, presents, dressing up. She played with her Magic Slate, her Barbie Doll Case and relished Monopoly. At Christmas, she baked cookies and gave them to her friends and teachers, wrapped in red and green cellophane. At Halloween, she dressed up as a princess, a pirate, and a ballerina. She loved babies and wanted to babysit."

The prosecutor asked, "How has she changed since the rape?"

"My daughter doesn't care about holidays, dressing up, baking cookies, or babysitting," the mother said. "Sally just sits and stares out the window like a zombie," she said, wiping tears from her eyes. "She isn't the same girl anymore."

The jury warmed to the mother, nodding and smiling, building a rapport with her and trusting her statements.

"What do you do about this?"

"I tell her I am here for her and will listen or hug her whenever she's ready." Deborah Howard left the witness stand weeping. When it was time for the summation, the prosecutor, Linda Rubin, began her closing statement. "He assaulted Sally and she resisted. He damaged this virginal child. He didn't care about her at all. He is a lech and must be punished. He assaulted this thirteen-year-old child, and

44

he didn't stop despite her pleas. There can only be one verdict."

The prosecution rested, and now it was time for the defense to present the case. The different physicians from Pearson's were put on the stand. They said it was to Larry's credit that he voluntarily came to the hospital seeking treatment for his problem. They recited all the different treatments they had given him. No promises were made that Larry was cured, but they told the court that he had become more aware of his issues. Larry chose not to testify in his defense.

Attorney Durenberger said, "This case is nuanced with so many different stories. One is the damage; you have heard about that. The other is a boy, Larry, who is fatherless and lonely with a mother who is overbearing and controlling. He lived in his uncle's house and then in a one-bedroom apartment without privacy. Larry was sad, going through puberty, and uneducated in the normal life of a young adolescent." Durenberger emphasized this by stopping and staring at all the jurors. Then he ended, "We cannot excuse him, but we must have compassion for a damaged young man. He needs help, both psychiatric help and love. Show Larry some love by sending him for treatment rather than incarcerating him where he will become more damaged than he already is."

Chapter Six

When the jury went out, a crowd of people gathered in front of the courthouse. Judge Fuller decided that Larry shouldn't be present when the verdict was read because his safety couldn't be assured. The jury took five hours to return a guilty verdict, and the news spread quickly; phones rang, and applause broke out at the luncheonette named Taffy's. It wasn't long before people danced down Main Street, passing the house on 2 Poppins Lane.

Crowds loved to discuss crime and sex and read about it. The media reveled in it. Scandalous behavior fascinated them. Newspaper sales increased, sensationalism entertained, and lurid headlines added a twist. Each trial turned into theater. The courthouse was a stage, the participants were the actors, and the citizens were the audience.

Larry was a sexual deviant. Susan heard her friends whispering about her cousin, but nothing was revealed about her and Ellen. When Flo and her son moved to Sagamore Way, neighbors speculated, but no one really knew why they'd gone. The truth was revealed only when Bertram Howard found him in the act. He caught the attention of the newspapers.

The next day, the judge pronounced his sentence. "Because Lawrence Fink is only eighteen years old, I'm going to advise that he go into protective custody because sex offenders are often harassed, attacked, and brutalized. I have given him credit for attending the program at Pearson's Hospital, where he participated in counseling, group therapy, and assorted mental health clinical treatments. I am recommending a prison designed for sexual abusers. I highly recommend he participate in an experimental treatment program for twelve to eighteen months to prevent recidivism. Lawrence Fink's best chance of changing his behavior is by attending this program, when available, five days a week. He has committed an awful crime, and he has to be punished. I have decided to sentence Lawrence Fink to ten years of incarceration instead of twenty. Perhaps when he gets out of prison, he will resume a healthy, normal life. That is my decision." Judge Henry Fuller got up from his seat and left the courtroom, his black robe flowing behind him.

Durenberger must have been disappointed because he failed to get Larry off, which was a long shot. He had made meticulous plans, and his team had worked hard. Larry stood like a zombie when the judge announced his sentence. He was escorted from the courtroom by the court officers and returned to his cell to await transfer to the prison where he would spend the next ten years. Finally, the family on Poppins Lane would be able to return home to their former lives and attempt to move on. Dad was exhausted from the ordeal, saying, "I am okay that he got only ten years and thrilled he is going to that experimental program."

Mama was relieved that the trial was over. "Maybe we can go back to a normal life."

Susan shook her head and considered the judge's decision. Then she turned to Ellen. "He's a lucky bastard. They never heard about what he did to the two of us."

Dom started to leave the courthouse but spotted the Stern family on his way out and stopped. Susan and Ellen were walking with their parents when they saw Dom, the tall, blond, good-looking man of nineteen. Despite herself, Susan pulled herself up straighter and taller, held her stomach in, and grinned. He walked with a swagger and a pack of cigarettes in his shirt pocket. "I know this isn't a good time to introduce myself, but I met Larry at Pearson's, and we became friends. I'm sorry he got convicted. If there's anything I can do, please consider me a friend. Dom, Dominic Sharp." He put out his hand, and Dad shook it.

"Thank you, Dom. I'm Dr. Max Stern, and I appreciate your sentiments."

"I'd like to chat with you, but this isn't the time or place," Dom said.

Susan said, "Why don't you come to dinner tonight?" She surprised herself by inviting him but looked at her parents for approval. She knew her parents didn't have endless parties or houseguests, but they would be interested in getting to know Dom better since he had spent time with Larry in the hospital.

"Of course. Why don't you come for dinner," said Mama, the hostess with a big heart. "Are you heading back home? Where do you live, Dom?"

"Just in Rhode Island, not that far. I'd love to come by. What time?"

"Come at 6 p.m. 2 Poppins Lane. You can't miss the house; it's a large pink Victorian on the corner of Main and Poppins, across from the high school."

"I'll see you then," he said. "Thanks."

The entire family gathered around the dinner table that night after Larry was sentenced. Odell, the maid, had put an extra leaf in the oval dining table to accommodate everyone. The table was set with a white cloth, napkins, a centerpiece of fresh flowers, and crystal glasses. Mama liked to dress things up, and this was a special night, not of celebration but of closure to a long, arduous journey. Susan could see that Dom was glad to be there and Dad was anxious to learn what Dom and Larry had discussed. Susan was attracted to Dom but could tell Mom was afraid of him. The rest of the family were just plain curious.

48

"I suppose you were in the hospital for a reason, weren't you?" Mama asked.

"Oh, yeah, I was there because I accidentally shot my sister, and they said I was temporarily insane. I wasn't insane; I just missed 'cause I just wanted to scare her. My sister, Barb, is my pal and usually helps me out with money, but for some reason, she resisted that day. I was trying to scare her. She wasn't hurt, thank goodness."

"My oh my, that's quite a story. I'm glad to hear your sister is okay," Mama said.

"You were damn lucky," Jeffrey added.

"Right about that," Dom exclaimed.

"How did you get to know Larry?" Dad asked as he passed the platter of roast beef to Dom. "Here, have a piece?"

"Thanks, this looks delicious." He took an end cut and a few onions.

"The food there wasn't very good, was it? Larry complained about it," Ellen said.

"He sure did," Dom agreed.

"So, how close were you and he?" Dad asked.

"We spent a lot of time chatting. He was nervous and distracted, of course, but I tried to talk to him about other stuff to get his mind off the trial." Dom cut his meat and stabbed a roasted potato.

"What kinds of things did you discuss?" Dad asked, taking a potato for himself.

"I told him about how the country wanted to take away our rights to have guns and discussed the more conservative part of the Republican Party. He was interested in learning about it as a liberal writer. Also, we discussed the Soviets launching Sputnik and how gas cost twenty-eight cents a gallon."

"Did he agree with your conservative views?" Dad asked.

49

"He was resistant at first; he didn't like the prejudice."

"I have to agree with him on that," Dad said.

"I know, you being Jewish and everything. I get it."

"You know Larry was working on his novel. Did he share with you what it was about?" Susan asked.

"No, I don't think he could concentrate on his novel writing. He was too depressed, Susan," Dom smiled at her.

She had put on a red blouse and lipstick before dinner and hoped she looked pretty.

"What else did you two talk about?" Dad asked.

"I told him about my gun collection and showed him how to assemble guns and disassemble them. I had a secret stash in my room, and I got him skilled at putting them together and taking them apart without looking. He liked that," Dom said, laughing.

"A secret stash?" Jeffrey asked, his eyes growing round.

"Yeah, buddy. I brought them in when I came, but the authorities found them and threw me out because I had them." Dom shrugged his shoulders and laughed.

"Yes, you took quite a risk," Mama said as she scowled and shook her head in dismay.

"I guess, but I'm here now, so nothing else happened," Dom replied.

Odell came into the dining room with homemade challah. "I forgot that I baked this today. Here, Dom, have some warm challah bread."

"Oh, this looks wonderful... Jewish bread; I never had any before."

"Oh, you're going to like it." Ellen laughed.

Everyone took a slice.

After Odell left, Dad asked, "Did Larry discuss what he had done to get him put there?"

"At first he didn't want to tell me. He was very

embarrassed because the population there doesn't support messing around with young girls and everything."

Susan and Ellen squeezed each other's hands under the table. No one else said a word.

"He told you eventually, though," Dad said, taking a sip of wine from his glass. "Here, have a little more wine, Dom."

"Thanks, Doctor."

"Did he tell you anything else?" Dad asked.

"Did he reveal to you if he had done this before?" Mama looked at Dad.

Dom waited a minute before he answered. "No, he didn't say anything else. He was pretty quiet about the subject."

Susan recalled Larry touching her. She remembered how he smelled, how he knew what he wanted, and how his hands felt on her skin.

Mother said, "Dom, did you have Odell's coleslaw? It's a family favorite."

"Oh, thanks, this is tasty. I'll have a little, but I'm enjoying your wonderful food. I've been working out in the gym and trying to eat a better diet.

"No kidding? I'm looking to exercise more and eat less junk food. Since I started running, I'm on a health kick." Susan smiled.

"Looks like it's working." Dom grinned back.

Susan pushed a lock of her hair behind her right ear. "Well, I lost fifteen pounds running when I first started; now, I run every day, about four miles, and eat cottage cheese and fruit for breakfast."

"That sounds great," Dom said. "I'm glad I came tonight and got to know your family. Larry made me curious about where he lived and what everyone was like."

"Did he talk about us much?" Susan glanced at her sister and nodded her head.

"Yeah, what did he say?" Ellen asked.

51

"That you were nice girls," Dom said.

"That's all? Just that we were nice?" Susan asked.

"That he liked you," Dom added, looking slightly uncomfortable.

"That's it?" Ellen squeezed Susan's hand again.

"Well, you know, we talked about so many things. Larry said you guys were very close. He said you liked to watch TV. I can't remember much else. I'm sorry," he said.

"What's your father do?" Mama asked.

"He made a lot of money in retail discount stores, retired early, and now he's bored. I think he may go into selling stocks."

"Stocks are hot now," Dad replied.

"That's what he thinks, too," Dom said.

"It's too bad Larry has to do ten years. Maybe we can get it reduced. What do you think?" Dad asked.

"I don't know much about the legal system, but he won't do well inside. He's not built for that population. I'd try if I were you, sir," Dom said.

"Yes, I'm going to," Dad agreed.

"Thanks for everything," Dom said. "I hope I see you folks again."

"Are you planning on visiting Larry?" Susan asked.

"I do plan on visiting. How about you?"

"No, I don't think so." She remembered how Larry had released his cum on her bedroom blanket. "No, I won't be going, but maybe you can stop by for dinner again."

"That would be nice. I'll call you. Give me your number, and we'll do something," Dom smiled.

"Sure thing," she said.

By the time Dom left, he said he'd keep in touch. Dom walked down the flagstone pathway, jumped into his Valiant, waved, and headed south towards Route 95 back to Rhode Island.

"What did you think of him?" Dad asked the family.

"I wouldn't be surprised if Larry didn't tell him all kinds of stuff. You know, all that time on your hands, nothing to do but talk," Mama said.

Dad said, "I bet you're right, Lily. He seemed like he had plenty to say about many things."

"He made me nervous. Too much of a risk taker," Mama said.

"I kind of liked him," Susan said, "but I don't trust him a hundred percent."

"It was pretty obvious that you liked him," Mama said. "Be careful, Susan."

Chapter Seven

Susan worried about her family and Larry's incarceration. She thought about how each person was a mosaic, and together, they made a pattern. However, each person has his or her individual pattern, desires, and path. Would they make a beautiful kaleidoscope because of all the colors and shapes? What would Larry do to the pattern? Susan shook her head and went out for a run. When she got home, she wrote a short story about people and patterns and thought about her sister and how different their paths were; her parents, Larry and Dom, each with their interests and styles. When she had it the way she liked it, Susan would bring it to Mrs. Norby and see what she thought.

After Larry went to prison, Flo went to sleep and never woke up. She couldn't live knowing her son was in prison. Unable to tolerate the nightmares of what could happen to him, Flo decided to go to heaven, where her late husband rested. It was a better choice for her.

Dad returned to the hospital, and his cronies seemed to forgive him for his troubles. Maybe they felt bad for him or understood how hard he had tried to do the right thing. They joined Max for lunch in the cafeteria, and the masseuse returned to give Dad his weekly rub down again. Mom received calls from women she hadn't seen and joined them for book club. Jeffrey joined a fraternity, had a girlfriend at the same school, and went out with her on the weekends. Ronnie was applying to college.

Dom went to visit Larry to see how he was doing.

"They attacked me and fucked my ass," Larry said. "What else do you want to know?"

Dom didn't know what to say but gave Larry the new addition of *American Rifleman Magazine*. "Here's something to read," Dom said. "If you get bored."

"The place is full of assholes; time moves slowly, and I'm tired," Larry said.

"Yeah, you don't have enough to do."

"What are you up to?"

Dom said he was putting in swimming pools. He had a good tan and looked handsome with blond streaks in his hair.

"Good thing you're not in here. They'd love your ass," Larry said.

"I thought the judge said you should get into some program and fix yourself. Hasn't your lawyer set this up, buddy?"

"He's working on it, but things here don't go quickly. I'm hoping to get into the program soon. I fuckin can't wait," Larry said.

"Maybe I can get you something to help your situation," Dom said.

"What?"

"Patience, buddy."

Mama and Dad decided to build an exercise room where Flo and Larry had resided. Carpenters, plumbers, painters, and other workers visited the house on Poppins Lane daily. Workers installed weights, exercise machines, mirrors, and a sound system. They enlarged the bathroom and put in a steam room and shower. When it was finished, Susan painted a mural on a wall with a female on a bike, two runners, and a woman who looked like Marilyn Monroe lifting weights. Every family member used the gym and got more into physical fitness. Mama started to push the Mediterranean diet and ate fewer starches. Odell learned a few new recipes.

"Come over and use our new gym with me," Susan, now fifteen, said over the phone when Dom called.

"You have a gym," he said. "That's heavy duty."

55

"Dad likes what he likes," she replied a bit sheepishly.

"Nothing wrong with that. A man after my own heart," he said.

Dom arrived in his Valiant with a gym bag. Susan noticed that he had thick thighs and a long torso. They worked out to music for an hour in the new gym. Susan did twenty leg lifts for her abs, Dom lifted weights with barbells, she did two fifteen repetitions on the thigh machine, and they held each other's legs when they did sit-ups. Susan was surprised at how strong Dom was, and Dom told Susan that her doing twenty push-ups was impressive. After they sat in the steam room and sweated, Dom took a shower, and Susan went to her room and cleaned up there. When they were finished, they walked downtown, and Susan brought him to Taffy's for a healthy lunch. They talked in the red crinkly booth and lingered.

"I visited your cousin," Dom said.

"Yeah, how's he doing? Not that I really care."

"He's suffering."

"Well, that's what happens when you're a creep."

"I guess you're right. He's suffering big time."

"I'd rather not talk about Larry, if you don't mind," said Susan.

"Sure, I'm sorry I brought it up," Dom said, reaching over and squeezing her hand.

They walked back to Poppins Lane and then drove to Cherry Island in Dom's Valiant so Susan could show him the beach and a vacant cottage the family was thinking of renting.

"It has perfect light, and I could paint here." Susan found the key under the mat and let him in.

"That sounds like a neat inspiration," Dom said as he walked around and inspected the rooms and the windows where the sunshine beamed in. "I thought you were going to college with Ellen."

56

"That's the problem; I can't decide."

"You're a gal with lots of ideas."

"My mind doesn't stop."

He walked over to her and gave her a big hug. "A fertile mind is a very significant asset."

Then they kissed a long lingering kiss, and Susan felt more undecided about college and the cottage on Cherry Island.

Susan was leaving the 1950s' female image behind and was turning into a feminist. Sensing that something was missing, she followed her inner voice. The same was true of Ellen. When Betty Friedan came out with the book *The Feminine Mystique*, Susan asked herself what was consciousness-raising; she went to a shrink and asked her too. Her mother didn't understand the concept, but Susan's mind exploded with the revolution. Where was her soul? Her mind? Her identity? Her autonomy? She didn't want to grow up suppressed and dissatisfied without freedom. Susan felt confused about what she was allowed to say and what she wasn't. When she was kicked under the table and didn't know why, she didn't understand what was happening to her freedom. She wanted to be herself in the most honest way.

Once the family gym was completed, Dad developed a new habit. He went upstairs around 6:30 a.m., got on the treadmill, placed the morning newspaper in front of him, and ran slowly or walked quickly for thirty minutes. One day, no sooner had he'd come out of a hot shower with a towel wrapped around his sturdy frame, the phone rang. It was the medium-security prison called Wellington, where Larry was incarcerated.

"Hello, Dr. Stern," asked a male voice.

"Yes, this is Dr. Stern."

"This is Head Warden McDonald at Wellington. I'm

calling to let you know your nephew Lawrence Fink was attacked last night at 2 a.m. and suffered a broken pelvis and mild concussion. We aren't sure who did this to him because he was supposed to be locked in his cell for the night. The guards found him on the floor in his cell, in a lot of pain. He refused to tell us who was responsible. We have him in the infirmary, and he will remain there for a few days."

"Jesus, who's in charge there?" Dad asked.

"We are looking into this, but Lawrence won't come clean."

"Come clean! You're not coming clean, sir. Maybe he's afraid to tell the truth for fear of reprisals. That place is dangerous, and you know it."

"We do the best we can. This is a difficult population," McDonald said.

"I thought my nephew was going to be put in some program for sex abusers. The judge ordered it. What's taking so long?" Dad asked.

"It's coming, but there are a few things we need to put in place before we can begin. Red tape."

"By the time you have it in place, my nephew could be crippled or dead. For God's sake, what's the holdup?"

"I told you it's just a few loose ends. I will let you know as soon as we have it ready."

"When can I see my nephew?"

"Today after twelve, sir."

"Thank you for calling." Dad hung up the phone, adjusted the towel around his waist, and sat on the bed. Lily reached over and squeezed his arm. She was still in bed and shook her head, thinking of Flo and how awful this entire ordeal had become.

"Oh, dear God, Max, it doesn't stop," Mama said as she slipped out of bed and put on her robe.

"They're going to kill him inside. They're fuckin going

to kill the kid," Dad said. "Lily, what are we going to do? They haven't done a damn thing the judge said. I'm calling Durenberger right now and tell him to get on top of this. We paid him all that money, and the kid is getting beaten up. I can't stand this." Dad started to get dressed for the day.

Larry was forced to stay in the infirmary for a week and not move. Dad told the entire family at dinner that Larry looked white with terror and ten pounds thinner. with terror and ten pounds thinner. Dad told the entire family at dinner, and they listened in silence. Durenberger called the warden and gave him hell. The judge was notified, and executed an order of protection, so Larry went into solitary until a program was ready for him. He sent this document to Max describing the program that would be set up for Larry and others.

Residential Sex Offender Treatment Program
Residential treatment involves high-intensity programming for a period of 12 to 18 months. This program is used at USP Marion in Illinois and soon the FMC Devens in Massachusetts. Participants benefit from a therapeutic community in a residential housing unit where they work to reduce their risk of further offending. Offenders receive treatment five days a week.

Dad murmured a sigh of relief and returned to the hospital, where he had several surgical cases.

When Dom visited Larry, he was allowed to see him for fifteen minutes, and the first thing he said was, "I brought you some dope. Give it to the guys who are attacking you. This will keep them off you." He slipped him a small plastic bag of brown powder, and Larry tucked it into his jumpsuit with his left arm.

"I don't know anything about this stuff. What is it?"

"It's heroin. There are all kinds of drugs in the joint, like speed, black beauties, and heroin. It makes junkies feel better, like they don't care or give a shit. Maybe you should snort something, and then it'll take the edge off things. Try it."

Dom spoke quickly, got up from the bench, and left. He wanted to leave Wellington without incident.

Things eased up inside and the warden got cracking on the new program that was supposed to protect Larry and teach him a few things about himself. It was a slow process, but everyone was on board.

At dinner, Dad said, "I think you girls should stay around Boston for college. With everything happening here with Larry, it would make things easier if I had everyone in the same area. There are great schools in the Boston area. This way your Mom and I won't have to travel to see you."

Jeff and Barry also transferred to Boston University to be nearer home. Barry decided he wanted to go to law school. Jeffrey looked into sports merchandising, selling equipment, announcing, and coaching.

Susan didn't know what would develop between Dom and her, if anything. And Barry. Then there was Larry in the background. She didn't like that Larry's situation still seemed to dominate her life, but Dad had a point, so she and Ellen decided to research a few local colleges and maybe visit them. Ellen and Susan often discussed Larry's disorder and wondered why he was compulsively promiscuous.

Ellen said, "He just likes to fuck."

"He's so screwed up. I don't think he has any hope," Susan said.

"Do you think someone screwed with him when he was younger?" Ellen said.

"It's possible, with his father gone and all. The experts say that happens. We'll never know unless he says."

"It's an interesting subject if you're not the ones getting fucked over."

"A lot of little girls get abused by stepfathers."

"You've been doing a lot of reading," Susan said.

"In a nursing book, this poor guy was messed up by his mother's boyfriend. He had to take some meds to keep him from having angry outbursts. It never could work. Rode a bike around town."

"Screwed for life," Susan said.

Susan wanted to paint and write, and the concept of helping people with problems was vital to her. She believed all this would come together in one big idea; she wasn't sure how or when, but she wasn't worried. Silently, she asked God to help her.

Chapter Eight

In the fall of 1957, Susan's older sister, Veronica, went to a small coed college in the western part of Massachusetts. She was a beautiful girl with an aquiline nose and a good figure who often wore hats to complete her outfit. Susan admired Veronica whom she called Ronnie, and watched her to learn about growing up. Mama and Ike, the family helper, drove her to the bucolic campus, settled her into a single room, and put up Elvis and Beatles posters. Ronnie organized her room with her record collection, large fashion books, paperback novels, and a hamper. Mama made her bed with hospital corners and white sheets she had brought from home, all ironed and crisp. Ronnie cried when Mama and Ike drove away but got over it and learned her way around the hilly campus.

Half the classes were too difficult for her, and she struggled to keep up. She knew nothing about Greek tragedy, and the professor, Dr. Grossman, spoke in a booming voice.

The names of the characters were too complicated to spell or pronounce. The school made Ronnie take another year of French because she did poorly on the entry-level test. The English class was studying Chaucer, which Ronnie hated, and she needed a tutor for math.

In no time, she got pregnant when she was drunk at a fraternity party. Dressed in a long red sweater dress that clung to her firm body, she could not resist the flirtations of the young, handsome studs, and she succumbed to one fellow's advances. Kurt was an engineering student headed to scientific success, so she was taken in. He brought her to his room in the frat house, where he made love to her on his unmade bed. They learned of her pregnancy when Ronnie missed her period and visited the local doctor. Kurt didn't look too happy when Ronnie insisted on telling her folks.

Mama was shocked and hysterical yelling, "Undo it, Max, undo it." Still, Dad whispered in Ronnie's ear, "It could've happened to anyone," and told her that she would have to marry the father-to-be and settle down.

"Ronnie, what are you going to do?"

"I don't want to go away to one of those places they send pregnant, unwed girls and then have to give up my child."

"Why do you want to have a baby now?" Susan asked.

"I don't, but I can't give up my kid. It would be too painful." She lowered her head and picked her cuticles.

"Oh, Ronnie, I feel terrible for you." Susan sat down on the bed and hugged her. She didn't want to throw away her dreams like Ronnie. It also seemed to Susan that sex got in the way of a lot of girl's lives.

"I hate the classes," Ronnie said. "Maybe I'm not smart enough."

She did what she was told because, in 1957, those were the rules, and she didn't want to give up the child or bring shame to their family. Abortions had just been legalized. After she left college before completing her freshman year, Ronnie and Kurt got married by a justice of the peace and settled into an apartment. She gave birth to a tow-headed girl who she named Amy. Ronnie hoped Kurt would become enamored with his new daughter and enjoy fatherhood, but as soon as Amy was born, he started to complain about not being able to go out and missing his fun weekends. Kurt got a job at an engineering company and earned an ample salary, so Ronnie stayed home and gave up her dreams of becoming a Bloomingdale buyer. Amy was fussy, but they gave her a pacifier and prayed it would do the trick.

On a Saturday, Ronnie asked Kurt to watch the baby because she wanted to go shopping and have a break when he was home. "I'll only be gone for a few hours but need free time. There's formula all prepared." She went out and did errands, window-shopped, got a haircut, and stopped for a cup of coffee and a corn muffin grilled with butter and topped with grape jelly. She enjoyed her freedom. When she returned, Kurt was not in the apartment. Baby Amy was crying in her crib and had a wet diaper. Ronnie waited and waited. When Kurt didn't return home after another two hours, she called her mother. "Kurt's not here. He left the baby alone."

"You're kidding? How long?"

"I came home four hours ago, and little Amy was howling."

"I'm sending your father right over."

When Kurt finally made it home, Ronnie told him her father was on his way over.

"Why did you call him?" Kurt asked.

"For Christ's sake, you left our child alone. I was frightened. Where the hell did you go?"

He hung his head and whispered, "I went to the race track."

"The race track?"

When Dad arrived and heard the story, he was furious. "What kind of bum leaves his baby alone and goes to bet on the ponies? You're a schmuck, Kurt."

Ronnie started to cry.

"Get rid of him, Ronnie. Get rid of him. He's a loser." Dad sat down in a chair and rubbed his hands over his eyes.

"It was a mistake. Can't you give me another chance?" Kurt cried.

"I don't care how smart you are. Any man who leaves his infant all alone and goes out to gamble is a fool and a loser. Get the fuck out of my daughter's home," Dad said.

"Ronnie, come on," Kurt pleaded. He looked at her with the same eyes that had wooed her at the fraternity party.

She shook her head. "No," and buried her face in her

hands, like her father had done, rocking herself back and forth in a chair.

Kurt packed up his books, clothes, and his mother's andirons.

Ronnie went to the kitchen and took a bottle of amber liquid from under the sink.

"What are you doing?" her father asked.

"I'm having a drink, Dad. I need something to take the sting off things."

Ronnie moved back into her old bedroom, and Mama fixed Amy's nursery. Now, there were sterilized bottles and pacifiers, not to mention a playpen and the smell of baby powder throughout the house.

Susan wondered how this new development would affect the family mosaic.

"Maybe you can work in one of the local shops and get to understand retail," Dad suggested. Ronnie got a babysitter and returned to her old job part-time twice a week at Monique's, a boutique in town. She loved the time with adults as she learned about the retail world. It was an ideal escape and a chance for her to partially live out her dream of working in retail.

"Want a little drinky-poo?" Lydia, the owner, asked at the end of the day.

"Why not?" she answered. Ronnie was secretly thrilled that her boss liked to have a drink after work. It became their ritual.

It started with the occasional nip after work and then progressed to adding a glass or more of wine with dinner. Soon, Ronnie found herself imbibing at lunch and dinner and watching television. Alcohol seemed to take the edge off, and it wasn't long before she began filling her coffee cup and thermos each day with vodka. When Chad, her second husband, who was a lawyer, threatened Ronnie with divorce if she didn't stop drinking, she got sober. She couldn't have two divorces. Working on a recovery plan, Ronnie regained her looks, which had started to fade from all the booze. After sobriety, she took long walks, biked, and often brought the children to the park. She and Chad went to a spa and stayed a week, where they learned about healthy eating, skincare, and meditation.

Dad bought the cottage down at Cherry Island, and Susan was thrilled. With all the family close by, Dad managed his responsibilities better. Mama noticed that Susan and Dom kept getting together. Even Odell commented, saying, "You sure like that boy."

When Dom met Susan for a date, he told her, "Poor Larry got hurt. Broken pelvis. I thought a guard hit him with his baton, but Larry said no."

"He can't stay, or he'll get killed there," Susan said. "He deserves this."

"Well, he told me a bit... he said he was dragged into the shower, guards stared the other way, and he came out with blood and stuff coming down the backs of his legs. He looked like his eyes had gone blank, the poor bastard."

"Let's change the subject. Let's go down to Cherry Island and look at the sunset. What do you say?" Susan smiled because she knew what would come next. The cottage was sparsely decorated, with only a twin bed in the bedroom with a large window. They fooled around and took off their clothes; Susan felt breathless with desire and could tell Dom was an experienced lover.

When they finished, he said, "You're my special one." As soon as he said those words, she knew...

"SPECIAL ONE! What does that mean... you have others?"

"Because that's how I feel," he said.

"No, bullshit, that's what Larry said to me, and you know it, you creep."

"What are you talking about? Are you nuts?" Dom asked.

"You prick." Susan leapt off the twin bed. She slammed the door, shrieked, and ran outside, her hair flying. He must have known about her and Larry. Larry must have told him. Feeling powerless, Susan hurled herself back inside the cottage and yelled, "Get the hell out of my house. Get out and never come near me or my family again."

Dom said, "You're a crazy cunt," and stormed off in his Valiant, leaving Susan all alone, without even a ride back home. She threw herself into the shower, turning it to the hottest she could stand, wanting to remove any scent of Dom's touch from her skin. She walked back to the road to try to find a phone and call someone at home to come and get her. Lily couldn't manage the two-mile ride to the beach; her mother was a bit pathetic. Ike, the black helper, came. Susan thought, thank God for him.

That night, Susan slept with Ellen, curling up into her body like they did sometimes as kids. They used to scratch each other's backs, draw letters, try to guess which ones, and until their eyes closed. She hugged her sister; Ellen knew Susan was hurting.

"You shouldn't have gone out with him," Ellen whispered.

Susan squeezed her eyes shut and bit her lip, hating herself for being such a fool.

Chapter Nine

Susan didn't want to end up like one of Mama's sisters. Of course, that was in the olden days, but poor Aunt Sadie had to marry a guy Grandma Bubby chose. Grandma Bubby had promised one of the daughters to an old boyfriend back in Russia and decided Sadie was the designated bride. Because Sadie was a good girl, a shy, blond, poetic child, she went to Newark, New Jersey, and married the Russian's son, who had opened a shoe store. Tuvia was a decent fellow, just dull. He counted his boxes every day and kept a close watch on the inventory.

The couple lived in a walk-up apartment in Newark, a working-class city that, at the time, was full of unemployed blacks. There was a high crime rate. People were afraid to stroll on the streets at night.

Sadie gave birth to three daughters and valiantly tried to ensure they each had careers so they wouldn't become a woman like her. Tuvia also prayed his daughters would be successful and not wind up as clerks in a shoe store. Beth, the oldest, studied to be a school teacher, Mildred became a paralegal, and Sheila graduated as a nurse. Sadie joined the ladies' group at the synagogue and prayed on Sabbath. She smiled, and people liked her.

When Sadie visited Mama on 2 Poppins Lane, she arrived on a Greyhound bus in her Ked sneakers, knocked on the kitchen door, and declared her arrival. The two sisters sat at the large dining table. Sadie drank tea and ate Mandell bread as she reported the details of her life. Ellen and Susan overheard Sadie's daunting statement, "Marriage is death."

Sadie was a good-natured woman who liked her few friends in the Newark synagogue and tried to make the best of her situation. She worked five days a week in the shoe store until she started getting dizzy spells. This went on for a few weeks, and then one day, Sadie fainted. Tuvia took her to the doctor, who said she had a brain tumor. The next time Sadie visited, she had a white bandage wrapped around her head. Susan, Ellen and Lily were shocked. That was the last time they saw their Aunt Sadie. Susan thought about this old-fashioned custom of arranged marriages and wondered how she would have felt if that had been done to her. Maybe her parents would have chosen a good match instead of a dud. Susan was on her way to college, and this custom was out of fashion.

Susan started a project in her communication class at her new school, Commonwealth University, in 1960. She decided to write a children's book, creating it entirely independently, including the story, cover design, and illustrations. She worked very hard on this assignment because she was diligent and persevering. Meanwhile, Ellen took classes in nursing and considered becoming a trauma nurse. Yet every time she studied something new, she'd get so excited that she'd switch majors.

Whenever the two sisters got together, Susan tried to encourage Ellen. "Maybe this is a better fit," Susan said. "It's good that you get excited. Soak it up." Then she'd hug her sister and tell them they were overdue for a haircut, so they would go downtown and find a place to get a trim. They still kept their hair straight but were more Chanel-looking than Buster Brown.

Susan hoped her dreams would come together, but she had her doubts. Another of Mama's siblings was a playwright who'd been married three times. Susan wanted nothing to do with three divorces, three big fights, horrid money troubles, dating again, the whole messy subject that she read about in the Daily News and other tabloids. The movie magazines were full of celebrities who had several divorces and breakups. Even businessmen, including a few of her uncles, had been through a divorce or two. Susan shook her head and almost put her head under a pillow at night, thinking of these disasters.

Dad made an appointment with Attorney Durenberger to talk to Judge Fuller. The judge was in his private office with his degrees and pictures on the walls, his robe on a hanger, and his body tall and erect behind his large desk.

"What can I help you with, Dr. Stern?" he asked.

"Thank you for seeing me, Judge. My nephew, Lawrence Fink, is being brutalized in prison, and I'm very concerned. At the end of the trial, when you sentenced him, you recommended a new type of treatment that was being tested for sexual molesters. Nothing has been implemented, and I'm worried that Larry will be dead or crippled before we can get him into a program."

"Yes, yes, I remember," Judge Fuller said, nodding. "Let me tell you, in a way, Larry is fortunate. This new program is a test run for sex offenders. The Federal government has been trying to find a way to treat them. The agenda I recommended for Larry is residential, lasts twelve to eighteen months, and is designed to prevent recidivism. It's still experimental. I'm going to urge them to accept Larry."

"That's kind of you, Judge Fuller. How many inmates will be in this start-up program?" Dad asked, trying not to show his excitement.

"Probably a dozen. No more because they haven't worked out the kinks; this is their first time doing it. But a great deal of effort has gone into the experimental course. It'll be five days a week because they recognize that sex offenders are a vulnerable population within the prison setting."

"That's so true; I couldn't agree more. Where will they be holding this program?" Dad asked.

"At Fort Devens in Ayers. All male offenders. They'll

have about one hundred inmates when we get the whole thing up and running."

"No kidding?" Dad started feeling better about Larry's future already.

"There will be rules, regulations, visiting times, and all kinds of matters you'll learn about."

"No doubt."

"Families and some friends can visit if they have a prior relationship with the inmate."

"And what about attorney visits?" Durenberger asked.

"Oh, don't worry, there will be a conference room for you to use, but you'll have to show your credentials. They're running a tight ship," Judge Fuller said.

"As they should, Judge," Attorney Durenberger said.

"They're hoping to reduce repeat arrests. Besides individual therapy, family meetings, and group sessions. Vocational training and financial education will give these men a chance for a new life, and putting Larry there will make you a part of the solution."

"Wonderful. Well done!" Dad said.

"I know Larry is only twenty-two, so we want to help and avoid him being assaulted in the adult prison. I want to treat him carefully," Judge Fuller added.

"Thank you very much," Dad said, shaking the Judge's hand. "You've given me a lot to be hopeful about."

"Let's see if they can determine why Larry is this way. I'd like to know, wouldn't you?" the Judge said.

"Yes."

Attorney Durenberger said, "Please notify me when we can expect this to begin."

"I will. I'll be anxious to learn how this new program helps these inmates. I will move this along and be in touch," Judge Fuller stood up. The meeting was over.

Susan was pleased that Larry would get a chance to

participate in this experimental agenda. Even though she still felt a lot of anger towards him, which she wrote about in her diary, she was excited to learn about this progressive initiative. She still had bad dreams which she discussed with her therapist. It was about time that they tried to improve people's lives. What was the point of just sticking someone in a cell and not treating them? Susan and Ellen were interested in this new therapeutic approach and wanted to learn why he had done these despicable things. He couldn't have just been born that way. One bad turn had changed Larry's life and affected so many. Kind-hearted at her core, Susan wanted to see if he could find his way back.

Susan's family was a colorful painting with a few black splotches. Her parents kept their problems hidden except if Mama had a few too many scotches and then she'd opened her mouth or misbehaved. Once, Susan was sitting and watching television, and Mama came and sat on Dad's lap and started to fondle and kiss him more seductively than Susan had ever witnessed. There was a bit of moaning, tongue-wagging, and wet kissing. It embarrassed Susan, and she wanted to say, "Stop it, Mama." But Susan squirmed in her seat, said nothing, and looked at Dad to see what he would do. He sat like a statue while Mama kept squirming in his lap. Finally, Mama got up and left the room. What a relief.

What provoked that misbehavior, Susan wondered? Perhaps Dad was screwing one of the nurses, and Mama was jealous. Mama had too much to drink; Dad probably felt guilty and didn't want to add to the problem in front of Susan, who was mortified at the interaction between her parents. Susan would never know because nobody talked. It was private, like Larry's sexual molestation of Ellen and her. Susan didn't understand marriage, and that made her nervous. The scene provoked her curiosity and disturbed her. Her mother was out of control for a reason.

Jeffrey and Barry decided to take the Red Cross training for lifeguards so they could work the summer after they graduated from college. They got a job at Cranes Beach in Ipswich, MA, worked eight-hour days, got tanned, and watched the swimmers diligently. Susan and Ellen visited the beach and loved that the guys were there doing their jobs.

"Let's go out tonight," Barry said when he spotted the girls during the break.

Later, after work, they all piled into Jeffrey's car and drove to Cherry Island to get fried clams and beer. They were so happy in the summertime. It was the best time of year for Susan.

No school and fantastic weather made the season special. Susan and Barry started to flirt, and Susan decided to consider Barry her boyfriend.

"Hey, come here, firecracker," Barry said. He hugged her tight, and she laughed with delight. Barry picked up a rubber ball, bigger than a baseball but smaller than a basketball, and tossed it to Susan. She caught it on the first try and threw the ball over the dunes into the sand. Back and forth, the ball flew between them. They laughed and jumped and threw the ball again. Sometimes it was wet, others sandy; back and forth, they scampered like young children and kept throwing the ball, having such a carefree, happy time with each other. She decided she liked him more and more.

"I sure like the summer," Barry said.

"Would you ever want to live in an all-sunny climate?" Susan asked.

"Naw, I'd miss the seasons. The autumn leaves in October are my favorite time of the year," Barry answered.

"I like spring too," she said.

He started to caress her shoulder. "I like you," he said.

"I know," she replied.

"A lot."

"I like you a lot too, Barry," Susan said. They stared at each other and took each other in.

"Someday, I'm going to be successful. I'm going to go to law school," he said.

"I'm not surprised."

"I love you, firecracker." Then he bent over and gave her a long, tender kiss. Susan wanted to weep with joy. Suddenly, she felt like she was going from girlhood to womanhood. As her breath got a little shorter, the air got hotter, and Barry held her gaze.

"Have you ever had a boyfriend?" Barry asked.

She touched her pinky to his finger, feeling closer to him, and said, "I never had a serious one." Barry kissed her, their lips locking, and she drew him nearer.

Inside the prison, Larry met another Jew. His name was Aaron Schwartz, and he was in for fraud. He had stolen multiple credit cards from elderly people, charging up thousands of dollars. The two inmates spent some time together talking about what it was like outside and dreaming about what they missed.

"I miss Sunday dinners with meatloaf and mashed potatoes," Aaron said.

"I miss long hot showers with plenty of soap," Larry replied. On and on they went, laughing together. Aaron was a determined young man, doubly determined to get out of prison early. He tried to reduce his sentence through good behavior, extra work details, brown-nosing the guards, lying, sneaking, speaking to his attorney every week, and even reading law books.

Larry was impressed. They went for walks around the inside yard, Larry gasping sometimes to keep up. They talked and walked until Larry's legs ached. He liked the camaraderie of their friendship, eating their meals together, and having a person who wanted to hang out with him. Aaron said he had grown up in a lovely house with a bay window and bookshelves full of novels. He and Larry both liked to read.

Despite this friendship, Larry was anxious to get into the new program. Who knew when someone would start messing with him again now that his injuries had healed and he was no longer in solitary. The drugs that Dom had given Larry helped keep certain men away, but now they wanted more, which put pressure on Larry. He was nervous and edgy, lost his appetite, and had difficulty sleeping some nights. Larry regretted his past sexual harassment, and he didn't know why he'd done it, except he knew he had been driven and hadn't cared about his victims.

Chapter Ten

Susan and Ellen got summer jobs when they had a school break. Ellen got a job at an old age home on Mountain Avenue, and Susan was employed at a daycare center on Irvington Way. Off they went with their lunch in brown paper bags and their faces scrubbed.

Susan took the number four bus, which dropped her off at the corner of Scot Road and Ray Street. The daycare center stood alone: a concrete box with a huge sign saying "Green Grove Daycare" and a picture of a stick-figure child jumping, looking like she was up in the air with her legs bent. The artwork was very primitive.

Susan was disappointed by the shabbiness of the daycare center.

The rooms looked tired. "We always wash our hands when we get here," a tall, plump woman said. "I'm Grace, and I'm the supervisor," she added. "I'm glad you're here; we need the extra hands," she continued. "You can put your stuff in there." She pointed to a locker with no lock on the wall. Grace had a strong voice and a Maine accent.

Susan looked around and saw a spacious table in the center of the room where they did arts and crafts. Most of the helpers and teachers were young and athletic looking. One man, Nate, the director, worked in an office, but Grace seemed to be in charge.

"Hi, I'm Peter. Glad you're aboard," a fit-looking fellow said. He was dressed in shorts and a tee shirt with the name of the daycare center, Green Grove, on the shirt in bright red block letters. "You can get one of these tee shirts in the storage closet, with the brooms, mops, and paper products."

"Thanks," she said. "I'm Susan, and it's my first day."

"The kids are a little rowdy. Some haven't been fed breakfast, some come from broken homes, some need a bath, and others are messed up. Otherwise, they're a great group of kids." He laughed in a way that told Susan he wasn't impressed with the population.

Susan nodded and walked towards the storage closet to get a tee.

The kids were a mix of cuties and chubbies, dirty-faced and cross-eyed. Susan counted them; there were twelve in her group. They ranged in age from three to five, with equal numbers of boys and girls. Peter was the teacher, and she was his helper. They all sat in a circle on the floor and listened to Peter tell them what they would do that day.

When she had a moment, Susan asked Peter, "What kind of homes do they live in?"

"Some are okay, a few live in trailers, and a couple of those ought to be condemned," he said as he squeezed his nose with his thumb and finger.

Susan took half of the group, three boys and three girls, and brought them into the art room. She started to pass out white paper and markers, put up pictures of birds and flowers, and suggested they copy or do their own thing. "Color a picture of something you like," she said. One little boy drew a vibrantly colored bird with very well-scaled feathers, a beak, and bright colors. It was an excellent copy of one of the photos she had posted.

She was so impressed that she approached him and said, "That's wonderful. Where did you learn to draw like that?"

"I don't know," he said, scrunching his slim shoulders. He had a head full of dark curls and was skinny. His picture was much closer to scale and more realistic than the other children's. The other kids drew smaller, less precise pictures. They were colorful but not nearly as well done.

"What's your name?" she asked.

"My name is Dickie, short for Richard."

"Dickie, you're very talented."

77

Then she went around the table and complimented the other kids to avoid playing favorites. She couldn't get the picture of the bird out of her mind. When it was lunchtime, she went over to Dickie and sat down next to him. "Have you always liked to draw?" she asked him.

"Oh yes, it's one of my favorite things to do," he answered.

"I like to draw and paint also," she said.

"Can we paint together?" he asked with his sunny face up to hers.

"I don't see why not, Dickie." Susan smiled at the little boy and added, "Maybe we can make extra time to do it."

As the days went on, Susan started to take Dickie into a corner of the art room and draw with him. Maybe it was nap time, but he was done napping. Maybe it was lunchtime, and he had finished eating. Perhaps they just figured out how to make time. Grace didn't object, and Peter thought it was neat.

Then one day, Susan said to Dickie, "Let's go into the storage closet and do a private project." She opened the door to the storage closet and brought Dickie inside. Anxiety came over her but she tried to ignore the feeling. She had markers, paper, and a few bird photos in her hand and then closed the door. Then she locked the door so no one could open it.

"It's crowded in here," he said.

"I'll make room. You wait." She rearranged the closet, stacked the paper goods on a shelf, put the brooms in a corner, and piled the daycare tees higher. "You sit here," she said as she pointed to a space on the floor. "Are you comfortable?"

Little Dickie made himself comfy and brought up his knees to his chest. "There, that's better," he said.

"Great. Here's some paper, markers, and pictures; you can draw something. What do you think?"

"Are we supposed to be in here?" Dickie asked.

"Sure, why not?"

"I don't know," he said.

She looked at this skinny little boy and thought about how easy it would be to hurt him, control him, touch him. He was a child, and he trusted her.

What was she thinking? She wanted to do it. Why? She had to be bad. To go crazy. To break the law.

Without thinking, she reached over and stroked the little boy on the shoulder, so innocent and unknowing, this child who liked to draw. This boy was exceptional, the way he drew a picture; she wanted to touch him, nice and easy. Nobody would know, just Dickie and her, their secret.

After a few pictures, Susan bent over the little boy and tentatively started, then the voice came, talking to her, warning her, telling her, no… Maybe I want to touch him, but no, I won't do that, I can't do that. It would ruin him, damage him – my little artist boy. I can't hurt him. Susan took a deep breath. *But she would like to do it. She must stop that nasty thinking. She was bad. She must sit up. Straighten up. Behave herself.*

"Let's go out and get some fresh air. Come, let's go get a cool drink," Susan said.

Dickie looked up with his red marker in his hand.

"Hurry now while the sun is out," Susan's heart was pounding.

Dickie dropped the marker. "That's a good boy," Susan said. Dickie stood up.

I'll take the crayons and markers. I have the papers, all the pictures."

Dickie picked up his picture.

"Great. Now, let's go and see what the other kids are doing."

That was better.

Dickie waited.

She mustn't ruin this sweet boy.

"We're friends," she said. Susan felt like she was watching herself do something.

"It's okay because we're buddies." It felt like a movie to her, like she was watching a movie of herself and Dickie, and she was two Susans. Like she was in a different world. Then she thought, I'm going crazy. I don't want to.

Hearing voices outside the closet door frightened her. She stopped, waiting, waiting, hoping the voices would go away. Her heart pounded, and she could hear it in her chest. No one knocked on the door or tried to open it. After a few minutes, she unlocked the door and said, "Let's play with the others." Dickie got up and walked out, and no one said a word. A group of children were singing together, as Grace played the piano. Peter was washing the paintbrushes and cleaning up. One of the other teachers showed her kids how to outline their hands. Not one seemed to notice that she had been in the closet.

As the days went on, Susan took Dickie into the room, even though she knew, she was being crazy again. At first, she'd give him a piece of candy or a special marker. She kept watching herself and observing her behavior. Her heart pounded. The pressure increased in her temples; she could hear voices, and she knew if she did anything terrible, people would know she was a bad person, a weirdo, a molester. She would get help. She wouldn't touch her sweet child. Then she smiled and gave him a hug.

"It's too crowded in here," Dickie said.

"I think we'll have to find a new place besides the storage closet," she said.

When his mother died, Larry didn't feel a huge loss or a void, only relief. Susan remembered how he had behaved.

80

He had been convicted and was distressed, and then he was motherless. Susan knew he was warped and wondered what had happened to him. She knew he had done something bad, miserable, and rotten to her, and now she was a sick person. Did Flo have a boyfriend who fucked him, was there a camp counselor, a Cub Scout leader, or a teacher? She believed she was now the same awful person as Larry and poor little Dickie was her victim. The chain continued, and now there was a more prominent, blacker splotch in the family mosaic. She had poured a fat, ugly spot into the mosaic, and there was no erasing it.

She feared she was damaged, crazed, and ruined because of Larry. Where would it end or wouldn't it? She hated herself, but she couldn't stop yet. She went to the kitchen and binged, shoving food into her mouth until she felt like bursting, but after trying that she stopped. Instead, she got under the covers in her bedroom and pretended she was sleeping. God wasn't going to help her; God was watching her ruin Dickie's life. She was behaving like she was a shoddy, atrocious, evil person. Sick individuals were ravaged and behaved like terrible people. Was it their fault? Whose fault was it, or did it matter? What matters is what happened. She watched herself touch Dickie, and she couldn't or wouldn't stop herself. Now, she had inked her story into her consciousness. Her mosaic was written and corroded. Her family was disgraced, and there was no expunging it.

Larry didn't move into the experimental program. He languished in jail because the program wasn't ready to admit him. The inmates approached him for some more dope. After Larry called Dom, Dom brought him some heroin in small plastic baggies. Larry gave them to the men again who had hurt him and hoped they would leave him alone. The guards were complicit if he gave them some dope. Larry just wanted to be left alone; his body couldn't take another attack. At twenty-four he was weak, soft, and frightened. He was a mess.

He looked through the wire mesh when Dom came, the smell of urine coming from the floor, the odor of people's bodies, and the openness of the prison with the defecating and the eating all surrounding them.

"Here, take this," Dom said as he slipped some dope through the holes of the wire mesh into Larry's hand. "Quick," Dom said. "Don't let them catch you."

The bulky guard with the nightstick stood in the corner; he was barrel-chested, had a gun in a leather holster, and wore a blue shirt with the name of the correctional institute on the pocket. Larry hated him and didn't want to be beaten with the baton.

"Hurry, hurry," Dom whispered.

The Green Grove daycare planned an outing to the beach. They were taking the kids to Cherry Island for a fun day, so they packed lunches, put together the bathing suits, put all the pails and shovels in a big duffel bag, and placed the permission slips in an envelope.

"Plenty of suntan lotion," Grace announced. "We don't want any sunburned kids."

They all went off in two vans with the Green Grove name on the side of the vehicles. The children, all twenty of them, were excited and thrilled. Even the director, Nate, came out of his office for the grand exit. "No screw-ups," he warned the staff. "I don't want any bad publicity. Get it," he said, puffing on his pipe.

"Don't worry, captain, we've got it covered," Grace said. She had a large straw hat on and a bathing suit under her Bermuda shorts and a tee.

82

The children chatted all the way into the van. Susan said, "Okay, kiddies, let's do it. Up you go into the van. Don't trip."

"Anyone forget to go to the bathroom?" Peter asked at the last minute.

Cindy, a little girl with glasses, said, "I need to go again."

They waited until Cindy returned. Peter was the driver in one van, and Grace was the other driver in a second van. Scattered helpers sang, "Row, row, row your boat," and the children chimed in.

Cherry Island was a few miles away, over the bridge and into the dunes by the ocean. It faced other coastal towns across the water. As the vans got closer, Susan saw the beaches jutting out. They turned right, parked, and poured out of the bus. The teachers loaded packs on their backs and tried to take at least one child's hand each. All the kids marched in single file into the dunes across the sand until Peter and Grace said, "Stop."

Spreading out the blankets, distributing the pails and shovels, and rubbing the suntan lotion onto each child's back and face took time, but it was a warm, balmy day, and the tide was out, so they relaxed.

Dickie looked at Susan and said, "Boy, I could draw a good picture here, couldn't I?"

"Absolutely."

Some of the kids ran into the water, and others started digging in the sand. They laughed and shouted. There were shells and sea glass to collect. After a while, the children declared they were hungry, so they sat on the blanket and ate jelly sandwiches and potato chips.

Susan wadded into the water and let the waves crash into her face. She smiled, thinking about when she and Barry had been to the ocean. After lunch, Dickie wanted to draw a picture, so Susan took him behind a dune and got him set up. "I'm taking Dickie back here 'cause he wants to draw a picture."

No one minded, and Grace said, "Go with our little Picasso. Do your thing."

They went behind the dunes and set up a large drawing pad and markers on a blanket. Susan and Dickie both started to draw, and they each checked each other's artwork.

"I like what you're doing there," Susan said. "Nice work." Then she put her hand on Dickie's back, scratching it lightly. "You like that?"

"It's okay," he said and giggled.

"Shhh," she warned.

"I can't draw when you do that," Dickie said.

"I'll stop," Susan said.

He put his little hand on her back and started to scratch it. "Do you like that?" he said.

"Maybe, a little."

Just as Dickie was scratching her back, Peter stuck his head around the dune.

"What are you doing, Susan?" he asked. "I thought you were drawing."

"I'm just..." she stuttered, "scratching each other's backs. No big deal!" Susan said.

Peter reprimanded her, "Stick to drawing pictures, girl."

"Of course."

Peter said, "Dickie, stop whatever you're doing this second." Dickie stood up, and all his markers fell into the sand, and he moved away. Susan's face turned red from embarrassment, and she knew she was saved from being in a nut house like Larry or worse.

Chapter Eleven

The *Georgetown Daily News* printed an article the following day about Green Grove Daycare having a successful beach outing at Cherry Island. The paper said that Green Grove took the children to have a day of swimming and fun, with lunch included. The director, Nate Corrigan said that he was very proud of the teachers and interns and added that all the children had a terrific time.

Susan feared she was in big trouble and went to see Mrs. Norby and explained the dilemma. "I didn't do anything bad, but the thoughts were there. I think I need to see a shrink."

"I see the problem, Susan. This is an opportunity to stop the chain of events. You must tell the entire story so the doctor hears what happened to you and Ellen, and then you'll receive help; be strong and explain what happened. You'll rise to the occasion."

Susan bent her head and whispered, "I couldn't help the urges. I knew it was wrong, but I didn't do it. I had a voice telling me no, so I didn't do it. I think I was temporarily insane. I believe that what Larry did to me made me crazy."

"A voice?" Mrs. Norby asked.

"It was like there were two Susans, me who wanted to do it and me who was watching me. I never had that happen before." She hung her head and shook it, embarrassed but truthful. Her hair was stringy and unwashed. She'd fallen into depression and mainly stayed in her room since the beach outing at the daycare and called in sick.

"This isn't the life I wanted. I can't be crazy or tormented. I wanted to help the poor, the people who lived in vermin-infested apartment houses with the stench of garbage in the halls, the drunks, the homeless, the junkies. I planned on writing about them and counseling them. Mrs. Norby, what should I do?" Susan said in near tears.

"You do whatever you must to get your head in the best place. It's a big deal," Mrs. Norby said. "First things first."

Susan got up from the chair by the fireplace and went home to her room, where she got under the sheets and covered her head. She knew she was in between being well and being crazy. Mrs. Norby had said, "First things first." She dragged herself into the shower and let the hot water pound her body. She would get healthy. Unlike Larry, she had a clear choice. She let the water clean her and take away her fear. Sitting inside the shower, she held her knees to her body and yelled, "God, help me."

A few days later, Barry came to see her at Poppins Lane, the place where Susan was first molested. He walked up the flagstone path and knocked on the door with the brass knocker. Waiting and getting no answer, he rang the doorbell. When Mama came to the door, she said, "Barry, what a nice surprise."

He came in and said, "Is Susan home?"

Mama called up to Susan's bedroom and got no response, so she climbed the stairs and said, "Barry's here to see you." Mama knew about Susan's visit to Mrs. Norby.

Susan shook her head.

"He's here to see you. Maybe it will be a good thing. Give him a chance, sweetheart."

So, Susan said, "Okay," and Barry came upstairs to her room. He sat in a chair and rubbed his hands together, and Susan sat on her bed. She said, "Barry, I'm in big trouble."

"Susan, I know you; something must have happened because I don't believe you would have done something bad," he said. There was a stillness in the room, and Susan wanted to tell Barry the truth. He was her boyfriend and she loved him.

"Barry, bad things happened in this house." She closed her eyes and whispered when she admitted this news.

"Larry molested both me and Ellen, but my parents didn't know until we told them, and that's why they moved Larry and Flo to the Sagamore Way apartment. No one knew, but when Larry molested that thirteen-year-old girl, he got caught." She spoke louder now and stared at him with wide eyes.

"I knew something had happened to you; I just knew it."

She sat up. Her hair was rumpled and she held a Kleenex. "He was awful, Barry. I can't get into it, but believe me, he didn't care. When I confronted him, he laughed at me; he was such a prick."

She started to cry, and Barry put his arms around her and kissed her. "I love you. We're going to work this out. It'll be better, you'll see."

Susan felt his warmth, and for the first time in a while, she felt some hope. She smiled at him, and he smiled his crooked grin. Even though he wasn't so handsome, she loved his kindness, devotion, and intelligence. He was a decent person, and he believed in her. She couldn't let him go. They took a walk outside and went to the park where the ducks swam in the water as the ping of tennis balls echoed. They sat by the pond, took their shoes off and lay down on the grass, dangling their feet in the water, talked, hugged, and cried.

The new program got started and Larry was moved to Fort Devens in Ayers, MA. He said goodbye to his friend Aaron and promised to write. They liked discussing Kennedy, Charles Manson, and Eichmann. "Let me know how you make out in that place. I'd be interested in hearing if it helps any," Aaron said.

Larry went in a van with the correctional institute name stamped on the door. When he got there, he was put in a room with another guy named Lorenzo, who looked like a prizefighter. They each had a desk and a twin bed with a mattress, sheets, and a blanket. There was a bathroom that all twelve inmates used. It was a far better deal than what he'd been used to. He took a shower, changed into fresh tan-colored inmate clothes, and went to the meeting room where all the selected men were gathered.

The group leader, Saul, had a short beard, and glasses, and was in his mid-forties. He looked okay. The guys in the room ranged from twenty to sixty. Some were in bad shape with pot bellies and a lot of grey, unkempt hair, and some were slim and pale with vacant eyes. All twelve of them stared at one another. No one could say anything about anyone else because they all had sexually abused children. They were scum, the bottom of the barrel, and they all had this huge defect, no matter what their background was or how much money they had.

Saul began by saying, "Just so you know, we are recording these sessions. This is our first try at this type of program so we need to keep precise notes. Let's proceed. All kinds of people are sexual abusers; they come in all shapes and sizes. Men with beards, college students, older men, young guys, men with muscles, and some skinny… junkies, actors, rabbis, doctors, lawyers, priests, ministers, novelists, monks, Cub Scout leaders, teachers, counselors, and politicians. Some sexual predators have attended substandard schools, and endured brutality, but some have grown up comfortable and well-fed. There are no distinctions, but I'll tell you, no lie can live forever."

On the blackboard behind Saul, these words were written.

As you know, sexual addicts make sex a priority more important than family, friends, and work. Sex becomes the organizing principle of your life, and you become willing to sacrifice what you cherish most to preserve and continue your unhealthy behavior. Men with sexual addiction often experience patterns of out-of-control sexual behavior.

"All you guys are sexual molesters but are fortunate to be in this new experimental program. We will talk about what happened to you, what you did, and how to stop doing it. Since you all have this problem in common, there is no need to bully anyone. You're all the same, so no need to pick on anyone. Get it? I hope so. I hope you'll bond, share, and become buddies. This program is designed to help you stop doing these unlawful things. Now, if each of you would introduce yourselves and say something about how you got here, that would be terrific. Who wants to start?"

Larry looked around but didn't say anything. Neither did anyone else for a while. They went around the room and when they got to Larry, he said, "I'm here because I raped a thirteen-year-old girl." No one said anything, but Larry knew he could say a lot more, even though he stopped. He wasn't all that comfortable. One guy said he'd fucked his sister's girlfriend, another said he messed with two little girls, and one person said that his uncle did him so he screwed his cousin. Oon and on it went, and they all were perverts; that was the essence of it.

Larry assessed the eleven men. Immediately, he liked the old over-the-hill actor with long gray hair and looked like he'd lived several lives. His skin was weathered, eyes hooded, and he sat with a French cigarette, Gitane, dangling unlit from his mouth and a newspaper in his lap. His name was Trevor; he talked about his father who beat him up, and his mother who'd been murdered. He'd risen to the top of his field but now was coming clean. "I know what it's like not to have a dad."

89

Saul said he wanted each of them to talk about the time they committed this illegal act and what was going through their minds at the time.

Larry wasn't sure what to say, but he tried. "I thought the girl was cute and I got friendly with her 'cause she lived next door. I wanted to fuck her. I took her key and came into her room at midnight. I liked young girls. Who wouldn't, right?"

Saul said, "That's a good start. Thanks, Larry."

The group was asked to write one page about themselves and bring it to the session the following day. They needed to get to know one another.

Larry wrote, "I grew up normal and had a mother and father. My dad was a medical assistant at the hospital. He never made it as a doctor, but he assisted in the surgery room and gave the instruments to the surgeon when needed. I loved my father, but he dropped dead at the age of forty-four when he was playing racquetball, and that changed my life. My mother had a strong personality and bossed me around. I did what she wanted so she'd leave me alone. She had boyfriends. I didn't like that, so I stayed in my room, wrote, and didn't do much else; I was a loner. Then we moved to Massachusetts, and I'm here now."

The inmates revealed their stories in dribs and drabs. Even though they had common problems, they were reluctant to talk about them. It took a few weeks of prodding, but Saul got them to open up. "As you know, we are recording each session. Now, let's proceed. I want to hear about what happened to you so we can trace this behavior. There is a chain," Saul said in week three. "We know this from our discussion and our studies. Nothing starts from nothing. I want each of you to tell one another what sexually perverted act was done to you to push you in this direction."

Larry hunched his shoulders and tried to disappear, but he knew that was useless. He and Lorenzo, his roommate, had already privately discussed what was happening and how everyone would have to tell their story. They were prepared, and Larry had been rehearsing his tale in his head at night before he went to sleep.

Larry's turn came. "When I was ten years old, my father had been gone for four years, and my mother had a boyfriend. His name was Charlie. He was some kind of salesman and he made decent money. He sold appliances, worked for Sears, and was always bragging about how many dishwashers or stoves he sold. Kenmore, that was the brand. My mother liked him and Charlie started paying some of our bills so life got a little better. More groceries, my mother was in a better mood. Charlie slept over and then it began. Because we had a small place, I had a tiny bedroom and it was in the middle of the night. Charlie came into my room and said, 'Hey kid, wake up.' I didn't understand at first what he was doing in my room. I was a pure innocent kid. The dude started pulling down my pajama bottoms. I go, 'What the hell,' but Charlie whispered, 'Keep your voice down. Shh.' "

Then he started messing with me, started shoving his dick into my asshole. I go, "Don't do that to me."

Charlie said, "Take it easy. Shh, don't make so much noise." He mounted me from behind.

"The agony was colossal. I wanted to yell, but instead, I held my pain in. Charlie entered me and went back and forth, moaning. I put my face into my pillow, muffling the sound coming from my mouth. The discomfort was enormous. I just wanted to get it over with. Finally, when the asshole finished, all this wetness started running down my inner thigh, blood and semen. Then he said, "Now, don't you say a word to your mother, kid. If she makes me leave, you won't have enough money for food. There won't be any steaks in the freezer. I pay the bills for the electricity and heat. You'll suffer big time, and it'll be all your fault. Your mom will be pissed. You hear me?"

"I just shoved my head down and buried my noggin and face back into the soft pillow.

The shooting pain inside of my body accumulated each fuckin time Charlie molested me. I couldn't outrun the throbbing. I tried to sleep at a friend's house, but that was only once in a while. Plus, I didn't have a lot of friends and there weren't any relatives around. One older cousin came; he was a lawyer and helped my mother with her taxes. He wasn't all that friendly and I didn't feel close to him. I was afraid to tell him. Finally, I complained that I was lonely and asked if we could move. When I was sixteen, we moved to my aunt and uncle's house up in Massachusetts."

After his talk, Trevor approached Larry and said, "Listen, I'm sixty-seven. Don't throw away your life. I'll help you if you want."

Trevor told his story, when it was his turn. "I became an actor and enjoyed success. Young gay men waited outside my door at night, waiting to be chosen. I preferred children because I had been sexually molested by my father's friends, sometimes two in one night. Maybe my father set it up. I never knew. I do know he beat me up, and I hated him. I went along because of my fear. When I was famous, I abused boys. It was my revenge."

When Dad came home and sat down with the family for dinner that night, he said, "I have something to share with you." The family looked at him and waited. Susan and Ellen were particularly interested, although the entire Stern group at the dinner table now knew about what Larry had done to them. Nobody discussed it, but they knew.

"Larry shared with the group at this new program what happened to him. It means that Flo had this boyfriend

92

named Charlie when Larry was ten, and while Flo slept, he came into Larry's room and sexually abused him. Larry was horrified, but Charlie threatened him and said if Flo kicked him out, Larry wouldn't be eating steaks, the electric bills wouldn't be paid, and his mother would be poor. So, Larry put up with this abuse. Sometimes, he'd go to a friend's house, but Larry never had a lot of friends, so he was stuck at home. Finally, he implored his mother to move, saying he was lonely." Dad shook his head in disgust.

Everyone just stared at one another without saying a word. Then Jeffrey said, "What a holy mess."

"No wonder," Mama said.

Susan and Ellen stared at each other, and then Susan said, "I thought about abusing Dickie," and she hung her head in shame.

Dad said, "We know that psychological problems can be very mixed and not everyone reacts the same way, but a large percentage repeat these behaviors. That seems like the pattern more often than not because I see it in the clinics. It's a mess."

"What to do now?" Mama asked.

"We are a sorry-looking family at this point, aren't we?" Jeffrey said.

"We are," Dad said.

"We could move away," Mama suggested.

Barry, Susan and Ellen nodded in agreement.

"We could, but I'm not sure," Dad said. "First, I have my practice at the hospital. Next, we have this house, which we all love. Third, we have our lives."

Mama said, "But we wouldn't be worried about what the citizens of Georgeport were saying about us."

Ellen said, "You know as bad as this is, we are all talking about these things for the first time. Before, not one of us discussed it, except maybe Susan and me, and even that was difficult at first."

Odell, the maid, popped her head in the door and said, "Mrs. Stern, do you want dinner served? I don't mean to be disrespectful, but I gotta know 'cause it's all cooked."

"Yes, Odell, please serve the food; whoever wants to eat can have some. We certainly can't skip our supper."

No one said a word as Odell served dinner. Everyone took something and started to eat.

Susan said, "Oh, you made my favorite thing, your delicious coleslaw. Thanks, Dell."

Odell smiled and shook her head, saying, "You are welcome, my child."

The dinner was fried chicken, potato salad, coleslaw, and homemade cornbread, and for a few minutes everyone ate in silence.

Dad said, "I have an idea. What if we came out and discussed this problem in the open?

"Then maybe we could generate enough support to create a unit in the hospital where people get treatment for this horrible problem. If we did this, we would feel better and be doing something good for the community. You know making lemonade. It would be huge and a great deal of work and courageous, but think about it."

"Do you mind if I have a glass of wine? Susan asked.

"Since when did you start drinking?" Lily asked.

"Mama, I've been having a meltdown. It's been stressful."

"You better keep it moderate," Dad said.

"Give me a break for now, okay?" Susan said.

Ronnie watched her take a drink and said, "Watch out, or you'll be going to AA with me."

"Let's get back to the topic on the table," Dad said. "And could you pass me the platter of chicken, Susan," he added.

Ellen said, "You know this is a fabulous idea, Dad. I think you have just saved this family."

"Your father is a very smart man, sweetheart. That is one of the reasons I married him."

That brought a smile to everyone's lips.

"What do we do first?" Dad asked.

Jeffrey said, "We make a list of our priorities and go through it, one by one."

"First, Larry has to go through the treatment program," Susan said. "That'll take twelve to eighteen months."

"Correct," Dad said.

"I have to get treatment," Susan said.

"You'll do it, my firecracker," Barry said. He was now officially Susan's steady boyfriend and ate regularly at their dinner table.

Everyone in the family wanted to work on the project.

"I know about addiction," Ronnie said, thinking of the man with the mustache who had turned around in his seat and warned her about how dangerous it was for her to be going off with strange men. Her neediness pushed her to take risks; she could have been raped, thrown on the side of the road, and left for dead. She needed to give back and help others.

"Maybe I will help draw up something," Jeffrey said. "Barry, you can help."

"We can draw up some working documents. We will brainstorm with Dad."

"Can we go play, Grandma?" Amy asked. "Louie and me are restless."

Mama smiled and said, "Of course." Then she called, "Odell, would you give the kids some cookies."

Susan found her calling. This is what she was meant to do. Could it be any clearer? Does God work in strange ways? She was going to learn and help others; that's her future.

Ellen said, "You'll need a trauma nurse. Trauma care will be my specialty."

"Isn't that amazing how you talked about trauma?" Susan said.

"And you said it would all work out. We're coming full circle."

The evening went on, and the discussion continued. It was the beginning of something important for the Stern family. Something very significant. Susan kept thinking of the family mosaic and how this was so unexpected. She had been so worried when Ronnie's life had gone off course. She couldn't believe that life could go in such unexpected directions; worse than you imagined. People were hurting you in unpredictable ways. Tricks, lies, disappointments, and enemies. Susan wondered what would happen next and saw how the family wanted to act. The excitement in the room was contagious, and the members of the Stern family talked with renewed vigor. She hadn't known what God had in store for her, but she anticipated how this family's mosaic was becoming a beautiful story.

PART TWO

Chapter Twelve

Dad went to see Judge Fuller, who was strongly interested in the treatment agenda. As soon as he settled in the judge's office, Dad said, "I want to raise money for the new unit at the hospital, a new clinic for treating sexual abuse and trauma, and counseling for both the offenders and victims."

"I think that's a sterling proposal. You know why I have been so interested in this subject?" Judge Fuller asked.

"No, but if you'd like to share, I'd like to hear," Dad said.

"A long time ago my brother had a little girl and they had this boy who lived next door who offered to babysit. He was very gentle and kind to their child and used to sit in the rocking chair and hold her. She loved it. My brother and his wife should have stopped it, but foolishly they let it continue. When their daughter was four years old, the boy started to touch her but told her not to tell. Of course, by then, she was very fond of him, so she didn't say a word."

"I don't like where this is going," Dad said.

"Well, they came home early one evening; his wife wasn't feeling well and found their daughter in her bedroom with her panties off."

"Oh no!"

"Right, my poor brother never got over the guilt. Their daughter has been in therapy all her life."

"I'm so sorry," Dad said.

"His wife's addicted to pills."

"It never stops," Dad said.

Dom jumped into his trusty Valiant and drove to Poppins Lane. Walking up the flagstone path, unannounced, Odell answered the door.

"What are you doing here?" she asked.

"Why, Dell, I just thought I'd stop by. See how everyone's doing."

"So, you can gloat?"

Susan was listening and smiled. That Odell was fearless, she thought.

"Why'd you say that? That's not nice," Dom said, with a smirk on his face.

"You're one charming son of a bitch, Dominic Sharp." Odel looked directly into his eyes.

"I'll pretend I didn't hear that. Is Susan here?"

"I'll go see," Odell said, leaving Dom at the door. When she spotted Susan, Odell asked, "What do you want me to do?"

Susan stood up and said; "Thanks, Dell. I'll take it from here."

As she went to the front door and stared through the screen at Dom, dressed in a black T-shirt and jeans, she said, "Go away. I have no interest in talking to you. If you return, I will take out a restraining order to keep you away."

He looked at her and shrugged his shoulders. "I just wanted to see how you were doing," Dom said. "I'm on my way to the gun shop in Pembroke."

"We have nothing to discuss. Go away."

"I'm sorry you feel that way, Susan."

"Why wouldn't I feel that way, Dom? You used me and hurt me. You're not my friend, and you know it. Now leave."

He turned, walked down the flagstone path, and drove away in his beat-up Valiant.

On his way back to Rhode Island, he stopped at a gun shop in Pembroke. He and the owner were buddies, and Dom liked to chat. Scottie was an old fellow who wore flannel shirts and had a fat cigar hanging from his mouth. They discussed the gun industry and what was new and hot in the market.

Dom bought some bullets and a new cleaning kit because he liked to keep his gun collection in the best of shape. Showing off his firearms was a big deal for Dom who had yet to figure out what he wanted to do with his life. He mostly liked bedding pretty girls, drinking Miller beer, living at home, and working at the swimming pool company.

On his way down Route 95, snow started to fall, making the roads slippery. It was March, but in New England, weather was fickle. The weather was getting worse, and it was close to five o'clock when folks headed home from work, so the highway became crowded.

The heat in the car kept Dom's hands warm. Maybe Dom was anticipating a tasty dinner at his suburban home with its modern kitchen.

Susan read the newspaper article later in the week. A woman who fought with her husband and wanted to leave him was having a problem getting away. She drank too much alcohol and got into her car, smoking cigarettes and cursing. She was driving too fast, lost control of her car, and swerved into oncoming traffic. She hit Dom's Valiant smack on the driver's side; he wasn't wearing a seatbelt. He was killed instantly. The woman's car rolled over, and she was killed. Other vehicles also became involved. It was a miserable scene, and as the traffic backed up, emergency vehicles arrived, taking folks to nearby hospitals while the highway patrol cleared the roadway. Dom's parents were later notified, and his sister, Barbara, was extremely distraught.

Susan shook her head and went into the kitchen and said to Odell, "You'll never guess what happened."

"What you talking about, girl?" Odell said as she scrambled an egg for Mama.

"Dominic Sharp was killed by a drunk driver on Rt. 95."

100

"You must be kidding," Odell said.

"No, he was here, we talked to him, and he left. Now he's dead," Susan said.

"Well, I'll be damned. That poor fellow. I guess we put the spook on him," Odell said.

"Life is full of surprises, isn't it?" Susan said.

"You got that right, girl," Odell said as she slipped the fluffy egg onto the plate and went to serve Mama in the dining room.

Dad attended a hospital board meeting with a group of ten people: doctors and a few administrators. They were all medical people and had a vested interest in the hospital in Georgeport. He stood up and announced, "I have a new proposal. I want to suggest that we start a program for sexually abused children and molesters, as well. I know this is a huge undertaking, but because of my family's experience, I would like to organize a new clinic to help this unfortunate population. If we raise money, we will become known for an excellent clinic and people will come from all over for help. I have already spoken to a few experts and my family is ready to get involved. I would like to hear your reaction to this idea." Dad looked around the conference table and then sat down.

"This is an excellent notion. I am very pleased because our community has taken a huge hit with the scandal, and this program would turn the citizens' opinions around. We could make it state of the art, get some experts to sit on the board, including a few well-known psychologists, and attract a lot of money. I am totally in favor," Dr. Donaldson, the past board president, said.

An attractive woman, Gail Collins, who had been the administrative assistant to Dr. Stern for six years, stood up. "I'm so pleased to hear of this program. I applaud Dr. Stern and want to help in any way I can. Here! Here!" She sat down, smiled, and then resumed her note-taking.

A doctor from the pediatric division, Dr. Longmore, stood up. He was young and full of energy. "I can't tell you how needed this is. A human, healing environment for little kids who have been abused this way is definitely necessary. We need to help the families and provide outpatient care, as well. I ache for all the children who have been sexually abused. This way, more families will come forward." A few people got up and went to the table where coffee and donuts were spread out. Some talked quietly among themselves and sat down with their refreshments.

The pediatrician continued, "I want a special section for pre-kindergarten children. I'm willing to head this up; put me down for this particular program. Thank you, Dr. Stern."

Dad nodded.

Dr. Frankel, a dental surgeon, asked, "Is anyone concerned about the reaction in Georgeport to a clinic on sex? Will the citizens worry molesters will go out and abuse their kids?"

"We'll have to do a huge ad campaign and reassure the community that, in the long run, this is good for them. I know this is a giant undertaking so I ask all of you to let me know in what way you would like to contribute. We need help, ideas, money, experts, and all kinds of guidance. It could take five years to get this clinic off the ground. I want to begin now." Dr. Stern said. Then he sat down and felt a profound exhaustion come over him. It had been a long journey to this point.

Dad decided to take a leave of absence and planned to visit a few facilities specializing in sexual molestation. He brought his assistant, Gail Collins, and told her to take copious notes. They'd only be as good as their research.

There was a clinic in the western part of the state, where a farmhouse was built, with a lovely meeting room, comfortable furniture, a fireplace, and a dining room with delicious food. He liked the feel and mood of the facility and wanted something like this for the Georgeport Regional Hospital. There were rooms for meetings, art therapy, family sessions, and individual counseling. Dad especially approved of the alert list for children, warning them what was inappropriate and what they should look out for. Outside, there were all kinds of recreational facilities: swimming, archery, and volleyball.

Susan began her therapy and went twice a week to Dr. Edwards. He had graduated from Harvard and practiced in Boston. She liked seeing him and decided she would open up and tell him whatever came to her. He listened but didn't say too much. When he spoke, he commended her. "You had the urge, but you didn't act. That was your healthy self, the voice that told you not to do this. You liked the child, you didn't want to hurt him; this was your conscience, the thriving part of your mind. I'm very pleased, Susan."

Larry continued his special program and went five days a week. He and Trevor became friends. Larry started smoking the French cigarette and the other men made fun of him. Larry didn't care.

Barry continued law school and planned to specialize in sexual offenders. "I'll charge thirty-five dollars per hour. If people are in trouble, they'll pay the going rate," he said. Susan loved it when he talked like this. She promised that when Dr. Edwards said she was well enough, she would marry Barry, but not before.

"I'm not messing up our lives until I feel this is under control. It's the only way, Bar," she said one evening when they were out to dinner.

"I know, I know, but we've been together a long time. I want a family. Don't you?"

"Yes, but I want a healthy family, not a fucked up one."

Barry laughed. "You're my firecracker. That's why I love you."

At another dinner six months later Susan commented, "The plans for the new clinic are coming along. They're going to put it over at Cameron Park. There are five acres that we can buy for the building, and it will have all kinds of rooms for recreation, residential rooms, and centers for parents and children. You should see the blueprints. Come over, and I will show you,"

"How far is it from the hospital?"

Three miles tops. The place is perfect. My father's very excited."

Barry said, "You know, there are a lot of ways daycare centers can prevent these horrendous events from happening. They could install surveillance cameras to monitor and evaluate all interactions between employees and children. Most daycare centers could perform extensive background checks, and some could implement policies that prevent employees from gaining private access to the children. Just think how different things will be when these policies are enforced."

"Excellent," Susan said, nodding.

"I hear Ronnie left school and is becoming an addiction counselor, and Ellen is studying to be a trauma nurse. And you're an Expressive Therapist. We've got the whole family practically involved. What an accomplishment. Don't you think?"

She looked down at her hands and blushed.

"Okay, Susan, pick a date for the wedding. I've waited long enough."

"Oh, I didn't tell you one more thing about Larry."

104

"Yes, yes, tell me." Barry raised his hands.

Susan knew he understood. "Larry will be moving to California to write for some studio that does television shows. He finally will become a real writer and get paid. Evidently, he submitted a script and they accepted it."

"Wonders will never cease, will they?"

"I've started running again," Susan said.

"You look great."

"Barry, I love you."

He smiled and took her hand across the table. He waited.

"Six months," she said. "In six months, we'll get married."

"Now you're talking."

Susan looked at him with a serious face. "I have one thing I must do before."

"What?" Barry said.

"I have to go see Dickie. I must go see his family and talk to them. I owe them a visit. Dickie is such a sweet boy, and I almost damaged him. It weighs on my mind every day." Susan looked down at the tabletop. "I talked to Dr. Edwards about this over and over again. The guilt's ripping me apart."

"I understand, but you didn't do anything wrong," Barry said. "They don't need to know everything in your head, Susan. If there's anything I can do, tell me." He reached out and took her hand.

"Just stand next to me."

"Always, sweetheart," he said as he kissed her hand.

Dickie Martine lived in a run-down house on the side of a country road. His mother, Inez, was a drunk and an overeater. She had a beautiful face, but her body was corpulent and she didn't care. Often, she would sit in a rocking chair, watch television, and eat chips and dip. Sometimes she smoked cigarettes and drank beer. While she was doing this, Dickie would play by himself. He loved to draw, and he also played with the three dogs that his mother kept. Twenty-seven-year-old Inez had been with Dickie's father for a few years before he left to go to Texas to work on a farm. Inez stayed in Massachusetts and decided to live on her own, except when her sister, Pamela, came to visit.

The house was dirty and unkempt. Dishes were stacked, unwashed, in the sink. The front lawn was littered with broken toys, and an old truck stood abandoned in the driveway. If they needed groceries, they would walk to the corner store, pay too much, and walk home. Dickie went to *Green Grove* daycare for just a short time but was sent home when the family couldn't afford to pay. Dickie didn't discuss much with his mother, and she was content hugging and kissing the child. When Dickie stopped going to daycare, he missed the place. He told his mother that he had liked his teacher, Miss Susan, and she drew pictures with him, and he had enjoyed his time with her. He liked the attention.

Susan drove to the shabby house, walked up to the front door, and knocked. Dickie opened the door, and Susan said, "Hi, Dickie, how're you doing?"

He stood behind the screen door and looked at her with huge brown eyes, saying nothing. Then he went and got his mother.

Inez looked like she'd been napping and rubbed her eyes.

"Hello, who're you?" she said.

"I'm the teacher from Green Grove. I'm Susan Stern, and I'd like to talk to you."

"Why?"

"I just want to speak to you for a few minutes. Please, just a couple of minutes, and then I'll go," Susan said.

Inez stood there with her hands on her wide hips. Susan

106

remained speechless. Then, after a minute, Inez opened the door and said, "Wanna come in?" Inez turned off the television, and Susan sat in a comfortable chair while Inez sat in the rocking chair. Dickie stood by the doorway and watched and listened.

"I like your son and I wanted to tell you this," Susan said, as she twisted her hands together and sweated.

"Yes. he is a fine little fellow," Inez said, lighting a cigarette. "Do you have children?"

"No."

"Someday, if you have a child, you'll see how it feels," Inez said.

Susan had tears in her eyes. "I'm sure you're right," she repeated.

Then Susan wiped her eyes with a tissue and turned to Dickie and said, "Dickie, I wanted to see you."

He looked at her, and then he ran away.

"Is there anything I can do to make your life easier?" Susan asked.

Inez hesitated and thought for a minute or two. Then she said, "You know Dickie liked drawing with you. Maybe you could come here and just sit with him for an hour once a week and draw pictures? I'll be here. I know he loved drawing with you because he told me."

Susan said, "If Dickie agrees, I'd be happy to do that."

"Dickie, come here baby. Mama wants to ask you a question," Inez yelled.

The child returned and looked at her from the doorway.

Inez explained what she had in mind. "Do you want this if I watch?"

He looked at Susan, and then he nodded his head.

"Let's try it," Inez said.

"I'll come on Fridays at three o'clock. Does that work for you?" Susan asked.

"Yes, very good."

Susan got up and left. She was relieved that the visit had gone as well as it had. She'd bring art supplies when she returned. Thank you, God, thank you, God, Susan said to herself.

Chapter Thirteen

Friday came, and Susan drove to Dickie's home. She had a bag of art supplies: markers, crayons, pictures of birds and cats, photos of kids playing in the sand, airplanes, and tigers. Susan carried a large pad of paper and a few small scissors that Dickie could handle. She was nervous and excited because she liked this child, had almost hurt the boy, and wanted more than anything to secure a healthy relationship with the youngster.

When she walked up the wooden steps to the screen door, Susan heard a voice and turned. "Hi, there," Pamela said as she brought the split wood for a fire. "Dickie's been waiting for you." Pamela wasn't much to look at, but she was sturdy as a boxer. Her hands were dirty, her cheeks smudged, and her face was sweaty. Her soiled white tee shirt stretched across her muscled body. She was the worker of the two sisters.

Susan walked into the house and saw Dickie standing by the table in the television room. He crossed his arms and didn't say anything.

"Hey, there, Dickie," Susan said. "I'm ready, and I see you are too! Let's get started."

Shyly, Dickie sat down and waited.

Inez said, "Hi," and then settled down to watch as Dickie and Susan began drawing.

They sat at the round table and scattered the supplies. Dickie's mother sat on the rocking chair after she lowered the television's volume, crossed her legs, and put her hands in her lap.

"Here, buddy, I brought some great pictures, and you can decide what you want to draw." She spread the photos out and showed them to the child. He smiled broadly, and they drew and drew. One picture was of a bird with a blue head and a pink breast; one was of three puppies on top of each other; one was of a rooster with a red crown, white breast, and a sloping back looking very serious. Susan smiled when Dickie said he couldn't decide what to paint first. They were off to a good start. Inez observed closely but then relaxed as time went by. Pamela stacked the wood near the fireplace with a slight smile.

Susan and Barry were married at 2 Poppins Lane in front of the mantel in the living room with the same rabbi who had married Ronnie and Chad. Barry wasn't Jewish, although he was fine with Rabbi Pressman, who came in his tuxedo and performed the ceremony. Susan wore a cream-colored dress, tea length, Ellen was the bridesmaid, and Jeffrey was the best man. Barry's folks attended; they looked modest but respectable. His father worked in the silver factory a mile away and wore a polyester suit from Sears & Roebuck, and his mother, a stout lady who baked and sewed for a living, dressed in a simple blue dress scattered with small pink flowers that she'd had made herself. Barry's siblings all came and stood erect and somber. The two brothers looked like Barry, and his sister, with auburn hair and freckles was the replica of the mother. They were warm to Susan, and she liked them because they were decent people. Susan loved Barry and knew he would be a fine husband. She couldn't ask for more because he was her best friend.

Mama made a delicious luncheon for the wedding guests and served crabmeat, chicken, and tuna salad. Odell scooped out a watermelon and filled it with fruit balls. The wedding cake was a pink champagne cake, Susan's choice, with buttercream icing.

The married couple took a one-week vacation to Quebec and Nova Scotia. Susan had brushed up on her French so she could converse, and Ellen, who was proficient, drilled her. The excitement was catchy, and everyone was happy because they felt they had turned a page in their family saga.

When Susan and Barry returned to Georgeport, they moved into an antique rented home on the south end; it had salmon-colored clapboards and crooked wide pine floors. A trestle and ivy were covering it as they walked in. The walkway was winding and twisted, and the picket fence was white and needed a fresh coat of paint. They could walk downtown, and Barry could stroll to his law office on the corner of Main and Mountain Ave. He set up his office with a sign that said, "Specializing in Sexual Abuse Cases," and before long, people were coming in to see him for all kinds of problems. There were a multitude of types of predicaments, such as rape, sexual molestation, improper touching, a slew of incidents such as athletes taking advantage of girls at high school, and presidents of companies expecting favors from secretaries. Barry was busy as ever, and Susan smiled when he came home and shook her head back and forth, listening to his stories.

She was also busy with her expressive therapy cases while waiting for the clinic to open at the Georgeport Regional Hospital. Putting together a sexual harassment clinic was more complicated than anyone imagined. Focusing on one population, college-age kids, Dad discovered that 18-34 year-olds was the highest risk group. There was a considerable tendency for both men and women to underreport. The schools urged the victims to find a safe place to report and document what happened. Then to seek help. There would be a hotline set up. The victims were warned that there was only a 72 to 96-hour time for collecting evidence. Schools were setting up security guards to patrol the campuses. They were offering transportation services.

Years later, when Susan looked at the history of the second women's liberation movement, she was reminded that in 1964, President Johnson passed Title VII to protect women in the workplace. Until then, women employees silently endured sexist treatment and they put up with lecherous bosses. Sexism was legally and socially addressed in the 1960s. Dr. Max Stern, however, was on the cutting edge. Husbands weren't charged for beating their wives. It was customary for women in families with one car to ask for permission from the "man of the house" to take it. The early 1960s was a period of changing times, but men still wore suits, ties, and crew cuts, and women wore gloves and had bouffant hairdos.

The birth control pill was approved by the FDA in 1960. After introducing "the Pill," within ten years, 80 percent of women were using some form of birth control. 1961, President Kennedy established a "Commission on the Status of Women." This was very important because it would address women's second-class treatment. Topics such as gender equality were subtly introduced.

In 1962, Dad was still compiling ideas for the new clinic. He insisted that the center would never disclose anyone's name, and men and women, young or old, would have privacy. He promoted training so that those who wanted to study at the center would have a low student-to-faculty ratio. The faculty would work full-time, and all would have doctorate degrees. For long-term treatment patients, the residents would bunk two in a room, make their beds, and dine in a cafeteria. They would try to keep the cost on the lower end of the spectrum and provide outpatient therapy. Dad reported on all these ideas when he returned to the Georgeport Regional Hospital board meeting. Everyone was impressed, and they started to break apart into various committees and create concrete plans for the new center.

It was an exciting time but also a time of intense work. "What shall we name it?" he asked them one day as they sat around the dining room table. Everyone had a different suggestion. Nothing was decided.

They needed a fundraiser, and Mama started to discuss ideas for the gala, which she wanted to hold at the Ritz Carlton in Boston. Dad said he would bring it all up at the next board meeting.

At the board meeting, Dad said, "First and foremost is picking a chairman of the event. We need someone who cares about the subject and wants to do an outstanding job. I suggest Dr. Longmore, the pediatrician."

The people gathered around the table cheered, and Dr. Longmore blushed. "Why, I would love to do this, and I do care tremendously about sexually abused children. Thank you." Dr. Longmore was a mid-forties doctor with a young-looking face and a family of two young children. He had graduated from Tufts Medical School, and his wife was a maternity nurse at the regional hospital. It was a perfect fit.

"Wait a second," Dr. Haas, an internist with a bald head who had a practice in the hospital, said, "I don't mean to be disrespectful, Dr. Longmore, and I know your interest in this subject is high. However, Dr. Stern has been the one who has gotten this entire program up and running and has done the lion's share of work, not to mention his reasons. I think, this time, our very first gala should be headed by Dr. Stern. Next, Dr. Longmore, you will have your turn. What do you think, everyone?"

The board agreed, and Dr. Longmore said, "By all means." Then, it was put to a vote, and Dad was unanimously elected.

Dad thanked everyone around the table, and then Dad's assistant, Gail Collins, said, "We need a date for the gala, folks." There was much discussion of when to have the gala before they picked Spring. Winters were hard in New

England, so they didn't want to tempt fate. Surely, by May, the weather would cooperate, and people would be in a giving mood.

Gail, said, "We need a date and a room in an affordable hotel. I'll make some calls, see what's available, and check the prices. Who'd like to help me, and what exact dates do we have that work? Another issue is what kind of event do we want? There could be a dinner dance or just a dinner or luncheon."

Mike Bloom, the accountant, added. "All this will affect the ticket price."

Dr. Haas said, "We need to form committees. Gail, will you list all the different types of committees we'll need?"

"Yes, I think we should stop for now so I can get to work. I'll find some helpers. Let's decide when to meet next. Maybe in two weeks. There are a lot of things to consider: designing the invitations, decorations, speakers, music, food and catering, color scheme, dancing, and raffles." She looked at Dad, who shook his head and decided at that moment to give his assistant a pay raise.

Chapter Fourteen

Susan loved her little house in the south end of town. Now that she and Barry were married, they thrived in the crooked house with the crooked floors and the crooked doors. They had a bedroom with a double bed and an armoire that they bought at the local furniture store on Mountain Avenue. The two of them had walked in, and an eager salesman approached them and showed them around, giving them all the information and prices.

Barry smiled politely. "We'd just like to look for a while, please." They wanted to browse and see whether they liked the same things. Susan wasn't sure because they had never gone shopping together before. Who knew whether they would agree? Luckily, they seemed to choose similar styles and decided they would only get what they needed, although they did buy the colorful ceramic rooster that Susan had fallen in love with for the kitchen counter.

Susan planted a small garden out back that had string beans and tomatoes, and Barry hung a new lighting fixture over the dining room table. He was very handy since he had grown up doing repairs with his father. Susan learned to cook, trying a new recipe every weekend when she had the time. She would open the large *Joy of Cooking* and see where her fingers landed. One Saturday, she baked an apple pie and enjoyed the scrumptious aroma of cinnamon and apples. She served it, warm with vanilla ice cream, She smiled when Barry asked for seconds. Another Saturday, she decided to try to cook beef stew, browning the small cubes of floured-coated meat in the skillet first and then adding all the vegetables with some tomato sauce. That was a huge success. Occasionally, she put too much pepper in the recipe and forgot to take the feathers out of the chicken for soup, but mostly, she was a fast learner.

She learned to look under the bed when she was cleaning when Barry showed her the dust bunnies, and she washed a few windows inside the living room but hated cleaning the bathtub. Barry washed the kitchen floor because he had done that for his mother on Little Street. Together, they blossomed in their little salmon-colored house close to town. In the evening, when the weather was warm, they strolled to the local pub. They liked visiting the pub, sitting at the bar, talking to the locals, and chatting with Earl the bartender, who knew everything about what was happening around Georgeport.

"I hear your Dad is working on a new clinic up at the hospital," said Earl one evening as he wiped the counter. He wore a tan apron, had a mustache, and had been at the "Joy Box Saloon" for fourteen years.

"Oh, yes. We're all involved. It'll be a wonderful addition," Susan said as she sipped her glass of Beaujolais Village.

Barry drank his beer and said, "It's a huge undertaking but well worth the effort."

"When do you think it'll be ready to open?" Earl asked.

"I don't know because there are many moving parts, but it's coming together, and my Dad doesn't want it to open until it's just right." She laughed and said, "He likes everything perfect."

"Well, he's providing a needed service. That's all I know," Earl said.

Susan didn't want to get into the subject too deeply. "I think everyone will benefit."

"Oh, you better believe it. I have a friend who had that situation with a buddy who took advantage of his daughter. It was terrible. Ruined the friendship, damaged the girl, and almost broke up the marriage. It was bad," Earl said as he wiped a glass and put it back on the shelf.

116

At home that night, Barry said, "It's the talk of the town, Sue."

They made love in the double bed and discussed having a baby, but not right away.

"Maybe after the clinic's opened," Barry said, "like a celebration baby." He laughed and kissed Susan on the head.

"Well, that sounds like a plan. I'll be relieved when it's opened."

There were discussions about who would talk at the gala, and Susan said she'd be willing to tell her story. "It's the least I can do for the family after all we've gone through. People need to know and get the history straight in case there is any doubt about what happened," she said. She'd tell the story of Larry and Ellen, too, allude to the tendency to repeat the offense, without mentioning Dickie, but just referring to the subject. "That will be enough to demonstrate the problem and show people how strong an urge it is."

Mama was excited about the gala and got involved in the preparations. The development office ran the gala benefit, and the chairman was very organized since Gail Collins micromanaged Dad. Mama couldn't help herself from being overly involved. "I heard it's easier to sell tables rather than individual tickets," she said one night at dinner. Local businesses were listed according to their popularity, and the tables were priced according to their proximity to the speakers.

"You know there are law firms, doctor's offices, and a lot of services that do very brisk business in town, and we should target them as well," Dad said as he took the plate of lasagna from Odell and served himself a portion. "This smells enticing," he said.

"Thank you, Doctor." Odell smiled.

"A lot of folks on the committees are soliciting donors. It's amazing how many people know someone in different kinds of careers. It's impressive," Mama said.

Dad said, "Tickets are selling. The Silver Company down by the north end of town, the large law office on the corner of Main and Mountain, and Farnell's Hardware Store all bought tables."

"Who's speaking?" Chad asked.

"Susan and me," Dad said.

"Who else are you having to speak, Dad?" Susan asked.

"Judge Fuller, believe it or not, has stepped forward and will tell the story of his brother's daughter. His family was affected, and he has a deep interest in this subject," Dad said.

"That's very impressive," Mama said, "having the judge as a speaker."

"We need to give each category of donors a special name, like gold, pearl, silver, crystal, etc. This way, we can list it in our brochure for gala night. Think of the different ones, okay?"

"Music?" Ronnie asked.

"Yes, a musical guest and a band. I'm afraid we can't get the Beatles."

There was some laughter.

"Changing the subject, how's Larry doing?" Barry asked as he took a piece of garlic bread from the basket on the table.

"Larry's okay. He took a class in creative writing at the special program, which met daily. It's a nine-month course, and six inmates have signed up. They put out a publication, and they got funding from the National Endowment for the Arts. He's ecstatic and submitted a story or script to a show on television. I believe he got accepted. Isn't that something?" Dad said.

"I can't believe that. What a turnaround." Jeffrey nodded, showing his pleasure. Jeffrey was working on the local radio station doing interviews and sports announcements.

"I wish his mother were alive to see this. Poor Flo, she just couldn't handle the tough times," Mama said.

Odell cleared the dishes and served a fruit bowl and homemade brown sugar cookies for dessert. "I'd like to attend the gala and hear the speeches. Is there any way I can get a seat?" She stood at the table in her maid's uniform and looked at Dad and then at Mama.

"I don't see why not," Dad said. "You certainly can attend. Lily, make sure Odell has a seat at the kids' table when they do the seating and table arrangements. Right up front so you can hear your girl, Susan," Dad said with a big grin.

Ellen said, "That's so cool, Deli. I'm glad you asked."

Odell grinned widely and said, "Thank you very much, Doctor. I'll buy a new dress for the occasion.

Mama took Odell shopping, helped her pick a dress, and paid for it. Odell was so excited she told all the other maids on the bus on the way to work. They were chatting away and told their employers, and suddenly, another group of people became interested in attending the gala. The *Georgeport Daily News* ran an article about all the preparations regarding the upcoming clinic in Cameron Park. One shop started selling special dresses "For the Gala" as it said in the window. Even Lydia at Monique's featured "Frocks for the Gala and the Charity." It was growing in popularity.

Susan began writing her speech for the gala. It wasn't easy because it was so personal, but she figured she'd bring it to Mrs. Norby for final approval when she was ready. Mama suggested that Susan take public speaking lessons to improve her effectiveness on the podium. Susan considered this idea and said she would.

When I was a young girl, I had no idea what life would have in store for me, she began writing. *I'd grown up in a nice family and enjoyed my life, and then, my cousin and aunt moved in. My teenage cousin started coming into my room and doing all sorts of things to me. I pretended to be asleep. That was the only way I could handle it,* she continued. *I decided to open my eyes. I couldn't stand pretending; I didn't know what else to do. I was only ten years old.*

Susan sat at her desk and stared at the paper. Her problem had been that she wanted to tell her parents, but the difficulty was being afraid to share this information with them.

I live in a world that kept me from telling my parents that my cousin was molesting me? Why couldn't I tell them about it? Fear, ignorance, lack of communication, the times, whatever it was, I was stranded in the middle of this cage, and if I did tell them, would they believe me and take my side? If someone was being sexually abused, did they fear they wouldn't be protected? Of course, they feared this. People reacted in so many different ways.

She wrote about the eating after each time Larry came into her room, the binging and hating herself, and how she looked, then running mile after mile, the nightmares that revisited her every night. Fantasies of killing Larry. No ten-year-old child should have to experience these thoughts. She didn't know what to do. Upon learning that Larry was doing the same thing to her sister just down the hall, she experienced feelings of jealousy, shame, embarrassment, anger, and hatred. It only got worse when Larry laughed and belittled her? Was she an object, a nothing? How could this happen in her pretty home? Then, she told Mrs. Norby.

Mama started hosting dinner parties for friends to tell them about the new clinic. They came in blue silk shirts, drove

120

Mercedes, and ate steak tips, which Odell had marinated in Wishbone Italian dressing and broiled to perfection. In addition to the steak tips, there were tiny roasted potatoes, string beans, almondine, and Odell's famous coleslaw.

"We have to help these children who are in pain and abused," Mama said to the guests with a glass of wine in her hand.

Susan and Barry talked to the diners. Susan's hair was styled in a new, bouncier manner, making her look more fashionable and attractive. Ronnie and Chad attended, too. The living room was decorated with fresh flowers and candy in a silver dish. Barry discussed business, law and abused children, of course. He was seeing more and more cases. Susan watched him raise his hands for emphasis and admired his natural movements and people skills. A born lawyer, Susan thought. Sitting erect but relaxed, he appeared confident and polite.

Dad was pleased to have these gatherings. Georgeport was a small city, and its citizens needed to be educated. What they were proposing would be a progressive plan, and for a small New England community with many old-time Yankees, it was revolutionary. "But look at Pearson's, look at Harvard, look at the schools in Boston, the hospitals, the knowledge, the respect for education," Dad said. "This is a perfect place if we just correctly introduce this idea."

Chapter Fifteen

At the end of the prison's program to address the distorted thinking of sexual molesters, Dad went to see Larry and his therapist, Saul, whom he liked. At dinner that night, he shared his impressions with the family. "Saul is a passionate, dynamic fellow who believes in social justice and wants to save the souls of these sexual deviants. Odell, he is a wonderful black man."

"That is so nice to hear," Odell said as she served dinner.

"He understands the power that sexual deviants feel," Dad said. "Saul told me, "'At least no one in this group had killed or mutilated their victims.'"

"He shared his background with me; he said he had a father who molested his sister. He was a beatnik in boots and a kinky black beard, a good guy, and a skilled therapist."

Mama said, "Does Larry seem improved?"

Larry completed twelve months of intensive rehab and learned what made him a sexual predator and how to avoid relapsing. It had been a grueling ordeal in many ways. It was tortuous, revealing himself, but the other guys couldn't smirk because they were just as bad. That made it easier. One guy said he'd had intercourse with his sister, and they had done it for years. His parents were both druggies, so they were always stoned and never bought groceries. He and the sister, a skinny girl two years his junior, slept together to keep one another warm, and then they started fooling around. It felt good; they needed each other, which became their routine. Larry said that the girl didn't want to get pregnant, so they figured out about condoms, and she avoided the baby business. This continued for years until they each wanted to fool around with other people and did. Eventually, one parent overdosed, the other went to jail, and the authorities wanted to put them in a foster home, but they ran away. Who needed that supervision after all their freedom?"

The family listened, and Susan said, "I can see why they didn't want to go into a foster home."

"Another kid wanted to screw his neighbor, so he tricked her into coming over when their parents were at work, and he would do it to her in the bedroom after school. He told her not to say anything and gave her candy and stuff to keep her quiet. She got pregnant, and he was sent to jail."

"I'm glad that kid got caught," Chad said.

"Can you believe this?" Ellen asked.

Dad told them that Larry said, "They were horny and didn't care about the rules. It was as simple as that. They looked at females as sex objects, nothing more. Most people respected the rules, but these men were mistreated or ignored, so they did what they wanted. It gave them a feeling of power."

Mama said, "I cannot believe how widespread this is."

"Larry looked well; I think he even gained a few pounds," Dad told the family.

"I'm glad, because he was too thin," Mama said.

"He picked up another hobby," Dad said, or as Larry put it, "Anything to keep my horny mind off pussy." The family laughed, and Mama blushed.

"Larry said his therapist suggested he use mental discipline. He should close his mind to unwanted thoughts," Dad continued.

Susan said, "I like that approach. It takes focus and work."

Yes, he was pretty honest with me. I was impressed," Dad said. "He took up a hobby, baking. He makes chocolate chip cookies, brownies, and coffee cake in their kitchen," Dad set a cake down at the dining room table. It looked tasty and everyone helped themselves to a small slice.

Odell gave out napkins and served coffee.

As they were eating, Dad continued, "Larry said sometimes he woke up with pressure on his chest. The therapist said it was repressed trauma. Stress can overwhelm the body and cause heart muscle weakness. He gave him exercises to do. As you know, he likes to write, so he kept at it until he wrote something decent and sent it to someone in Hollywood who looked at it. He said it wasn't bad."

Susan said, "Larry has talent. Does he want to go to Hollywood and try writing for television or the movies?"

"Well, Larry doesn't have much going for him. California is nice and warm. After all the snow in New England, when he gets released from prison and the program, he told me he's heading west to Hollywood. Of course, he'll go to meetings every week. AA is fine as long as they are twelve-step meetings."

"At this point, he's all set up through letters with a one-room place in a house rented from an elderly lady. The woman sent a diagram. It wasn't much, but there was a bathroom down the hall, and he'll write in his room, and it's on the bus line to the studio where he can bring his writing. The pay's poor, but he'll persevere and eat at McDonalds, and little by little, he'll earn a living of sorts. If he messes up, he'll return to prison, which should keep him honest." Dad looked at everyone around the table.

Barry said, "It's a beginning. That's all we can hope for."

Dad said, "I'll send him a few extra bucks so he doesn't starve."

"You're a good man, Pop," Barry said.

"Larry likes being a writer and not getting in trouble. He doesn't want much, just some recognition in his writing and no more jail time. That's enough for him."

"Listen, he's lucky to get out," Ellen said. "He's led a useless, destructive life. He needs a job and maybe a few bucks in the bank. Maybe he can get health insurance and stuff like that eventually."

"He mentioned Dom and said he felt bad that 'the poor bastard got killed on the highway.' Larry doesn't have time for guns, and his parole forbids him from owning firearms. He said he got nervous whenever he saw a man with a badge."

"I had a teenager in an emergency who was date raped," Ellen said. She now worked at the Georgeport Regional Hospital and was doing trauma work. "It's pretty heavy duty when we get a case like that. There are all kinds of procedures we have to do to collect evidence," Ellen added.

"I'm very proud of you, Ellie," Dad said. They smiled at each other.

"Sorry to change the subject, but does anyone want to come hear me speak at AA? I'm giving my talk next week on my second anniversary of being sober," Ronnie announced.

Everyone clapped and gave high fives.

Jeffrey wasn't at dinner because he was working, but he got the report from Mama. The Sterns were a closely-knit family. Everyone was involved in the clinic project and Larry's welfare.

"Odell, you should make a coffee cake. This one was delicious," Mama said as she got up.

Thinking about the family tapestry, Susan realized that each member made unique and distinct contributions to the kaleidoscope of stories. The world was multifaceted. You could be a combination fighter and a poet, a bully and a gardener, a rabbi and a child molester. Thousands of allegations have been made against priests. The clergy blamed it on the sexual revolution in the 1960s. The church called it sexual permissiveness.

Susan knew that kings used to treat children like sexual

125

playthings. From the research she started after she spoke to Mrs. Norby, she learned about the slow and uneven progress that had taken place in recognizing sexual abuse. In 1953, Kinsey reported that a quarter of the girls under fourteen had been sexually abused. Molestation went on at summer and day camps by nurses, daycare workers, and youth sports organizers.

Dozens of female patients accused gynecologists of sexual abuse. It went on in the best of hospitals and clinics from Boston to Los Angeles. Susan read literature from the library and thought about the number of people walking around with knowledge and guilt about these activities. That is the tapestry we have and after she learned these facts about priests and kings and the prevalence of abuse, Susan felt released from the innocent, naïve, dark ages.

Since Penny Long was the biggest donor, Dad named one of the buildings after her. He asked her which part of the program appealed to her personally. She said that she was committed to the children who had been molested and abused sexually. Dad said he would name the building for treating the victims "The Penny Long Treatment Center." The members of the board all agreed and said they were thrilled to have this woman's donation of five million dollars. It would make their project more legitimate and famous.

Mama wanted to meet Penny Long, so Dad and Mama went to Manhattan and had dinner with her at the four-star restaurant, Chloe's on Fifth Avenue. They sat in a red leather booth at a table covered with a white tablecloth. The waiters wore black tuxedos. Mama was so excited that she purchased a new dress for the occasion. Penny Long was wearing a beautiful blue sheath, her blond hair in a chignon. She was a woman in her late fifties and looked charming and refined.

She explained her position. "I have wanted to do what you are doing, Max. All my life, I wondered about children who got abused the way I was. I couldn't say a word when I was young because my mother needed the boarders' money to pay the bills. So, I dared not stop that. We wouldn't have had groceries or electricity. Now, I want to give back. This is my way of helping other children," she said as she looked at Dad and Mama, her blue eyes peering over her half glasses.

"We're thrilled that you've come forward, Penny. Lily and I have wrestled with this problem personally, first with a nephew and our daughters. You have no idea how much energy and time we have put into this. Your donation is monumental to the clinic." Dad looked at Penny and lifted his wine glass. "I toast you, my friend. Evil wins when good people do nothing."

They ordered steaks and sat at the table for a long time, sharing life experiences. Mama and Penny clicked and decided to see one another again in New York for a shopping spree. Dad explained about the gala and what was expected of Penny.

"Oh, I won't have a problem speaking. I'm a born show-off." She laughed. "Remember when I was in the high school play, Oklahoma?" she asked Max.

They laughed and talked about some of their old classmates. One kid had been on a state championship team. Someone's daughter, Sandy, had sat in front of Dad from kindergarten to twelfth grade. None of it mattered to them now. They had both moved on with their lives. It was a warm evening, and later, Dad and Mama reported all of this to the family, like they did on many other occasions. Before they headed home, Dad and Mama visited the Mt. Sinai Hospital and talked to the head of pediatrics.

"What's the situation with child sexual abuse?" Dad asked.

A young Asian doctor sat down, wearing her blue surgical gown and cap. "I'm Dr. Joy Klum," she said as she took a thick manilla folder in her hands and opened it. "We have seen children killed and desecrated in addition to being sexually molested. There were nails and pins in their bodies," she added as she referred to her notes in the file.

Dad took a deep breath. Mama couldn't speak.

"Do you ever wonder why they do this to the children?" Dad asked Dr. Klum.

For a moment, her eyes looked down. She had a kind face. A picture of a child was on her desk; she was a mother. "I try to focus on who they are, not why they did it. But I think they do it because they like it."

"Is it that simple and straightforward?" Dad asked.

"Evil is simple," she said.

Chapter Sixteen

The local newspaper, *Georgeport Daily News*, ran Susan's profile, which began on page one and spread over a full page inside. They used her high school graduation picture and a photograph taken at the beach on Cherry Island the day the school made that visit with Dickie. The caption said, "The Doctor's Daughter." The piece, said Susan, was one of four children and Larry Fink's cousin. There was a small photo of Ellen.

On the night of the gala at the Delmont Hotel, uniformed valets were ready to serve the guests. Susan was wearing makeup and wore a long teal gown. The grand ballroom had a high ceiling with an overhead light fixture that sparkled. People swarmed around, including folks they knew. Susan was nervous, but she had gone to the public speaking professional and had a few lessons on projection, elocution and pace. In addition, she and Mrs. Norby reviewed her speech several times and took out repetitions. "I think you did a fine job, Susan. It will be very moving," Mrs. Norby said.

The evening started with drinks, hors d'oeuvres, and music. People danced, and there was much talking and observing of others. The fact that this was serious led people to discuss matters in more reverent tones. They were about to do something worthy, helpful, newsworthy, and courageous. They were leaders and were changing the world in a small but significant way. Their voices were excited and respectful.

Rock and roll music and a male star imitating Elvis Presley kept the crowd entertained. Dressed in tight pants and hair falling into his eyes, the singer shook his hips and sang *Heartbreak Hotel.* The crowd went wild and danced up a storm, jitterbugging and twisting until they fell from exhaustion.

When it was time for the speakers to get up and the crowd to quiet down, everyone sat at their tables with their checkbooks out in case they felt inspired to donate some more. Judge Fuller sat at the podium with his wife, who looked regal in a pale blue gown. Mama, stunning in a garnet frock, sat next to Dad. Susan and Penny Long sat next to each other at the main table.

Odell sat with the rest of the members of the Stern family, and she glowed in her pink dress on her large frame against her dark skin. Mrs. Norby and her husband also sat at that table.

"I am flattered to be here," Odell said when someone approached her. She stood with a drink of sherry in her hand and nodded. "This is a fine night in Georgeport," she added. "It's a wonderful night."

Dr. Haas and Dr. Longmore both went to the tables for the doctors. Susan sat at the podium and took a deep breath. She would tell her story to the town, and they would learn the truth, and then they would understand. The Sterns would show them that they were decent people and anyone could have this happen, not just Jewish people who owned a pink Victorian house and a red Cadillac convertible.

Gail Collins, Dad's assistant, was wearing a navy blue gown with decolletage and looked lovely. A ten-piece band provided music. Dad looked handsome in a tuxedo, and Mama was radiant. Susan danced with Barry and smiled at everyone.

"Nervous?" Barry asked.

"Petrified." Susan thought about how she would put herself out there, be her real self, and speak from her heart.

"My little firecracker will do just fine," he said as he spun her around the dance floor.

When the band began playing the twist, Odell got up by herself, turned her wide hips in the hot pink dress, and

130

swayed back and forth. People stopped and watched and clapped. Light on her feet, Odell twirled around, grinning widely. There was a young, handsome man in a white dinner jacket who reminded Susan of Dom. He was dancing the twist in a clumsy way but drunk and happy. She turned her face away.

The overhead lights blinked, and people went to sit at their assigned tables. Dad got up at the podium to speak.

"I am here tonight to mark a highlight for our community. We are about to tackle a problem that has been ignored for much too long. I am talking about the sexual abuse of children, our children. Georgeport will no longer tolerate this horrid behavior. People all over, in other towns and cities, should stop ignoring this damaging crime. We must protect our youngsters. We are decent, caring folks; we must step up to the plate and say, 'Enough is enough.' Here in Georgeport, Massachusetts, we are going to build a life-altering clinic to treat the victims of sexual molestation and try to rehabilitate the abusers. Now in the 1960s, we must begin! I ask you for your support!"

Everyone in the room rose and applauded.

"There are envelopes on your plates, and we ask you to donate. Now, our first speaker is my daughter, Susan. She and her sister, Ellen, were sexually abused." There were gasps from the audience, mutterings, whispers, and nodding of heads. "Please listen to her story."

Susan rose, stepped to the podium, and adjusted the microphone.

"When I was born, I cried in the dark, afraid, because I didn't know what had happened to me. When I became a young girl, I had no idea what was in store for me. Just as all of us don't know, I had no clue. My life seemed fine at first. I lived with my nice family and had a comfortable home. I had siblings and caring parents. Life was flowers

131

and hopscotch and Dick and Jane. Then our cousin, Larry, and his mother came to live with us. His dad had died, and Larry had been lonely. He moved in, lived on the third floor, and was quiet."

People in the audience whispered to one another. Susan heard bodies moving, but she stayed focused. "Then my world and my sister's Ellen's world changed. Larry was sixteen years old, I was ten, and Ellen was nine. As I said, my cousin was a recluse most of the time. Once, he took us for ice cream sodas at the local luncheonette. Then Larry started coming into my bedroom at night when I was asleep. He would slip into my room in his pajamas, take off his glasses, and get on top of me. He'd start rocking back and forth while I pretended to be asleep. I kept my eyes closed because I didn't know what else to do, and, at ten years old, I was scared."

Susan hesitated and then said, "What I am about to say might upset you, but I have to go on." Waiting for a moment to collect her breath, she caught Barry's eyes. He nodded his head in approval.

"Larry got so worked up that he released himself all over my sheets. I had to clean it up so the maid wouldn't find it in the morning. I opened my eyes. I couldn't stand it anymore. Larry looked at me and said, 'Oh, my special one, you're awake.' I asked him why he called me his special one, and he replied that I was his very special girl, and that was why he couldn't help but come into my room every night. I thought that was flattering but odd because even I knew, at the tender age of ten, what he was doing was wrong. He was my cousin, and I was just a child. We had intercourse after I stopped pretending to be asleep; it was painful and upsetting. I was unprepared for this."

Again, the people in the audience whispered and moved. Susan heard the shuffling.

132

"After Larry left my bedroom at night, I went to the kitchen. My emotions were in turmoil, and to calm myself down, I started to binge. I ate hordes of food, got fatter, and felt very bad about myself. I couldn't stop, and I couldn't look at myself in the mirror. Then one night, Ellen, my sister, who slept down the hall, said to me that Larry was coming into her room and fooling around with her. I replied that he was doing the same thing to me. I said, 'He calls me his special one.' Ellen laughed and said, 'That's what he calls me.' "

There were gasps from the audience and chairs moving. Susan stayed on script.

"I was furious, hurt, outraged, shocked, and upset. I ran to Larry's room, knocked on his door, and told him how angry I was. He laughed at me and called me a baby. He didn't care. He was cruel, condescending, and indifferent."

Again, Susan stopped and looked at the audience. Then she said, "I so wanted to be healthy and normal, so I ended my binging and started running. Every single day, I ran a little more each morning. I kept a dream journal. I had nightmares. I dreamt of stabbing Larry with the kitchen knife. I wanted to tell my parents, but the words wouldn't come out. I thought about telling my brother. I was unable to. I finally talked to my friend and teacher, Mrs. Norby. She lived down the street and had helped me with my writing. I went to see her and asked her to keep my secret, and told her everything. She rescued me and had my Mama come to her house, and together with my sister, we devised a plan to get Larry out of the house. Mrs. Norby explained what Larry was doing to me was illegal, and he could go to prison for twenty years. My parents helped him and his mother move to an apartment. Then Larry raped the thirteen-year-old girl in the next-door apartment, got his jaw broken by the father, and got arrested."

She took a deep breath and told herself to go on.

"As you can imagine, this entire part of my life has been a terrible ordeal. From my nice, comfortable home life, I became a living wreck. No one knows what's in store for them, and let me tell you, this is not something any young girl should have to endure. If I had been able to articulate this abuse to my parents, things would have been a lot better, but I was afraid to tell them. I was ashamed, and I was scared."

The crowd again nodded their collective heads.

"We, as a community, need to bring this crime out in the open and teach young girls to speak up about sexual abuse. Girls have a right to protect their bodies and boundaries. I beg you to contribute and help move this indecent maltreatment into the open. Thank you very much."

The audience stood up, cheered, clapped, and nodded. Many audience members wrote checks that evening. Susan sat down, and Barry kissed her and whispered, "You knocked it out of the park, woman."

Then Dad introduced Judge Fuller, who came to the podium and looked tall, serious, and imposing. "We are honored and proud to have the esteemed judge come here and speak at our gala. He is a Boston University Law School graduate and has advocated for women's rights and equality for all people. The highly admired Judge Fuller," Dad said clapping his hands and beaming.

The judge looked handsome when he rose in his dark suit and gold tie. "Small towns are full of secrets. Some teachers take advantage, priests sabotage, and doctors use their power unfairly. I am a judge, and I have seen a great deal of this behavior and secrets in community after community. There are sinners in the church, among world leaders, and in the trailer parks. I came here to tell you about my niece, my brother's daughter, who was traumatized by being raped and sodomized by a neighbor. It broke our hearts. The neighbor was a young boy who babysat and then took a shine to our little girl, Caroline. He seduced her with compliments and gifts. She fell for him and let him do inappropriate things to her. To be unable to speak to your parents about such matters is wrong and emotionally crippling for a child. This cannot go on. My niece didn't tell because she was frightened and threatened. Let me tell you, we need to educate our daughters to speak up and stand up. These human beings were severely mistreated. This is the twentieth century, and it is time to turn the clock forward. I am a judge and have been on the bench a long time, and I have seen and heard terrible secrets. Please give your money to this new clinic so we can start to end this malady."

The audience rose and applauded.

He escorted Penny to the podium. "Here is our Platinum Donor, Mrs. Penny Long, from New York City. She has a history of giving and has decided we at Georgeport Regional Hospital deserved a large gift for our 'Penny Long Children's Treatment Center'."

Penny stood erect and coiffed when she got to the podium in her blue palettes, slim fitting Bob Mackie dress with sparkles. She took the microphone off the holder and held it in her bejeweled hand. She gazed at the audience and said, "I am here because I have wanted to make a difference all my life. I grew up in Brooklyn, New York, in a tenement. My father was an alcoholic and deserted us. My mother took in borders, and we scraped by. The boarders molested me, one after another. I said nothing because we needed their money to pay the rent and keep food in the refrigerator to feed the children. There were six of us. I had to stay silent, or we would have starved. Needless to say, I had a traumatic childhood. I got married, and my ex-husband made a great deal of money in television production, producing some very successful shows. When I heard about what Dr. Max Stern, my brilliant high school classmate, was doing up here in Georgeport, Massachusetts, I wanted to make a difference so girls don't have to stay silent and perverts and rapists won't keep getting away with abuse and molestation. Sexual predators are damaging girls for life and keep repeating and reoffending. I want to help stop this illegal, abusive behavior. I have come here tonight to beg you to please open up your hearts and pocketbooks. This clinic will be monumental and begin a trend in psychology and social behavior. I believe in this because I have suffered, and I know what these victims feel. Thank you very much."

"Bravo," people shouted. "Yeah," the doctors and nurse screamed. "Kudos," said the businessmen and chairmen of the boards. Gail Collins clapped and hugged Dad. Then she hugged Mama. Susan thought maybe Gail was too enthusiastic because she had kissed Dad on his lips. Even so, the evening was a huge success, and Dad and Mama were thrilled. The doctors at the hospital were ecstatic, and the nurses and the staff were delighted. Susan, Barry, and all the other family members kissed one another and knew that their efforts had not been in vain.

Then, they and their partners kicked off their shoes and celebrated. They were on their way, and the Boston Globe and the New York Times both ran articles in their newspapers the following day.

Larry was in California and had already settled in his apartment. He met his landlady, and she showed him around. He had a twin bed with a thin mattress, a dresser, and a desk with a large lamp. Larry wrote to Dad and Mama and told them about his new digs.

"It's pretty good, nothing fancy, but adequate."

He went to the television station office and was hired as a staff writer. He was thrilled, returned to his room, sat at his desk with the light beaming down, and tried to generate creative ideas. When he wasn't in his apartment, he visited McDonald's, relaxed there, and wrote while he ate. Larry was content after jail and relieved to be free. His sentence had been reduced, and he was released because he'd completed his reform classes and the program.

"I don't miss New England's fickle climate," he wrote in his letter.

Writing once a week to 2 Poppins Lane, he reported his progress. Trying to keep his mind disciplined and focused, he kept his head down despite all the comely young females when he walked around the area. He didn't want to be sent back to prison and lose his freedom; didn't, didn't, didn't.

Then he got a script accepted about a guy, kind of like Dom, who shot his sister because she wouldn't lend him money. The sister wasn't hurt badly, but the Dom character was put in a mental hospital where he met another outpatient, a sexual pervert. The producer liked the character and told Larry to expand it. Larry got spiffed up after getting the dinner invitation at the producer's house in a section of Hollywood set behind a high ridge of trees called Morning Lane. There was a staff of help, an outdoor kitchen, and a beautiful daughter. The producer's daughter was Lucy, a comely blond teenager with a well-developed chest. Naturally, Larry took a liking to her. During the evening, they flirted with each other. Then, she showed him her room with a collection of books, plays, and records of the most popular singers and authors. Larry was fascinated, and Lucy played some of her favorite songs. Larry borrowed a few plays he liked, one by Tennessee Williams and one by Arthur Miller.

"I'll bring them back in a few weeks. Do you mind?" Larry said.

"Oh, no, that's fine, Lar. Whenever you're done with them; I'm in no rush," Lucy said.

After eighteen months of construction, with delays in between, changes made, and new hires, the clinic would open ahead of schedule. The architect was a nice guy from Boston, and he met with the building committee and listened to their requests. Money kept pouring in. They eliminated one elevator to the roof for fear of suicide attempts and added another bathroom to the girls' dorm because they knew how females like to primp.

On the day of the opening, large crowds pressed into the bright red ribbons across the entrance. Photographers stood in front, and the press was behind them. The podium was set up, and Dad and Mama were there, along with several of the other doctors and board members. Bank presidents, leading businessmen, and Judge Fuller were in attendance. Gail Collins, stood on the side with her pad and pencil. People crowded around, and the weather boasted blue skies and seventy degrees.

"Today, we open the 'Penny Long Children's Treatment Center' at Georgeport Regional Hospital," Dad said with a wide grin. "We are thrilled that this day has arrived. Due to the generosity of this wonderful woman and all the other contributions from various caring folks, we have this great new clinic. It will help so many children. We have a state-of-the-art facility with top-notch design, meeting rooms, conference rooms, therapy rooms, residential rooms, and doctor and nurses' stations. There is a gym, a cafeteria, and even spaces for families. Doubtless, a lot of time and effort has been put into this clinic's planning. The registration building is constructed in a farmhouse style because I wanted to give a homey, inviting feeling to people coming here for the first time. There is a fireplace, cozy chairs, and

138

warm decor. I hope you like it. We also have classrooms for those who are being trained. In addition, there's a modern art room and a drama center." Dad paused and then looked up. "Penny, please cut the ribbon."

She stepped right up and cut the red ribbon, everyone applauded, and flashbulbs went off. Waving and smiling, she had pictures taken, and they went to the front page of the *Georgeport Daily News*. The television ran the event on their six o'clock news, and people talked at Taffy's and all the local watering holes. On Sunday, the sermons were about helping the abused children, and the visiting rabbi talked about it when he spoke at Friday night's sabbath service in the white synagogue on Old Point Road. Dad and Mama went to the service and prayed to the good Lord, thanking him for helping with their efforts. After the service, the small congregation had challah and kosher wine, and the attendees shook Dad's hand and complimented the Sterns for their contribution to the community.

"Lily, we worked so hard for this to come to pass. I think it is only fitting that we go and thank God for his help," Dad had said.

With a new chapeau from Lord & Taylor on her head and a fresh hairdo from Eleanor's, Mama took Dad's arm, went with him, and prayed from the good book. She sang the old Jewish songs she had sung as a girl; Dad put on a tallis over his shoulders, a religious shawl symbolizing his connection to God. They bowed their heads and said their thanks to God for all the help. It was a fine day for the Stern family. It was a very fine day.

PART THREE

Chapter Seventeen

Susan and Barry were expecting twins. The excitement in the Stern family was palpable. Mama had to know every detail of Susan's obstetrician visits, and Odell learned how to knit booties and blankets. Ellen couldn't contain her enthusiasm. In addition, she had met a doctor at the Georgeport Regional Hospital, an Israeli neurosurgeon, Zev Hirschberg, and they were dating. Ellen served as the surgical nurse when Zev performed surgery on a woman who needed a cyst removed that was pressing on her sciatic nerve. She stood in the operating room and expertly gave him each instrument he needed. "You're good, Ellen," he said afterward.

Susan and Barry's twins, one boy, Michael, and one girl, Michelle, were adorable. The nursery was painted pink and blue, with two cribs, changing tables, and two high chairs. Odell came over, helped with the babies, cooked food, and put it in the freezer. Mama slipped her a few extra twenties for her added hours. Susan was exhausted from getting up at night, and Barry tried to help, but with two screaming infants, neither parent got much rest. When they discovered pacifiers at the drug store, things finally quieted down. The twins were healthy and grew rapidly, and Dad and Mama smiled with giddiness whenever their new grandchildren visited.

Ellen and Zev visited the salmon-colored house with the crooked floors and loved what Susan and Barry had done with the nursery. The room had a wallpaper fence about five feet high that encircled it, music playing on the mobile, and smelled of Johnson and Johnson baby powder. Susan wanted Ellen to get married soon so they could have children around the same age. They whispered about it when no one was around.

"I'm working on it, sis," Ellen said. "Give me time."

Ronnie's children, Amy and Louis, were thrilled with their new cousins and wanted Ronnie to have another baby. They were one big growing family, and Mama decided to make a playroom out of half the gym by removing the steam and sauna rooms on the third floor. Later, she filled the space with toys, child-safe ladders, a wooden kiddy gym, and trampoline mats.

Jeffrey had a girlfriend, Deborah, so everyone seemed to be moving along. When Zev popped the question to Ellen on an evening they had gone to their favorite steak house on Stuart Street in Boston, he placed a round diamond with two sapphire baguettes on each side on her finger. The Sterns started to plan Ellen's wedding, and things got busier.

The wedding for Ellen and Zev would be in Georgeport at the new hotel that opened to accommodate everyone coming into town now that the clinic was starting to get busy. The Harris Inn Hotel was handsome, with gardens, a restaurant, and a large lawn. Red-jacketed valets and bellhops helped with the cars, the baggage, and the check-in. There was a vast Oriental rug, antiques, a fireplace with porcelain plates on the mantel, vases with fresh flowers, and paintings completing the decor. The hotel had a ballroom, which was a perfect size for the one hundred and fifty people.

Zev's family lived in Brookline and moved from Tel Aviv when Zev was seven years old. They were warmhearted, hugging people and kissing all the relatives when they arrived and again when they left. Dad and Mama had to adjust to this more affectionate style. Zev's parents were very touchy-feely and liked squeezing Ellen's cheek when they saw her.

Ellen's wedding dress was strapless and beguiling with a mantilla over her dark hair like a Spanish princess. Zev, a handsome man, resembled a movie star. The rabbi was conservative and said the prayer for bread at the wedding over three challahs. The married couple broke the glass for good luck under the chuppah, and the family danced until midnight, singing Israeli and American songs and doing Hebrew dances. They lifted the bride and the groom in the air as was the custom while all the guests sang and danced. It was a festive, joyous occasion, and everyone cried with happiness. The married couple went to Hawaii for two weeks on their honeymoon and stayed at the Royal Hawaiian, painted pink and smelling of native flowers.

Larry returned the two plays to Lucy two weeks after he had borrowed them. He continued his script, including a scene where the Dom character and the sexual abuser hid a stash of guns in their room and practiced assembling and reassembling them in record time. The producer praised the plot. As Larry swam in the pool, Lucy was sunbathing in her yellow bikini. He had seen her working in the producer's office, but seeing her in this setting aroused him.

"Do you want to take a walk?" Larry asked Lucy as he stood with a vodka tonic in his hand.

Lucy rose from her chaise lounge and said, "Sure, why not?"

They walked around the grounds and sat by the pool, where a waterfall gushed high spurts of curving water.

"You look pretty," Larry said, sipping his drink.

"Thanks, Lar. That's very nice of you to say." Lucy sat on the lounge and spread her long legs out in front of him.

"When you do that, it turns me on," Larry said.

"Do what, Lar?"

"You know, spread your legs out like that," he said, finishing his vodka tonic. "I think I need another drink. Want one?"

"Sure, just don't let my father see you."

Larry returned with two vodka tonics, and Lucy drank a large gulp. "Yummy," she said.

After a short time, he lured her upstairs into her bedroom when no one was watching.

They closed the door, Lucy put on a Janis Joplin record, and Larry kissed her. Then he got on top of her and threw her yellow bikini top onto the floor. She was a seductive girl, and she knew it. He made love to her and enjoyed every second. Lucy was sixteen, and Larry was twenty-four.

After a while, the producer looked for Larry, searched indoors, and finally found Larry asleep in Lucy's bed. Since he'd had too much to drink, he'd simply passed out. Lucy, not accustomed to booze, was sleeping right next to him, stark naked.

"What do you think you're doing in my daughter's bed, Larry?" The producer yelled.

Larry scrambled up and kept crossing and uncrossing his legs. Then he put on his shirt and started picking off lint on the sleeve.

"Speak," the producer yelled.

He finally said, "I don't know."

"You don't know?" the producer said. "I think you know damn well what you're doing."

Lucy ran to the bathroom to put on some clothes.

"You and I are finished, Larry. I'm calling 911, so you'd better stay here and not go anywhere," the producer said.

Larry was arrested and spent the night in jail.

The following day, the producer officially fired Larry.

He said, "I can't tolerate you sexually molesting my daughter, so I'm firing you. It's too bad, kid, but you blew it," he said as Larry stood there and hung his head.

"There's no way you can give me another chance?" he murmured.

"Listen, you're good, but not great. I don't need this trouble. My daughter is precious to me. Now pack your stuff and get out of my face."

Larry signed the release and returned to his small room. Since this was his second arrest, he figured he was headed to prison. The entire writing project went down the drain. Larry was facing charges, and the court informed Dad since he was the relative named in case of emergency on Larry's working contract. All the diligent effort went south. Dad was heartsick when he found out and cried in the bathroom when Mama wasn't looking. He felt defeated and depleted. With the clinic opened, he didn't want the world to know.

"How can we avoid this coming out?" he asked Mama as the family gathered around the dining table.

"He's only one case, not a reflection of the clinic's work," Mama said.

"But we were supposed to cure these offenders," Dad said.

"No, you were helping the victims and trying to cure the offenders, but there were no guarantees," Susan said. "Like any addiction, child molesters sometimes relapse."

"I'll have to write a response to have it ready. Surely, someone will ask," Dad said.

"Let me help you, Pop. I see many cases and can write," Barry said.

"It's not the clinic's fault. We just opened. Larry was one of the reasons we built the clinic," Mama said enthusiastically.

"You're right. We must emphasize this," Dad said, putting his hands over his face and shaking his head.

"Can I bring some refreshments?" Odell asked.

"A pot of coffee and a few sandwiches would be nice, Odell. Thank you," Mama said, lighting her Chesterfield cigarette.

"Is Larry coming back here?" Ellen asked.

146

"God, I don't know. Where else will he go?" Mama said.

"He's not coming here, sweetheart. He's been arrested, and he will be jailed in California. I'll have to go out there," Dad said.

"Mama, I have to go home in a bit and take care of the twins," Susan said.

"Of course, go when you have to."

Odell brought sandwiches, and everyone took one. The coffee was hot, but the mood was somber.

"I'm going to California to see about Larry. I'll take Gail with me because I need an assistant. Barry, if you can spare the time, will you join me? I don't know what's going to happen, but Larry is all alone, and I can't stay here and do nothing. It's just not right," Dad said, looking at Barry and hoping for help.

"Let me know when you want to leave, and I'll clear my schedule. I have a few matters to take care of. How long do you think you'll be out there?" Barry asked.

"I'm not sure, but even if you come for a few days and then return, it would be a big help," Dad said.

"No problem, Pop," Barry said. He loved his new father-in-law and wouldn't let him down.

Susan grabbed half of the sandwich, kissed Barry, and left.

Dad, Gail, and Barry flew to California. They found Larry in jail, awaiting trial for sexually abusing and raping a minor. Barry spoke to the attorney, who agreed that Larry was going away for twenty years. It was his second offense on record. After Barry had collected the facts, he explained the charges to Dad, who said, "I'm going to stay through the trial to show support for my nephew. I want Gail to stay, too."

Dad took Gail's luggage and placed it with his, directing

147

the bellhop to put it in the taxi cab. Then he put his arm around her. Whispering something in her ear, she blushed. It was obvious that Dad and Gail were involved with one another. Barry left, and when he got home, he told Susan what he thought.

"Pop didn't need her. He wanted her to stay. They're having an affair, Susan."

Susan felt disappointed with her father, but it was not up to her to say anything. She remembered that night when Mama had gotten so drunk and how she had acted so seductively with Dad. Yes, he fooled around. He wasn't perfect, and Susan had to accept this. Painful and disappointing, Susan had a hard time dismissing it.

Dad and Gail stayed one more week in California and watched as Larry was found guilty and sentenced. He was incarcerated in a prison near Sausalito, California. Before he left, Dad spoke to him.

"I tried to help you, son," Dad said.

"I know you did. I guess I'm too damaged to be fixed."

"I hope you'll be okay in jail."

"I'll survive."

"I'll put a few bucks in your account," Dad said.

"Thanks. I appreciate it."

Dad and Gail stayed a few more days at the Beverly Hills Hilton Hotel to enjoy the balmy seventy degree weather before getting on a plane east. Mama was home drinking scotch, smoking, and popping Valium. She sat in the dinette where she had her phone, pen, pad, and ashtray. The small room was decorated in a French provincial design with a cherry cabinet, cafe curtains, and red shades. Mama and the decorator had put great thought into the space. This was where Mama liked to sit when she was alone, thinking, ruminating, and wondering about her life. That night, after she'd had too much to drink, she dialed the

Beverly Hills number where Dad was staying. She said, "Dr. Max Stern, please."

When the phone rang, it was late in California, and Gail answered it.

"I'd like to speak to my husband," Mama said in her inebriated voice. It was two in the morning back in Georgeport.

Dad got on the phone and said, "Hello."

"Who is that woman?" Mama asked.

"That is my assistant, Gail Collins," Dad said.

"Why is she in your room at this hour of the night?" Mama asked.

"She travels with me, Lily," Dad said.

"Well, isn't that cozy? You're a son of a bitch, Max." The phone went dead.

Mama told Susan what happened the next morning. Susan didn't know what to say. It didn't come as a surprise, but she still felt shocked when Mama explained the whole situation. He was having an affair with his secretary. The faithful, uncomplaining, efficient assistant, Gail, a woman in her late thirties, attractive, blond, unmarried, and probably in love with the good doctor. Maybe waiting for him to leave his wife, maybe not. How many years, no one knew? She had worked for Dad for six years, and Dad had bragged when Gail had her fifth anniversary, saying, "I gave Gail her yearly salary as a gift," pretending to be this generous boss. Susan had wondered about the present, and now she knew. Her Dad had opened a sexual abuse clinic and was now cheating on his wife. Susan struggled with what loyalty meant and the meaning of love.

The grandkids came over, and Odell baked cookies. They went upstairs and played in the new playroom. Mama gave them each a dollar and a lollypop. The twins fought, but they crawled into bed together at night and slept with their arms around each other. Ronnie's kids were thrilled

149

that their mother had a new baby, a little girl whom Amy dressed up and fussed over. Maybe she'd love hats, too. Taking up running kept Ronnie committed to staying sober, and she trained for the ten-mile race in Georgeport, which was held yearly and started at the high school, right across from 2 Poppins Lane.

The new clinic was admitting more and more victimized children. They stayed in the rooms, received therapy, and took back their lives. The usual length of stay was one month, but some were there for as long as six months. It depended on the case. People came from all over, even a few from Europe. It was a bonus to Georgeport, and this coastal magnet grew. Locals and tourists visited the clinic's open house to see the shops, go to the beach, eat at the restaurants, and go on a tour of the city. The value of homes increased, and Georgeport and the surrounding towns became a more desirable place to live.

Dad thought about divorcing Mama and confided in Jeffrey, but Mama cleverly gave Dad no ammunition, behaved in the kindest, most accommodating manner, and never raised her voice. Mama had supported the clinic and acted as the perfect hostess, so Dad felt guilty about a divorce. None of the family knew what would happen and tip-toed around the subject.

"What do you think, Susan?" Ellen asked when she returned from her honeymoon.

"Oh, God, I don't know; I'm not happy about this, but we don't have much to say on the subject. Maybe Gail is pressuring him? Who knows?"

"She probably doesn't want to just stay his mistress," Ellen said.

"I hope people don't look badly at the clinic now that Dad is fooling around with his secretary," Susan said.

"Our family keeps attracting publicity," Ellen said, shaking her head.

"First, we were worried about our reputation when Larry got arrested; now, we are worried about Dad and his mistress."

Dad became more casual about being seen with Gail Collins. One night, when Barry was out to dinner with new clients at a high-end restaurant in Boston, he spotted his father-in-law dining with Gail. They were sitting in a booth, and Dad had his hand over Gail's. Barry didn't say anything, but when Dad and Gail left the restaurant, Barry and Dad nodded to each other. No one said a thing, just a simple nod between two men who knew one another.

Barry told Susan when he got home that night. She hung her head and vowed to herself to never forgive her father. The male prerogative and double standards ate at her, adding to her anger about sexual abuse and other liberties that the male sex enjoyed in the culture. Some things she could never accept, and this was one of them. She knew this from the bottom of her heart.

Susan again thought about the family mosaic and how Dad's affair with Gail Collins would tarnish the design. Is this how life is? Are all people juggling the good and the bad? She had thought the sexual abuse was a large scar, and now the unfaithful marriage and the hurt that Mama felt because of the way Dad was behaving made her see the situation in a new light. Dad changed after Mama called the night Dad and Gail were at the Beverly Hills Hilton. Susan shook her head and tried to understand, but she couldn't. She disliked her father's conduct, was embarrassed about it, and honestly thought he was being cruel. This was a side of her father she had never seen. Where was the respect, she thought, like the famous black singer Aretha Franklin's song, *Respect*?

151

How interesting that Dad was showing this side of his personality. Was Gail pressuring him? Was he a selfish man? Why had she not seen this before? What had Mama done to add to this situation? Susan decided to talk to Ellen. They'd take a long, brisk walk, and discuss it.

Chapter Eighteen

The wife of Dad's colleague, Dr. Sofferman, a woman named Sylvia, called Mom and said, "Lily, I wanted to speak to you."

"Yes?"

"I just feel like us girls should stick together," Sylvia said.

"Go on."

"Your husband has been bringing his paramour, Gail Collins, to several social gatherings."

"Really?" Mama said.

"Yes. There was a card party at Dr. Letterman's, and Max came with Gail. Of course, no one said anything, but we were surprised he didn't bring you."

"Yes, that was unusual," Mama said.

"You know how we like to split up and have our separate card games, but you don't play?"

"Right, but no one minds," Mama said.

"Yes, that's true."

There was a long silence.

"This Gail is quite the gin rummy player. She joined right in and played all night. What do you think of that?"

"I don't know what to say," Mama gulped.

"Exactly."

Another silence.

"I just wanted you to know. It seemed in poor taste, but you know men; they're a little dense, don't you think?"

"I couldn't agree more," Mama said.

"We women should stick together."

"Thank you for calling."

"You're welcome."

Mama hung up the phone and felt numb. After all the support she had given her husband, she couldn't believe this was how he was treating her.

As the two sisters headed towards Cameron Park, they

walked their children in strollers over the bumpy sidewalks. The day was clear, and the little ones were dressed for the weather, so everyone was content.

"I'm so disappointed in Dad," Susan started.

Ellen nodded. "Can you believe it?"

"Only because I heard it," Susan said. "He's as bad as other men. Here I had him on a pedestal."

Ellen said, "Well, he's done many good things, but he's falling way short on this subject."

As they walked, they spotted their father's red Cadillac convertible parked down by the new clinic but over to the side of the new farmhouse. They figured he was checking things out until they saw that Dad was inside the car with Gail Collins. They were in deep conversation, sitting close, and she looked like she was crying.

They didn't want to interrupt, so they pushed their strollers toward the duck pond. The children loved throwing bread to the ducks and hearing them quack.

"I wonder what that's all about," Ellen said.

Looking at their father again before turning, they said in unison, "Not good."

Mama lived with this arrangement because Dad never filed for divorce, and Mama never wanted one. She liked the prominence of being the wife of the doctor who created the sexual abuse clinic.

Of course, she continued to spend money and even had a small room where she stored her evening gowns for all the functions they attended. She'd met Eleanor Roosevelt, Golda Meir, and other celebrities. When her brother married a Ford model, Mama learned how to walk. Susan and Ellen marveled as Moma walked across the kitchen's blue tile floor, tucking in her ass and flattening her stomach saying. "Who's that walking down the street?"

The clinic saw many victims and helped a myriad of

young girls. The entire Stern family participated in one form or another. Gail Collins got pregnant and gave birth to a son. Dad paid child support. Mama said that was the right thing to do. Eventually, she and her son, Max Jr., moved away and lived in Florida near her sister. Dad visited on a regular schedule.

Time Magazine did a piece on the clinic, and Larry got stabbed while in prison. Proud and distressed, the family absorbed this news in one month. Barry was named one of the best attorneys for sex abuse cases in Massachusetts in the *North Shore Magazine*, which made Susan feel thrilled that she had chosen him for her husband. Susan wanted more kids but thought she should wait. She prepared by moving into a larger house off Main Street. It sat on top of a hill with a long driveway. She had to hire someone to help her keep it clean and neat since she was busy with children and her part-time job as an expressive therapist at the clinic. On top of this, she wrote her memoir, which was on the Boston Globe's best-seller list. She was Barry's firecracker, for sure!

She knew from her research that once a person manifested the behavior of a sexual predator, he was highly unlikely to discontinue it. Intervals occurred when he used self-control, and his behavior improved. He could go decades without an event. She analyzed sexual abuse of youngsters and discussed it with Barry, who had a lot of cases. She did research, collecting names, backgrounds, descriptions of families, education, and careers. She was intrigued by all this. Cousins were interesting to her. She never forgot Larry and how he came into her room and rocked on top of her when she was ten. She never forgot how she pretended to be asleep for two months. Larry remained in prison, but Susan always feared for her children.

She and Barry talked candidly to their kids about being careful speaking up and never being afraid to tell them about anybody who tried to touch them in their private areas. She bought books about this and found appropriate children's stories to read at night before bedtime. "You have to be careful," Susan said to her twins. "Your body is yours alone, and no one has the right to touch it if you don't want them to. Period. Amen."

They smiled at their mother's enthusiasm and shook their heads up and down.

Susan turned twenty-five in 1969, and she had a party. The Stern family gathered around the large dining table at 2, Poppins Lane, and crepe paper streamers were hung with different-colored balloons. All the clan members came, and Odell set up a separate table for all the excited little kids, dressed in their party clothes and blowing horns. There were a few high chairs, diapers, bibs, and rattles to accommodate this large crowd.

Susan wore a beautiful red dress and high heels even though she was feeding and overseeing her brood. She believed in dressing for the occasion. Odell made her favorite foods: roast beef with onions, double-baked potatoes, and coleslaw. A carrot cake with cream cheese icing sat on the table with Susan's name on it. Drinks were set up on the bar, and Beaujolais Villages accompanied the meal.

After everyone had eaten and the children went up to the playroom with the babysitter that Mama hired, Susan decided to speak.

"I want to say that this family has turned into the talk show of Georgeport. First, we have Larry, the pervert; now we have Dad with the baby born out of wedlock and a strained arrangement in his marriage. I want to say it makes me uncomfortable. It's my birthday, and I want to discuss it."

The room was silent, and everyone looked at one another.

"You're such a troublemaker," Jeffrey said.

"Shut up," Susan said.

Mama said, "I agree with you, Susan; we are the talk of the town in a strange and unflattering way."

Dad looked up and said, "I know you must all hate me now."

"Well, Dad, you're not making us comfortable or proud," Ellen said.

"Okay, we should talk about this," Jeffrey added. He picked up his napkin and wiped his face because he was sweating.

"Yes, we must. We didn't discuss things when Ellen and I were getting molested by Larry fifteen years ago. We have to be different now. Come on!" Susan said as she looked around the table.

Most of the family nodded in agreement.

"I'm fairly new to the family, but it has been my experience that holding feelings inside is unhealthy," Barry said.

"Listen, I know you all are pissed at me and I understand. Marriages are complicated," Dad said. He started to get up.

"Where are you going, Dad?" Susan asked.

"I don't want to be attacked," he said.

"Don't leave, Pop," Barry said. Dad sat back down.

"At least Gail and the kid have moved to Florida," Ellen said.

"Really," Ronnie said. "I hated it when she lived here; there was so much gossip."

"That will help things," Dad said.

"I must confess that I am relieved. It was too embarrassing." Mama lit a Chesterfield.

Susan said, "Well, it's my birthday, and I wanted to say we should be able to talk about this like civilized people. Dad, you want to have a second family, and Mama goes along with this arrangement, so we get to say whatever we

157

feel. We are your kids." She smiled and nodded her head. "It feels better to talk."

"I know it's strange, but this is the arrangement for now. I'm here with your mother, and Gail is down there, okay?" Dad looked for approval.

"We disapprove but accept this as a better setup. At least Mama doesn't have to bump into her and the boy in the supermarket. Come on, Dad, what's happened to you?" Susan asked.

"I don't know, but I was trying to live my life," he said.

"I don't get why you brought her to that card game either," Ellen added.

"Yeah, that was a low blow," Susan said.

"I know you think that, but Gail likes to play gin rummy."

"I believe you ought to communicate with Mama before you do this kind of thing," Ellen suggested.

"Okay, you're right, you're right," Dad said.

After a while, the conversation drifted to other subjects. Odell brought more coffee and sweets, and people got up and wandered around the house. It was a beginning, and Susan was pleased she had started an open dialogue. It felt settled, but Susan didn't think she would solve everything in one conversation. At least she had opened the door. Fifteen years ago, she couldn't even open her mouth.

When they are small, youngsters put their parents on a pedestal. Then, the parents fail them, and the children fail the parents, too. Some parents are good, and some are not so good. Some are worse than that – some are mean. Children, too. Children try to survive and adjust. When the parents die, kids go to their graves and tell them the truth, but it's too late. The children's hearts are hardened and cannot be repaired. They try to live their lives as best they can, but it takes a long time to get over the disappointment.

158

Chapter Nineteen

Susan kept researching sexual abuse and discovered that there were quite a few females who also sexually molested young children. This seemed like society's last taboo, but mothers molested their biological daughters or other children in their care, sometimes out of jealousy. This abuse was much more likely to take place in families rather than outsiders.

Since so many sexually abused children went unreported, Susan realized she would never really know how much of this pattern went on. She understood that historically, males forced young girls into prostitution for economic reasons as well as bringing them to sex parties and raffling them off. The more she read, the more upset she became.

Sex trafficking had been going on for over one thousand years, and California was the number one state where it took place. Record keeping in the United States began between 1860 to World War I. It was human trafficking for purposes of sexual exploitation or modern slavery. In the 1960s, Susan learned that more attention was being paid to the problem because of the new wave of feminism; this gave her hope.

Poverty was a huge contributor to sexual exploitation when girls were desperate to find work. Mothers pushed sex on their daughters with their boyfriends in exchange for housing. Susan said a prayer for her good fortune, and yet Larry, her cousin, molested her and Ellen, so she knew anything could happen. As an art therapist, she had her clients draw pictures of traumatic situations they had experienced. One child drew an ashtray full of cigarette butts on the coffee table. He recalled his mother's boyfriend having sex with her on the sofa late one night.

Susan and Barry talked to their children and taught them

about pornography and what to do if they saw it. "Playing doctor is normal," Susan said to the twins, "but not if the other child is more than two years older than you."

She knew that ninety percent of sexual abuse took place with people known to the victims. It could be a babysitter, a babysitter's boyfriend, an older sibling at a friend's sleepover, or a family friend. Susan had an open door policy in her home, no secrets, and would ask the twins, "What was your least favorite part of your day?" She wasn't taking any chances with her children and hoped her words would be enough.

Gail Collins decided to visit. Even though Dad went to Florida to see Max Jr., she wanted to see some of her old friends and family. She hopped on a plane with Max Jr., who was now two years old and returned to Georgeport. Staying with one of her close friends was no problem. The Stern family was upset when they learned Gail would be in town for a full week. Mama decided she would take it in stride.

One afternoon Mama, Susan, Ellen and Ellen's six-month-old son, Hank, were having lunch at Taffy's. Mama spotted Gail and her little boy and gasped. The child had dark curly hair, deep brown eyes, and a dimple on his left cheek. Ellen asked, "What's the matter, Mama?" as Hank sat in an infant seat and chewed on a biscuit.

"You'll never guess who is sitting over there to your right… Gail Collins and her son."

Ellen glanced over and said, "My, oh my."

"The child looks like your father: the spitting image," Mama said, wiping her lips with a napkin.

"Yeah, you're right, he does," said Susan.

"I think I want to go. Let's finish up and leave. Do you mind?"

"No, it's okay; I'm almost done. The baby doesn't need a thing. He's fine."

160

They got up from the booth, and while they were paying the bill, Gail looked over and saw Mama. For a minute, the two women stared at one another. Mama, Ellen, and the baby left immediately. Mama put a pill in her mouth. "I can't take this. I thought she'd stay in Florida, not visit here."

"I was worried that something like this would happen, Mama."

"Am I being foolish?"

"No, not at all. Are you going to be all right?" Ellen asked.

"I don't know what to do." They continued to walk down the street to the car. "I should divorce your father and move away. Why, I could live anywhere I wanted. You kids could come and visit me. I'd buy a big enough house, and you all would come.

"You absolutely could," Ellen said.

"I should go talk to Chad. He does divorces."

"It wouldn't hurt."

"Oh, it's such a big decision," Mama said, sighing. "I've been with your father so many years. Will I be okay all alone?"

"You don't have to be unhappy. Don't underestimate yourself."

Mama smiled and squeezed Ellen's hand.

Mama went to see Chad and had a long chat. She decided she'd go ahead with the divorce if she got a generous settlement, which she would, Chad said, because of the length of her marriage.

"I need a new life. I don't want to live with this indignity. Your father can do what he wants. I'm moving on. Maybe I'll go back to school and get a master's degree. Maybe I'll get a job. Maybe I'll travel. I haven't decided, but I certainly will do something. I'm a modern woman," she said with emphasis. She put her hands over her face, muffled her sobs,

161

and then said, releasing her fingers, "God, I will do this." All the children loved hearing her talk this way, in her new affirmative, positive way.

Except for Amy, the oldest grandchild, who called and said, "Grandma, you're going to ruin our family. I hate this idea."

"I'm unhappy, sweetheart," Mama said.

"We'll never be together again; all our wonderful family dinners."

"Oh, please don't make me feel guilty."

Susan said, "Mama, are you sure you want to do this? You love seeing the grandchildren."

"I know I do, and it makes me angry to be away from them, but I can't let your father insult me. I hated seeing Gail and that baby," she said.

"I know it must hurt terribly."

"It's like a knife in my heart."

"I know, I can just imagine. Do what you want, Mama."

Mama went to see a shrink and talked it out, and with tears in her eyes, she packed her bags at 2 Poppins Lane. She didn't sob or talk on the phone excessively like other women often do when they were going through a marital breakup. She didn't drink more or pop more pills, but she did go through the memorabilia she and Dad had collected from trips and anniversaries. The gold-plated flatware matched the fine china that her Aunt Doris had given them when they'd married. There was an oil painting they'd purchased in Santa Fe of a colorful sunset, there were jewels he'd given her like a tennis bracelet of diamonds and sapphires, a full-length mink coat, and her set of fashionable expensive luggage.

Mama tried to be strong and didn't think about replacing Dad with a new younger man to escort her to dinner or compliment her. Avoiding the many temptations of a

162

rejected partner, she soldiered on and looked forward to turning the page. When you're thirty-one and substituted by a twenty-one-year-old, a woman feels discarded almost before she's old. However, when you're fifty-six, and replaced by a gal who's thirty-six, it feels even worse. Mama, who was losing her looks even with all her scheduled pampering, was displaced by a female two decades younger; and shouldered her indignities like a fighter. It was such a classic accepted rejection; people shrugged their heads and rolled their eyes.

Dad talked to Mama and said, "I still love you. Lily, but I fell in love with Gail. Sometimes that happens. I never meant to hurt you. Please, let's stay civil for the sake of the children. I'll give you whatever you want. Just send me the papers."

Mama decided to create a commercial enterprise with her new, close friend, Penny Long. After meeting several times in New York, going shopping, walking down Fifth Avenue, and admiring the windows, they discussed their ideas for a business over long lunches at upscale restaurants while they ate salads and sipped wine and realized they both had shared ambitions.

"We need to do something original and dramatic," Penny said, sipping her wine.

"It must be lucrative and useful," Mama added.

"For women."

"On the east coast."

"Yes, it's more convenient."

"We'll have to work hard."

"Neither one of us is lazy."

"Catering, parties."

"We know so much about entertaining."

"Plants, flowers."

"Absolutely."

The waiter brought the check, and they split the bill. They purchased a large farmhouse up in Bedford, New York, and began a gourmet home goods business. Selling all kinds of high-end crockery, tablecloths, wreaths, and copper pots; they prospered. With their wonderful decorating notions and recipes, they went into catering for parties. They hired some cooks and emphasized entertaining. Then they expanded their business with more decor like pine tables, gardening supplies, rocking chairs, cookbooks, and published their magazine, *Come Into My Home*. People bought the magazine with brightly colored pictures, which showed up at hair salons and doctor's offices. They went to the market at four in the morning to buy the best ingredients and opened their own cafe and cooking school. Weddings were next.

Penny and Mama got along terrifically. Penny was a force and inspiration for Mama, who became more independent. Once a year, the two women would make an appearance at the Penny Long Children's Treatment Center in Georgeport, and the *Georgeport Daily News* would run a story about how these two bright women met.

At an annual fundraising luncheon that the clinic sponsored, Penny spoke to all the admiring women, and Mama added a few words about how hard the family had worked to create this top-notch sexual abuse center. Dad sat in the audience and clapped loudly. Triumphant and proud of the two women, he stood and applauded. Gail Collins was in the audience and clapped politely. She understood that Dad was both glad and relieved that Mama and Penny were successful. There was a raffle, and the winner won an espresso machine from *Penlily*, Penny, and Mama's business in Bedford.

When the ladies weren't working in the gourmet home goods center, they traveled to Europe for new finds. Paris,

La Province, Rome, and Monaco were some of their favorite stops along the way. Dropping into Monte Carlo, they met wealthy middle-aged men, but neither woman was interested in being tied down. Instead, they went to a spa and spent a few days getting massaged and spruced up so they could return to Bedford rested and ready to work hard.

Susan was thrilled that Mama had created a new life and didn't sit around anymore drunk, drugged, and angry over Gail Collins.

"She's so much better off now," she said to Ellen.

"Oh, gosh, yes. I couldn't agree more. Frankly, I never thought she'd do it."

"She transitioned right out of the 1950s, didn't she?" Susan said with her lips turned up into a wide grin. They walked hand in hand down the cobblestone streets of Georgeport and felt the wind in their hair. October leaves were golden in Massachusetts at that time of year, putting beaming smiles on the sisters' faces.

Larry floundered inside the prison and had a difficult time. After months of depression, he finally decided to try his hand at writing again. Even if he wrote from prison, he could submit something to some producer back in Hollywood. He also wrote to his old pal Aaron Schwartz from the last jail he was in and told him how he'd screwed up big time. Aaron was sympathetic and told him to try again. "At least if you're inside, you can't succumb to any temptation. Give it a try," his friend wrote.

Larry worked on his television script daily, which he knew was the only way to finish something. In the library, he sat and wrote and tried to think up clever ideas. Finally, he sent a manuscript to a different producer he had heard about. Then he waited.

After two months, he received a response that said.

Dear Larry,
I like your stuff. It's got punch and wit, and it would
work. I'm going to run it by a tryout audience and let
you know.
Thanks,
Lou Gordon

A few weeks later, he received a response that said the guy was going to use it on a sitcom and would pay Larry $500 for each episode. Larry knew it was cheap, but he was so excited he didn't care. It gave him something to do and made him feel good. He wrote to Dad, who was pleased and told Larry to put the money in his commissary account and leave it there. "Save it for a rainy day," Dad said.

Aaron Schwartz, the guy he befriended in prison, came and visited Larry and brought him some magazines, candy bars, a few paperback novels, and a new hairbrush. Their visit went well. Aaron had made some money in a credit card scam but told Larry not to tell anyone.

"Who am I going to tell in here?" Larry said.

Aaron laughed and said, "How the hell do I know?" Aaron looked older and greyer.

"When will you come back?" Larry asked, lonely for visitors.

"Maybe next week. I took a place close by."

"Why?"

"I'm going to try to write a book by myself. I got a cabin up in Sausalito pretty close to here," he said.

"Come back and show me," Larry said.

"Yeah, maybe we could collaborate," Aaron said.

Larry smiled and thought about having two projects. "Sounds like a plan to me, buddy," he said with a wide smile on his face.

When Susan heard about Larry's new writing gig in prison, she laughed. "Well, if this is the way he has to work, then that's the way it is," she said to her father when he reported back.

Time moved on, and when the family met around the dinner table at 2 Poppins Lane, they all discussed the new events. Odell was getting too old to work, so she sent her niece, Trudy, to take her place. Dad still owned the house and lived there with Gail and Max Jr., who was growing up. The third floor still had a gym, but Dad had turned part into a large suite for Max with a bedroom, a room for study, and a room to do hobbies. He was into stamps, sports, and photography.

The people at the table were all excited to be there because it was Dad's sixtieth birthday.

Not everyone was pleased with what Dad had done with Gail, but they wanted to stay together and try to remain loyal. The best part for most of the kids was Mama being in business with Penny.

Dad looked distinguished with salt and pepper hair. Gail was still a blond, and she was three months pregnant with a baby girl. When Dad learned this, Gail and he slipped off and got legally married. Ronnie came with all three children and Chad. Susan and Barry were there with their two sets of twins. Ellen and Zev were there with two kids. Jeffrey and his new wife attended with an infant. The children were seated at a nearby but different table. Trudy, a slim pert woman, expertly orchestrated the entire dinner. Odell had trained her well.

Dad said, "I'm so pleased that you all could make it tonight. Sixty years old... I can't believe it. Well, we're here. Let's drink to that," he lifted his wine glass.

"Here, here," everyone replied and drank with him.

"Our clinic's doing well, Pop," Barry said. "We have a record number of patients this month," he continued.

"And I love that we're training new clinicians," Dad said. "That's so important," he added.

Trudy carved a golden turkey on the table while everyone talked. It had a cranberry necklace.

Susan said, "That looks delicious, Trudy."

"Just wait 'til you taste it," Trudy said.

"Mama's in Europe with Penny buying up straw baskets and caviar," Ellen reported.

"That's great," Dad said.

"Please pass the rolls," Ellen said. "Oh, you made garlic bread. Trudy, I love you."

"Max, what have you been up to?" Dad asked.

"I've been taking pictures down at Cameron Park and trying to get some cool shots of the clinic, Daddy." He was a precocious boy who was advanced for his age.

"That's fantastic," Gail said.

"Maybe we can make a new brochure," Dad said.

Everyone ate, and the food was wonderful.

"I miss Mama," Susan said.

Ellen said, "We all miss her."

There was stillness at the table. Gail blushed and kept eating and staring at her plate.

"Maybe Mama's traveling around and picking up men in Paris," Amy said.

There was some laughter around the table.

"Listen, let's cheer up. It's my birthday," Dad said.

Ronnie said, "Mama is off doing what she wants, and she and Penny are having a blast in Paris. Don't feel bad for her."

"Your mother is a businesswoman, and she's making a lot of money and becoming famous," Barry said.

Dad clapped. "That she is. I heard those two ladies will be on the cover of some magazine."

"Thank God for progress. Here, here." Susan lifted her

glass and she kissed Barry on his cheek. "Well, we should blow up the photograph when it comes out, frame it, and hang it in the clinic."

"That's a fine plan," Dad agreed.

Gail said, "Why not? It may inspire the young girls." She supported feminism and was pleased to hear about their success.

Susan and Ellen looked at each other and winked. "I agree, Gail," Susan said.

"I can't wait to hear all about her trip," Ronnie said.

"You know Mama loves the grandkids, so we must invite her over when she gets back from Paris. We'll have a party, and all the grandkids will be here, and she'll stay for a few days so she can see everyone and get to know our children better. She can sleep at our house for a couple of days and visit with the twins," Susan said.

"That's an excellent idea," Ellen said.

"I love it," said Ronnie.

"Kids, who wants to sing for Grandpa for his birthday?" Dad asked.

Susan's twins stood up, and so did Ronnie's kids, Amy and Lou, and they sang *Happy Birthday*, *Take Me Out to the Ballgame*, and *By the Sea*.

A few of the little kids got up and danced for their grandpa. Little chubby toddlers twisted and turned. Everyone laughed with pleasure.

"Oh, I'm a lucky man," Dad said, smiling and wiping tears from his eyes.

Then Trudy brought the birthday pie, blueberry with vanilla ice cream, and set it down.

Everyone clapped and cheered.

169

Chapter Twenty

A young gal and her parents parked in the lot next to the farmhouse in Cameron Park. The farmhouse was a rustic building, and the furniture was homey and welcoming, the way Dad had imagined it. People felt comfortable when they entered. There was a fire going, fresh flowers on various tables, and soft chairs. As they stepped up to the registration desk, Susan watched. The girl was about eleven years old and was thin and pale. Her hair was stringy, and she carried an old rag doll in her right hand. Her parents looked tired. The mother, Sydney, wore a shirtwaist and styled her hair in a page boy. Her husband, Mick, wore a mechanic's shirt and had an English accent. He told the Penny Long Children's Treatment Center secretary, "We want to admit our daughter, Anita."

The secretary, trained in such matters, said, "What is her last name?"

The parents sat down and filled out the extensive forms while the child sat silently. The receptionist escorted the three of them into a small room where they chatted with the social worker, Laura Katz, who was trained in sexual abuse. She had a master's degree and worked as a social worker for fifteen years. Today, Susan was observing because she wanted to learn more about the admitting process, and this case interested her.

"Susan will be joining us today. She is an expressive therapist," Laura Katz said. Laura looked at Anita. "Tell me what happened to you. Why are you here today?"

She looked at her parents, and then she said quietly, "My brother messed with me."

"When did this happen?"

"This past year." Anita squirmed in her seat.

"How old is your brother?"

"He's two years older than me, he's thirteen."

The interview lasted forty-five minutes, and the parents signed the forms so Anita could stay at the clinic. Anita got a bed in a room with another girl who was ten years old and had checked in the week before. The parents helped her settle into her room, stayed for lunch, and ate in the cafeteria with Anita, the social worker, and Susan before they kissed their daughter goodbye and left.

"Please come for the family session in four days. It's very important. If you can bring your son, that would be terrific," Laura was clearly trying to make the parents feel comfortable.

Anita cried a little when her parents left, but it only lasted a few minutes, then she was okay. Susan gave her a hug, and her roommate, Taylor, befriended Anita, which helped.

"What name is your doll?" Taylor asked.

"Phoebe," Anita said.

"Oh, I like that name," Taylor said.

Susan took Anita into an art room and they drew pictures. Anita made a drawing of her in bed with her brother, Mitchell, standing over her.

"That's a very good picture. Tell me about this," Susan asked.

"That's my brother. In the middle of the night, when he came into my room, he unbuttoned my pajamas on top," Anita said.

"When did this start?"

"Well, first, he touched me on my chest when I was playing touch football outside with him and his friends. He had never done that before, so I stopped playing with them."

"Did you say anything to him?"

"No, I never said anything. I just stopped playing touch football." Anita hung her head.

171

"So, then he started coming into your room afterward?"

"Yes."

"What happened?"

"I rolled over because I didn't want him to undress me."

"But you didn't say anything, like, 'Stop that'?"

"No, I was too embarrassed."

"No one ever told you about speaking up?"

"Well, yes, but not about this kind of thing. It was too private." She put a finger in her mouth and chewed on a cuticle.

"I get it." Susan thought about Larry and how she'd kept her eyes closed.

The drawing had a lot of detail; there was a black and white clock with a cat's face, a dish holding a bunch of barrettes, a doll resembling Phoebe, and a blanket on the bed that Anita colored light green.

"This is excellent. I like that you recalled so many details."

"It is my bedroom, so I know how it looks," Anita said.

"Of course."

Laura Katz invited Susan to attend the family session, the following day after she told Laura about the content and description of Anita's drawing. Laura felt this backup evidence would help secure the brother's admission that he was guilty of raping his younger sister.

The next day, the parents brought their son, Mitchell, a seventh-grade student to the family session. He squirmed in his seat and stared at the ceiling, but he had come. He was short and resembled a football player with broad shoulders and thick, messy hair.

Laura welcomed everyone into the family room, which had sofas and chairs and a water fountain. On the side table was a carafe of coffee with a plate of cookies.

"I'm glad you all could make it today," Laura said. She

172

wore a long skirt and peasant blouse. "Mitchell, it's good of you to join us today. Your sister, Anita, is troubled because of some things that went on between you," Laura started.

"Okay, okay, I know what you're talking about," Mitchell said in a gruff way.

"I know you're uncomfortable, but this is important. You do want to help your sister, don't you?" Laura said, bending her head toward him.

"I'm here, aren't I?" Mitchell said.

"And that's good," Laura answered. "Mitchell, tell me what happened?"

"Nothing much. One night, I went into her room and just wanted to look at her. No big deal," he said.

"It was the middle of the night, wasn't it? Couldn't you sleep?" Laura asked.

"Yeah, I woke up and wasn't able to fall back to sleep, so I went into Anita's room."

"Why did you do that? Weren't you afraid of waking her up?" Laura asked.

"I wasn't thinking all that. I was half asleep," he said.

"But you unbuttoned her pajama top, so you had to know what you were doing," Laura said. Anita stared at her brother and held her breath. Susan squeezed Anita's hand.

Suddenly, Mitchell rose from his chair and stomped out of the room, announcing, "I'm not doing this."

The parents, Anita and Laura, sat there and said nothing. Then Mick, the father, a tall, burly man with thinning hair, said, "I was afraid this would happen. Let me go out and talk to him." The mother got up, poured herself a cup of coffee, and took a cookie off the plate. A few minutes later, the father and Mitchell returned to the family room.

Laura said. "I'm glad you rejoined us."

"Listen, I went into her room because I was curious

173

about how she looked naked and I wanted to check her out," Mitchell said.

"Hadn't you seen pictures of naked girls before?" Laura asked.

"Yeah, yeah, but I couldn't help myself," Mitchell said, turning a slight shade of pink.

"You couldn't help yourself," Mick yelled. "You couldn't help yourself. What kind of boy did I raise? This is your kid sister. You're supposed to protect her."

Susan studied Mitchell as he turned pinker from shame and just sat there rubbing his hands together.

"Do you know that Anita has been having nightmares?" Laura said.

"I'm going to leave again," Mitchell said. He started to get up. Susan held her breath.

"No, you're not. You were a jerk. You did things to her a brother should never do," Mick said. "Just stay right there." They talked for another twenty minutes about touching and fondling and discussed what had happened.

Anita said, "I knew he'd come back the next night. When he did, I pushed his hand away when he went to unbutton my top."

"Yes?" Laura said.

Anita continued, "Mitchell said, 'Don't fight me.' "

"I wouldn't listen, so I pushed his hand away again. I moved, but he pulled me back."

"Go on," Laura said.

"I told him to stop," Anita said. "I said it twice." There was silence in the room, and Mitchell squirmed in his seat. He started to get up but sat back down. Susan wondered what would have happened if she and Larry had done family therapy. Would he have got up and left the room?

"Then he shoved himself into me with his penis, and I yelled in pain. It hurt, and I bled." Anita stared at her brother.

174

No one said a word. Mick turned red in the face.

"Afterwards, I punched him and screamed for him to get out," Anita said.

Laura looked at the parents and asked them, "What happened next?"

Sydney said, "She stayed in her room and pretended to have the flu. I brought her soup and toast, but she couldn't sleep, wouldn't eat, and she felt exhausted."

Then Mick said, "After two days, I told my wife to take Anita to see a doctor."

Laura asked the family group, "Do you want to continue?"

Anita wept, and her mother consoled her, but they nodded their heads. "Yes."

They continued the family meeting, and Laura nodded as they talked.

Sydney said, "It didn't take long to figure out Anita had been raped, and the only person it could be was Mitchell." Laura understood their predicament and made notations.

"The doctor did a genital exam collecting what was necessary for lab work and explained to Anita what he was doing. He was very gentle," Sylvia said. "Later, he got a DNA sample from Mitchell."

"I yelled at Mitchell and couldn't believe he'd done that to his kid sister," Mick said. They had come to the clinic after a month of Anita's depression and nightmares. They didn't know what else to do.

"I believe Mitchell should stay in the clinic and get some therapy," Laura suggested. "This is very important."

"I'm not staying here," Mitchell said.

"If I say you're staying, kiddo, you're staying," Mick said. "You're getting some help with your thinking. You need some straightening out, son."

By the end of the meeting, the parents signed Mitchell up

for one month and said they'd return with his clothes. "It may take longer than one month to help Mitchell," Laura said.

Sydney said, "It's a beginning. Let's see how it goes."

"Why do some kids respect females and others don't?" Susan asked Barry that night at dinner.

"That's the sixty-four thousand dollar question. Why do some boys not care, and others use restraint? I believe that this is because some boys think of females as sex objects, just there to please you, then I suppose you don't care. It's hard to believe," he said. The older twins, Michael and Michelle, listened as their parents spoke.

"I would never do that to my sister because I love her," Michael said.

"Of course you wouldn't," said Susan.

Mitchell was an unwilling patient. He came because his parents insisted, and they hoped he'd begin to acknowledge his illness. Sitting among the other boys who had abused females, he heard their stories; he couldn't sleep, wouldn't eat, and he felt exhausted. Mitchell was in the denial phase. He refused to see how he'd treated his sister, as if she had no rights, boundaries, or say. His desire overcame any acknowledgment that Anita had rights. Susan watched through a one-way window as they worked with Mitchell to change his thinking. It was like consciousness-raising. A male therapist named Ed said to Mitchell, "Tell me, Mitchell, what do you think of girls?"

"I like girls, especially cute ones," he said.

"When did you start to think about girls as cute or hot?" Ed said.

"I don't know, maybe a year or so ago."

"Have you been dreaming about them?"

"No, but I get horny when I see a girl I like," Mitchell said.

"What do you think when you see one you like?" Ed asked.

176

"I think how I want to touch her, feel her up, fuck her," Mitchell said.

"Do you think girls are in this world to please you?"

"Yeah, kind of."

"Do you ever think of girls as people, like boys, with ambitions, dreams, ideas?"

"Sometimes, but mostly for sex."

"Do you know girls have dreams too? Maybe one wants to attend a school and become a doctor or a lawyer. Did you ever think that?" Ed asked.

"I guess, but not much," Mitchell said.

"My wife is a psychiatrist. She went to medical school, studied, and became a doctor," Ed said.

"That's cool," Mitchell said.

"Did you ever think that your sister may have dreams and ambitions?"

"No, not much," Mitchell said.

"I have to tell you that girls have dreams just like us guys," Ed said. Mitchell nodded.

"They're people, just like us guys, and they have rights. What do you think of females having rights?"

"I don't know. I guess I never thought of it that way." Mitchell raised his eyebrows.

"Yeah, they're just like us guys. Some want to grow up and get married and have kids, some want to travel the world, and some want to become famous actresses. All kinds of things," Ed said.

Mitchell said, "I never thought of females in that way."

"Well, you ought to start thinking of girls differently 'cause they're people just like us fellows. One more thing I need to ask you, Mitchell; what if one of your friends wanted to fuck his sister? Let's just say he did. What would you tell him?" Ed said. Mitchell hung his head. "Come on. Does one of your friends have a kid sister?"

177

"Yeah, Charlie has a sister named Jen."

"Okay. Charlie wants to bop Jenny. There you go. What are you going to say to him?" Ed asked.

"Well, I guess I'd say, 'Are you sure about this?' "

"Really? Why not?"

"Stop! No, I know where you're going with this, stop."

"What's the difference? You bopped Anita. Charlie wants to do it to Jen," Ed said.

"He shouldn't," Mitchell said.

"But you did."

"Yeah, I know. I know."

"What's the difference?" Ed said.

"Stop, I get it. Stop already," Mitchell screamed. "I shouldn't have done it, but I couldn't stop. I was too fucking horny. I didn't care that she was my sister." He sat in his chair and sobbed. "I'm a creep!"

Susan looked through the window and thought about Larry.

Ed said, "You're starting to get it, Mitchell. I want you to think about why you didn't stop like you were telling your buddy, Charlie. I want you to think if you even gave it a minute's thought and then said, 'No, I'm doing it.' Between now and the next meeting, think about it. Okay, buddy?" Ed said.

Mitchell said, "Okay."

"Come here," Ed said. He put his arms around Mitchell and said, "You're going to get it. It just takes time, kid."

The following day, Anita came into the family therapy room. Her parents were sitting in two chairs, side by side. Laura, Susan, and Mitchell were there with the parents.

Susan said to Mitchell, "Your sister drew this picture. Do you remember this?"

"Yeah, that's me coming into her room," he said.

"So, you recognize it?"

178

"Yes, that's me and her in her room"

"What were you thinking when you came into her room?"

"I'd rather not say. It's kind of embarrassing."

Susan sat down with the drawing, and then Laura asked, "Does anyone want to speak?"

Anita walked up to her brother and said, "Please stand up, Mitchell." Looking at her brother straight in the face, she said, "I'm a person! See me?" Mitchell stared at her. "Who gave you a right to take my virginity?" she said. She stood right in front of Mitchell and wouldn't back down.

Mitchell stood there, looked down, then up, and stuttered, "I didn't think. I honestly didn't think."

She hit him, first on the face, then on his shoulder, and started to cry. "I hate you!"

Her parents watched because Laura had asked them not to interrupt earlier. Tears fell from Anita's eyes. Laura stood up and said nothing. Mitchell tried to hug Anita, but she resisted. When she'd worn herself out with the sobs, he stretched out his arms again, put them around her thin shoulders, and kissed her cheeks.

"I'm so sorry. Can you ever forgive me?" There were tears on Mitchell's cheeks.

Laura gave Anita a tissue.

Mitchell repeated, "Please don't hate me. Can you ever forgive me?" After Mitchell begged her to forgive him, Anita doubled over and buried her face in her hands. A few minutes passed, and then she wiped her face.

Sydney and Mick held hands, squeezing tightly, and then Anita said, "Mitchell, you're my brother, but why did you do this to me?"

"I'm an idiot. I'm a fool, an unfeeling selfish prick. I don't know. I wasn't thinking. Fuck," he said.

The clinic's doctor then learned that Anita was pregnant. Her parents were mortified, and Mitchell was embarrassed by

179

the scandal. Laura said they would have to take care of the problem. The parents found a doctor who performed abortions in Washington, D.C., for a medically necessary situation. Anita was very nauseous and sick. She vomited daily. In 1964, Anita entered the doctor's office, put on the Johnnie, got up on the table, and let the physician do whatever he needed to do to get rid of the fetus. She didn't want to have her brother's child. Everyone agreed. When it was over, Anita returned to Penny Long Children's Treatment Center to continue her recovery. Mitchell stayed in the other section for the abusers and also continued with therapy and family sessions.

Anita told Laura and Susan, "Thank God I'm not pregnant. At least I'll have a normal life."

"Tell me some of the things you want to do with your life?" Laura asked.

"I want to be like Gloria Steinem. I'm sick of girls being behind guys. I'm going to be a leader, write articles, march, go to Washington, D.C., and help women. That's what I want to do when I get older."

Laura and Susan both clapped their hands, and Laura said, "Well, that's a fabulous idea. I'm proud of you. You've grown so much. Do you know that, Anita?"

"I couldn't have done it without both of your help. You each explained to me about standing up for myself. I never understood that before. "They hugged one another, and then Laura and Susan discussed the case after the session was over.

"We're beginning to make a difference," Laura said. "It's amazing."

"Tonight, I'm going to report to my family. We have dinner together and discuss the clinic. My father will be thrilled. All our efforts are beginning to pay off. Good job," she said, as she hugged Laura.

That evening, when the Stern family gathered around the table, Susan shared her festive mood as she told Anita's story. The entire group listened intently. Dad was smiling.

"It's so satisfying to have a positive outcome to a situation that could have gone south. Way south. Everyone involved did a great job. Wait until I call Penny Long and share this with her," Dad said as he sipped red wine. Trudy served dinner. It was Italian, spaghetti and meatballs, salad, and garlic bread. One of the family's favorite meals.

"Is everything to everyone's liking?" Trudy asked.

Dad said, "You tell Odell that you are carrying on her style and tradition in the best way."

Chapter Twenty-One

Work never stopped at the clinic, and Susan was on top of the list of new clients. A twenty-six-year-old young man, Burt Rudin, came to the clinic after he was arrested. His family wanted him to get treatment, and he agreed after he was discovered. Burt had enrolled in a high school as a junior with false documents. He had never been popular with the girls because he was only five feet four inches tall and weighed one hundred and twenty pounds. He had a huge inferiority complex. He went to Southside High School in Fall River to seduce some young girls into having sex with him. He had a forged birth certificate, fake immunization records, a phony transcript, and other counterfeit documents. The high school let him enter as a junior. After he got acclimated, he convinced the young girls, who were fourteen years old, to pose for sexually explicit photographs, and he paid them, as Susan learned later from Joe Cohen, a therapist who did the intake.

The police reported that Burt took them to his small room on the wrong side of town because, after living with a mother who beat him and a dad who was a deadbeat, he was desperate to be loved. He knew how to charm these young coeds since he was older than the typical high school kid. He'd been reading magazines and practicing in front of a mirror.

He would say, "Hi, what's your name?"

"Maggie."

"Cute name. What year are you?" Burt asked as he stared at her breasts.

"I'm a sophomore. Are you new?" she said as she looked down at his crotch.

"Yeah, just got here. Can I buy you a Coke after school?" Maggie looked at him and hesitated. "Come on. I'm a good guy, and I'm new."

"Okay."

After half an hour at the local coffee shop, he touched her face softly. "May I take your picture? You're adorable."

"I don't know." Maggie blushed.

"You're so hot," Burt smiled.

"Sure."

"Come on back to my place. Just for a few photos."

At his place, he gave Maggie a red teddy. "Could you put this on?" She came out of the bathroom in the teddy and looked shy. "Aw, you're beautiful," he said. "Lie on the bed and put your arms above your head."

Maggie did what he said. Then she moaned. "Excellent. You're a hot number, Maggie." Burt clicked his camera. "I like what you're doing, Maggie."

He took a few more shots. "Great. That's enough for today." Maggie jumped up and giggled. "You're a natural," he said.

Maggie told her friend, Kathy, what she'd done. "You're never going to believe this, but I did sexy photos with the new kid, Burt."

"Oh, my goodness. You, hottie," Kathy said.

"It was so fun. I may do it again. I liked it."

Burt saw her the next day and said, "Want to come over again?"

Back at his place, he touched her when she got on his bed in the red teddy. "Moan like you did yesterday," Burt whispered.

Maggie moaned.

"Oh, I love it when you do that. You turn me on," Burt said. He put his hand on her thigh. They kissed, and then Burt slowly slid her teddy off. They had intercourse, nice and easy, and Maggie groaned some more. Then she whimpered. "I love your moaning; I love it," he said as he came and then licked her ear lobe.

183

Several times, he had sexual intercourse with underage girls. When one confessed to her friend, and the word got out, it was just a matter of time before Burt was arrested. His mother insisted he get help, and somehow, with funds from the town and the high school, he got into the clinic and was admitted for a two-month stay. After he got settled, he spent a lot of time in the gym, lifting weights to build his body into a more muscled version of a male. "I hate the way I look," he told Joe Cohen.

"You're not going to grow anymore, Burt. You know this, don't you?"

"I know. I'm twenty-six, so I won't be growing any taller."

"You can get more muscles, but your height is pretty much set. It would help if you learned to accept yourself. You know that, don't you?"

"I know. I know." He looked at himself in the mirror.

"Well, let's think of some ways you can like yourself more," Joe said.

"I don't know."

"Tell me a few things that you do like about yourself."

"I like that I can draw pretty well."

"Let me set you up with Susan for some expressive therapy. That's a start," Joe said.

After reading Burt's chart and talking with Joe Cohen, Susan met with Burt and they drew pictures together. Just like Susan had drawn pictures with Dickie. She brought photos, and he copied them. He had talent. Then Susan asked him if he wanted to draw something original. Maybe he had a picture in his mind he wanted to create. Burt drew a picture of a comely woman in a G-string with large breasts, long blond hair, and red lips.

Susan said, "That's a lovely drawing. Tell me, why this?"

184

"She's my fantasy woman. I wish I could take her to bed," Burt said.

"Can you think of anything besides a sexy female? What else comes to your mind?"

Then Burt drew a table with a family sitting around it, having supper. He took his time and put in details, including a father with a short beard, a mother wearing an apron, and a sister with a ribbon tied in her hair.

"That's a very nice picture, Burt. Tell me about it," said Susan.

"It's the family I wish I had, and we're all together, sitting there having a home-cooked meal my mom prepared," he said. "We're talking about the new Disney World that opened in Florida."

"I like this a lot," Susan said. "Nice."

It wasn't long before Burt spotted Anita in the clinic. At eleven years old, she was a petite, thin girl, and he decided that she was a perfect size for him.

"Hi there," he said when they were in line at the cafeteria.

"Hi," she said, holding up her grey tray to block her body.

"What are you getting to eat today?"

"Oh, I don't know. Maybe a burger. What about you?"

"Probably the same. They're pretty good here, don't you think?"

"Yeah, the food's not bad," she said.

Standing behind the two patients, Susan listened to their conversation.

She followed them as they got their lunch and sat down together. She sat near the table and tried to listen. It was unusual that a boy, who was an offender, would be dining with the victims, but they were painting that day and had to make an exception.

185

"How long you here for?" Burt asked Anita.

"Well, I'm not sure. I started with a month, but it's gotten more complicated," Anita said. "I wasn't quite ready to go home. What about you?" she said as she poured ketchup on her hamburger.

"I don't know. I got arrested. I guess I'll leave when they let me out," he said.

Susan wondered how motivated he was. He sure didn't sound it.

"What did you do?"

"I pretended I was a high school kid and registered and then I bopped a few girls and got caught," he said.

"Well, if you don't mind me saying, you don't sound very sorry," Anita said.

"It's just the way I talk. Napoleon complex," he said, laughing.

"Yeah, you are pretty small for a guy," Anita said.

"I know, it's messed with my head," Burt said as he took a healthy bite of his burger.

Susan liked the conversation because he sounded genuine now. Remembering how Dom had seduced her when they were at the dinner table, Susan tried to listen carefully. Burt was being honest about himself, unlike that creep Dom.

They were all excited because Mama was coming home. Trudy was busy making party preparations. "My mother is fussy. Do your best," Susan said.

Lily had a new life and was away, and Susan feared she'd hardly see her anymore. Knowing their family was a bit odd, she accepted this fact and cherished her life with her beloved Barry. She went home and looked at photo albums to see how her mother had looked when she was younger. She studied the pictures, amazed at how happy the

186

family was before her parents got divorced. There was a photo of her riding a pony and one of Mama dressed in a new cocktail dress.

Mama's plane landed at Logan Airport in Boston. Susan went to pick her up and was thrilled to hear her mother's voice when she said, "Hello, sweetie." It almost felt like too much. Susan wondered if she and Mama could take a trip together. She had to ask her about that.

They didn't say too much on their way to 2 Poppins Lane. Mama talked about how beautiful Paris was. When Susan opened the Victorian house door, only Trudy was there, and Mama warmly greeted her. Mama wanted to walk through the house, through all the rooms on the first floor, out the kitchen door, and around the backyard. Susan knew no one was home and wondered if Mama was checking out any changes in her old house. Susan watched as Mama twisted her hands together as she strolled around.

At last, Mama said, "Can we talk?"

Susan sat down and made a gesture to Mama.

"I'm so glad you're here," Susan said.

"I've been so many places," Mama said. "My head is swimming."

"I know. You have a whole new life."

"It's amazing. I can't wait to see the twins. "Two sets of twins!" she said, laughing.

"You'll see all the babies, Mama." Pictures of all the children were already on the walls.

"Yes."

"You look wonderful," Susan said. Mom had a new hairdo and a Gucci scarf around her neck.

"I'm a little nervous," Mama said. She took a pill out of her bag and popped it in her mouth. "This is harder than I thought." Susan squeezed her mother's hand.

Dad came home and tried to find the right words. There

was a silence at first between the two of them. Susan watched Dad walk toward Mama, sit down, and talk quietly. Susan let them have a few minutes alone because she was sure that they needed some time. She went inside the kitchen and helped Trudy. Soon, other people arrived; sons-in-law, babies, people holding bottles and toys. Everyone relaxed and the family filled up the rooms. Gail Collins walked in with her two children. Max Jr. still looked exactly like his father.

"Please don't be mad at me for marrying Max," Gail said to Mama after a few minutes.

"I'm okay now because I have a new life," Mama said as she controlled her unspoken tension. She was right. She was resilient and wanted to make the children proud. Trudy brought Mama a cup of tea and brown sugar cookies. The grandkids kissed Mama, and then many of them played outside. When twilight fell, they came back inside.

Trudy set the table and another for the kids. Coffee was fresh; drinks were served, and paper plates were in the corner cupboard in case they ran out of dishes. Everyone was quieter than usual, tense and tentative, talking in front of Mama and Gail. They ate a sumptuous meal. Trudy cooked a brisket with roasted potatoes and a noodle pudding with raisins. After a while, the family started to relax, spoke more freely, and helped themselves to warm challah with butter. They chatted with each other and ate for a few minutes before having coffee and dessert. The kids asked Mama a slew of questions, and she answered each one.

"Penny and I are learning so many new things. I am thrilled to be doing this. People write us letters and stop us on the street. It's exciting," she said.

Dad went outside with Gail for a few minutes. When they returned, their facial expressions looked more relaxed.

Susan and Ellen hugged and smiled at one another. They stood in the hallway. It was dark outside now.

"It's okay, isn't it?" Susan said.

"She'll be here a week."

"We'll have time." They were both hoping to have quality visits with Mama.

"Anything can happen," Ellen said, a bit nervous.

"Fingers crossed, sis." Then they hugged one another and felt better.

There was laughter in the house and the sounds of children giggling. Soft music played in the background. Mama took off her shoes, got down on the rug, and romped with the little ones. Max Jr. took pictures. Everyone surrounded Mom. When it was late, Mama wanted to go to Susan and Barry's house to sleep. The twins were ecstatic. Everyone kissed goodbye, and they made plans for the week. "Tomorrow, Max, take me to the new clinic, please," Mama said to her ex-husband as she was at the door.

"It would be my pleasure. You'll be proud, Lily. All our work paid off."

"I'm sure. I need pictures to show Penny."

"No problem," Max Jr. said. "I'm the photographer in the family!"

Lily bristled slightly.

Everyone was smiling at 2 Poppins Lane.

During the week, Mama didn't stop. She visited the clinic and loved everything she saw. The children's rooms with beds and closets were spacious and inviting. The rooms for the abusers were perfect. The therapy, the art and drama centers, the cafeteria, and the farmhouse with the inviting fireplace all impressed her. She loved the setting in Cameron Park with the duck pond.

"Max, it's just the way we imagined, isn't it?" Mama said.

189

She visited each grandchild and child, overlooking no one. Mama confirmed their addresses and phone numbers and asked them what they wanted. She promised to send presents and postcards and then asked her daughters if they wanted to visit *Penlily* in Bedford. "You must come and see what Penny and I are doing. It is really terrific," she said. Businesswoman that she was, she took out her calendar and penciled in some possible dates. Susan hugged her mother and asked her if there was any possibility that Ellen and she could go away with Mom.

"Oh, I'd love that. Maybe next time I go to Paris, we could all go. Would you like that?" she asked.

"Mama, what a question! Of course, we'd like to go. My bag is already packed," Susan said. She hugged and kissed her mother.

Susan drove Mama back to Logan at the end of the busy week and put her on the plane back to New York, Westchester Airport, which was close to Bedford.

"Thank you for the wonderful week. I'm coming back soon," Mama said as they parted at the gate. Tears were in her eyes, but she smiled broadly.

"Life is complicated, isn't it, Mama?" Susan said. She looked at her mom for wisdom.

"I'm afraid it is."

"Call me anytime."

"And you too, sweetie."

Off she went, Gucci scarf, new hairdo, and all. Susan was proud of her mother and believed she had inherited her mother's resilience.

The next day, a Boy Scout victim entered the clinic. He was eighteen years old and was coming in because his Boy Scout leader had been molesting him since he was eight years old.

"You have to give me some help," he said. He was a tall, dark-haired, handsome boy who had repeatedly tried to tell his parents about this scout leader but couldn't get the words out.

"Tell me what happened," the girl at the front desk said.

"I've been molested for ten years, and now that I'm an adult, I'm coming into this clinic for help," he said.

"Okay, why don't you fill these forms out," she said as she gave him the clipboard.

His name was West Williamson and he grew up in a rural town of five thousand people.

He had joined the Scouts at his father's urging when he was eight. His dad was unkind and picked on West, so West thought he might find another male figure more congenial to him. His leader was named David Care, and he was an attractive-looking man in his late twenties. He took West under his wing. That was the beginning of a nightmare.

He and Laura went into the therapy room and chatted so Laura, the social worker, could do a proper intake. Susan watched and listened from the one-way mirror because she was intrigued by this case. "Tell me about what brings you here," Laura said, putting one leg over the other.

"For ten years, I've endured sexual abuse by my scout leader and never told anyone. Now I'm a mess. I have nightmares, I can't concentrate, I have hardly any friends, and I can't date. I need help, big time," as he sat in the chair and twisted his hands together.

Laura asked, "Why did you wait so long?" as Susan listened.

"My parents are old-fashioned, and I just couldn't tell them. When I complained about going to the Scouts, my father said, 'Do whatever David Care says,' so I was stuck."

"Do your folks know you're here now?"

"No, I figured I could come alone now that I was eighteen."

"Tell me, what kinds of things happened to you?"

"He made me touch him, give him blow jobs, he raped me, he masturbated in front of me, stuff like that."

"And this started when you were eight?"

"Right."

"What else did you do with this man?"

"He taught me to shoot guns. We went camping and fishing, he gave me treats, and he taught me archery."

"And you never told your parents about the sex?" Laura asked again.

"No."

"Did you tell anyone?" She shook her head in disbelief.

"Never."

"How do you sleep?"

"I don't." He said, yawned as he rubbed his forehead.

"Bad dreams?"

"I have nightmares and flashbacks, and I lie in bed and go over what happened. I can't even eat."

"I want you to stay here for three months," Laura said compassionately. "You need a lot of help and therapy. I'm going to set you up with a doctor for a physical check-up."

He smiled. "I'm so relieved to be here."

"Do you have any hobbies you enjoy?" Laura asked.

"I like plays, the theater, acting. It's like taking myself out of my life and becoming somebody else."

"I'm going to have you do drama therapy with our expressive therapist, Susan. This will help you get these suppressed feelings out. I'm sure you have a great deal of anger."

Susan nodded her head "yes," behind the mirror. She was interested in this Boy Scout patient and met him the next day.

192

"I hear you like acting," she said when they met. She wanted to design a scene where West could release his feelings. After reviewing his chart, she asked, "Who do you want to be, yourself or David Care?"

"I'll be him, and you be me, and then we'll switch."

She could see that he was enthusiastic and wanted to begin.

West said, "Let's lie down on the floor, you this way, me that way."

They got down on the floor and waited.

West said, "I want to touch you on your privates."

"I don't want you to do that," Susan said.

"Then I'll touch myself," West said. "Maybe I'll unzip my pants."

Susan said, "I really don't like this at all."

"West said, "Well, I'm going to jerk myself off." He pretends to unzip his fly.

"I don't want to do this," Susan said.

West said, "It doesn't matter because this is what I'm going to do." His hand is on his zipper.

Susan stopped and said, "Okay. That was great. Now, you be yourself, and I'll be David."

West said, "I don't like this," acting as himself in this scene.

"Do what I tell you, or you're going to get into trouble," Susan said.

"I hate you're touching me. You're a pervert," West said. He tried to roll away.

Susan said, "I want you to give me a blow job." She reached out to roll him toward her.

"I'm just a kid and don't want to do that. It's disgusting. You're ugly," West cried, his hands over his face.

"How dare you say that to me, you spoiled brat," Susan said.

"I want to go home. I'm going to tell on you. You're sick," West screamed. He tried to sit up.

"No one will believe you. Everyone loves me," Susan said.

West started to weep, deep sobs, and Susan hugged him.

"Don't touch me, you sick fucker; keep your hands off of me, or I'll kill you," West yelled.

Chapter Twenty-Two

Larry wrote a letter to Susan and Ellen. He wanted to say he was sorry for what he'd done to them. It had been a long time since they were very young, but Larry felt he needed to apologize. They probably didn't want to hear from him and probably thought he was a real creep. It was more for himself; he needed to get it off his chest. I am a writer, he thought. Why couldn't I write something?

Dear Susan and Ellen,

I don't know what to say, but I want to apologize. I did some terrible things to you. You didn't deserve any of it. I'm sorry I'm a sick man; I don't think I will ever be okay, but at least I know that I have a problem. I don't think I will ever get over it. Some people have tried, the doctors, therapists, and group discussions, but it returns, and I can't resist. I'm better off in jail. In jail, I can write and create and feel useful.

I will never be able to say enough about how much I regret hurting you both. I guess I did it because I'm sick, selfish, and weak. That is no excuse, but it's what I got from group therapy. You are my cousins and nice girls. I shouldn't have ever done that. I couldn't resist. And then I spoke to you without any remorse. I was a prick; I admit it.

We may never see one another again unless you come out west and visit me here. If you want to see me face-to-face, I will put your names on the list. You can write to me. I know I damaged you both and caused you a lot of pain. I know what I have done to you, and I am deeply sorry.
Your cousin,
Larry Fink

Larry sent a copy to each of the sisters. He addressed them both to 2 Poppins Lane, since he didn't know their new addresses. They received the letters and read them a number of times. Then the two sisters met for coffee, talked. Susan sipped her coffee. "I can't believe he wrote us."

"After all this time, I wonder what came over him." Ellen added cream to her coffee.

"He probably feels guilty. Poor fucker."

"Well, at least he apologized and really admitted he did it, and he was sorry."

"He also said he's uncurable after all that work they did on him," Susan said. "Unbelievable."

"Well, we know what the recovery rate is. He's hardcore." Ellen took her napkin, rolled it up in a ball, and threw it with a look of disgust.

"Do we want to go see him?" Susan asked. "I actually wouldn't mind seeing him." Susan searched Ellen's face for some clue about what she really felt.

"I suppose, but what would it accomplish, sis?"

"I guess I'd like to see the inside of the prison and maybe talk to him about why he can't help himself resist the compulsion."

"All good things, but how will we get free right now? We're too busy, don't you think?"

"I agree, but he just wrote to us after all these years. We might learn something if we go when he's in the mood to talk. Besides, we may never have this opportunity again."

"Okay, let's say we fly out there and stay for two days. We'll arrange it with babysitters and stay in a hotel near the prison. What do you think?"

"I say we can do it."

They paid their bill, and each went on their way. After a bit of research, a few phone calls, a chat with Dad, and adjusting their schedules, they were set to go.

Barry said, "I think this is a big breakthrough. I fully support your going, Sue. I hired a baby nurse to watch the new twins. Don't worry about anything. Keep detailed notes. I want to hear everything."

"Okay, but..."

"Don't worry about the twins; I'm on top of it." He kissed her on her head.

Zev was supportive also and told Ellen to go with Glick, a Yiddish word he used when he wanted to say good luck. "I hope you don't get too upset. That's all I'm worried about."

Dad said, "I spoke to the prison, and it's all arranged. Larry has been informed. He's excited, and I think it'll be interesting. Susan, it would help if you considered giving a talk to the clinic afterward and sharing what you learned. We need to hear what transpired."

The plane was large, their seats were comfortable, and as it took off. Susan's nerves leaped into her heart. Susan was thirty-two, Ellen thirty-one; Larry molested them when they were ten and nine, and the memories still surged through them – twenty years since they'd even seen their cousin or had a talk.

The prison was in Salinas Valley, one of the notorious prisons for sexual offenders. Other prisoners killed these sexual offenders at a very high rate, even with special housing to protect them. Private investigators, lawyers, and bail bondsmen occupied the surrounding rental properties. A taxi drove them to the motel, and they settled in. The weather was hot; they were sweating and nervous. They changed their clothes and took a cab to the prison, but discovered they couldn't see Larry until his Saturday group therapy was over. Then they strolled through the town and stopped at a small cafe that had Formica tables and chrome chairs with red plastic seats.

Once they returned to the prison, they saw tattooed men of varying ethnicities in the yard as armed guards supervised. On edge, Ellen and Susan took deep breaths as they approached the glass door of the visitor's center. Susan and Ellen squeezed each other's hand as a heavy-set guard with a gun on his hip and a walkie-talkie led them through a long hall inside the prison. They came to the waiting area, and the guard told them to sit while he checked their credentials. They left their handbags with another guard. As their hearts beat faster, arm in arm, they were led into a visitor's area with small tables and a few chairs at each station. Larry walked in wearing a tan prison jumpsuit. At thirty-seven, he looked older and paler to Susan, like he hadn't spent much time outdoors. His body was soft but thin, and he looked tired. After he sat down across from the sisters, who had beads of sweat across their foreheads, they stared at one another. Guards were stationed all over the room, and no one was allowed to touch.

"Hi there," Susan said. She tried to grin.

"How you doing, Larry?" Ellen asked.

"I still recognize you both," he said, partially smiling.

"How're you doing in here?"

"Well, it's a prison, so it's not much fun, but they leave me alone now."

"We got your letter. It surprised us," Ellen said.

"I needed to apologize. I was so bad to you both. A real jerk."

"That's an understatement," Susan agreed, being brave.

"Really, Larry. Telling us that we were both special. You were really mean," Ellen said.

"You're right. I'm a sick man, and I was sick then, and I am ashamed of my behavior, but I can't seem to overcome it."

"Why do you think it's so hard?" Ellen asked.

198

"I don't know, I've tried and tried, but I can't kick it."
He was staring at the concrete wall behind the two women.

"Too bad. Some people do, but not many," Susan said.

"That doesn't mean I don't feel bad," Larry answered.
"I know I was a prick and treated you so shabbily." He hung
his head and looked ashamed.

"We appreciated the letter," Ellen commented.

"Why do you think some men treat children so
offensively?" Susan asked. "You've been to groups and
heard what the guys say, Larry. Tell us what you think?"
She touched the notebook in her pocket.

"Some males just don't care about kids as people.
They're just toys or sex objects for their pleasure, pure and
simple. No respect."

"Why?" Ellen inquired.

"The guys feel powerless and weak, and they take it out
on the youngsters. It makes them feel powerful for that
minute. That's their solution to their inability to feel
strong."

"Why are they so weak?" Susan asked.

"They were fucked over, damaged, ruined, and they
can't get on top of it, so since there's nothing more than a
temporary solution, they use revenge. Children are objects
to use," Larry said.

Susan and Ellen looked at each other and nodded.

"Do you mind if I write this down?" Susan asked.

"No."

"What do you do in here?" Ellen inquired.

"I write TV shows, I collaborate on a book with my
friend, and sometimes I write letters," he said. "Group
therapy, library. They pay me one dollar and twenty-five
cents a week to work in the library." He laughed.

"No kidding?" Ellen said.

"What's going on in your lives?" Larry inquired.

"Well, the family opened a sexual abuse clinic for children who have been molested. That was the positive thing that came out of the whole mess," Susan said.

"I'm glad I was good for something." For a few seconds, his face looked relieved and younger.

"It's doing very well and affiliated with the local hospital in Georgeport. Dad started it," Ellen commented.

"Your father is a good man. He helped me a lot."

The guard came over and said, "You have five minutes."

"We'd like to come tomorrow. We're just here for two days. Okay?" Susan asked.

"Sure."

"Can we bring you anything? Are you allowed?" Ellen asked.

"No, I'm all set. They're pretty strict."

"We'll see you tomorrow, and we'll talk more. Okay?" Susan said, smiling.

"Right," Larry said.

"Until tomorrow," Ellen said.

They left the way they came, hopped in a cab, and asked the cabbie to take them to a cafe in town. They needed to unwind. It was a heavy-duty day. When they got to the cafe, which had a green awning and was old and tired but clean, they slipped into a booth and ordered grilled cheese sandwiches.

"Well, what did you think?" Susan asked.

"I think that's as good as it gets with Larry," Ellen said.

"You're probably right."

"We came all this way to hear what we know," Ellen said.

"We came all this way to hear him say he tried, but he can't get better, yet he's sorry about it," Susan said.

"Let's eat; I'm starving," Ellen announced.

200

The next day, the two sisters went back to the prison. When they sat down in the visitor's room, Larry appeared. He smiled at them and said, "It's good seeing you again."

"What's your novel about?" Ellen asked.

"It's about a heist by some bad guys that goes south. My buddy and I are having a good time dreaming up the characters, mostly deadbeats and punks, but we love brainstorming. They're planning a bank robbery with a guy driving the van. They think they can get away with it, but, of course, they don't. But we love all the action," he said, smiling.

"Larry, why do you think you became a predator? What happened to you when you were younger?" Susan asked, being brave again.

He stared into his lap for a minute. Then he said, "My mom had a boyfriend who worked at Sears and lived with us. Mom liked him, plus he paid for things like food and electricity, and he made our life easier. He knew he was secure. So, he started coming into my bedroom when I was like eight or nine and fucking me. I was appalled, and it hurt like hell, but he didn't care because he knew Flo wouldn't want him to leave. We were eating steaks instead of Spaghetti-o's. My Mom even got her hair done. He told me to keep quiet and say nothing, or Mom would be pissed, and we'd be poor. So, I sucked it up. I was miserable, had stomach aches, couldn't study, didn't have many friends, and tried to stay away from him, but I was just a kid. I was stuck and it went on and on for a few years."

The sisters knew the story, but hearing Larry tell it really got to them. They both nodded and stared at him with understanding.

"How'd you get your Mom to move?" Ellen asked.

"I begged her. I said I was lonely. That did it. She really loved me and didn't want me to be miserable and have no friends. So, we came to your home, and I went crazy. You were the victims. That's the ugly true story." He hung his head and stared at his cuffed hands.

"You never thought to tell your mother afterward?" Susan asked.

"She would have felt guilty." He shook his head and said, "Who am I kidding? She would have been horrified. It was a Catch-22, as they say. Being a helpless kid is very bad. Where could I go? I was stuck in the situation."

"I know how hard it is to tell your parents. I had a very hard time until my neighbor helped us. She had Mama come over, and she told her. Did that program help you any?"

"Oh, God, it opened my eyes, and I tried to stop, but when I saw a sexy young girl, I would give in. My resolve would go right out the window. I was only good if I lived like a monk or in jail. Otherwise, my discipline fell apart."

"I guess they still have a lot of work to do to figure out how to help abusers. It is so deep-seated," Ellen said. "We're working hard at the clinic, but know everyone cannot be cured."

"We may need you on the team to give us ideas on how to cure people. What do you think, Larry? Could you send me ideas of how to get perpetrators to get over this illness?" Susan wondered.

"I'd love to help, and if you want me to write down whatever I think would help guys from doing it again, I'll try. I'd love to help in the cure." He smiled.

"That's an excellent idea," Ellen said, clasping her hands. "You write down ideas you think could help, and we'll see if they work. Since you have this problem, maybe you'll understand their minds better than we do. Your thoughts would be appreciated."

"I'll give you our clinic address, and you can write to

us. This is a beginning." Susan scribbled their Georgeport address in Cameron Park and gave Larry the paper after getting a nod from the guard. Their visit was coming to an end. They couldn't hug Larry or shake his hand, but they said they were glad they had made the trip.

Susan grinned at him. "This is the beginning of a new chapter, Larry. Thank you for reaching out to us."

Ellen nodded. "It's a milestone. You did a meaningful thing by writing to us."

Later, Dad called Susan and Ellen to see how things were going with their visit with Larry.

"We had a good talk, but he said he wasn't able to get over his tendencies to abuse, so he is a lost cause. He did sound repentant and apologized to both of us, but he admitted he can't recover from his compunctions."

"That's too bad, but that's what I figured. He's had so much therapy and so many chances. It's too bad," Dad replied.

"He's pretty okay writing his TV shows and working on a novel. I don't think he's miserable. It's not great, but it's as good as it gets for someone like him, Dad," Ellen said.

"We went back for one last visit. At least we've repaired our relationship with him to the point where we can be honest," Susan admitted.

"That's a big deal," Ellen said.

"Then it was a worthwhile visit. Say hello to him from me and tell him to keep working on his TV shows and putting his money in the bank account," Dad said.

They hung up after saying they'd see him soon.

Seeing Larry and hearing his offer to help made the trip worthwhile. Now, the sisters were anxious to get back to their families. When they got to the airport, they checked their bags and got their boarding passes.

"Time for a quick drink?" Susan asked. They went to the Irish pub and ordered beers from the good-looking bartender.

"I'm so thirsty," Ellen said.

The bartender smiled. "You girls sisters?"

"Yeah," Susan said. "Do we look that much alike?"

"Same look and style," as he wiped the bar top.

"Can you tell which of us is older?" Ellen said.

"You're not twins, are you?" he asked.

"Almost," Ellen said, laughing.

"Irish twins," he said. You're the older one," he pointed to Susan.

"Good guesser!" Ellen laughed.

The next morning, they were both back in their own kitchens, sipping fresh coffee.

Chapter Twenty-Three

The clinic continued to see all types of sexual abuse cases of children. One family came in with their son, who a priest had abused. Another family brought in a girl who a school teacher had molested. Another family brought in their mentally disabled child who a caregiver was molesting. Another was a young boy who his father abused. A rabbi sexually mistreated an eight-year-old child, and the ultra-orthodox community turned against the person who reported it. Coverups in the Orthodox community were rampant, and the sexual abuse often went unreported.

Estimating actual recidivism rates in sexual abuse cases is nearly impossible since many go unreported. Susan learned from her research that rape victims often don't tell authorities. Child molesters remain at risk to re-offend long after their releases. There are many sexual misdeeds. Some people say molesters who offend males are more likely to re-offend than those who offend females. Some people say incest is less likely to be repeated than rape. Sex abuse is a term used for minors; sexual assault is used to describe acts against adults. The therapists at the clinic tell all victims that the sooner they get to the clinic or doctor, the better.

Susan's first case after she returned from visiting Larry was a young girl who her Uncle Becker had sexually abused while he was visiting and staying with the family. He was a big guy who did auto mechanic and trucking jobs, had no wife, one kid he never saw, and was the girl's mother's brother. He stayed with the family for several months while he looked for a new job.

The girl, Hillary Hunt, who was ten years old, came to her mother and said, "Mom, Uncle Becker is coming into my room and putting his finger in me. I don't like it. Can you please tell him to stop?"

Susan was amazed that the child told her mother and wanted to talk to her about the case. "Tell me, Hillary, how did you get the courage to tell your mother?"

"His finger was big, and I hated the feeling. It hurt me," Hillary said. "Plus, Uncle Becker didn't smell good. He wore shirts that smelled like starch, and his breath was bad from smoking cigars. The whole thing was gross," she said.

"Would you like to draw a picture of this?" Susan asked.

"Yeah, sure. I like to draw."

The drawing depicted the girl in her bed with this burly man sitting on the edge of her bed while he had his finger between the child's legs. A cat was on the floor, a doll at the end of the bed, and a huge and scary-looking uncle.

"How long did this go on before you spoke up?" Susan asked.

"He did it three times, and then I decided I couldn't take it. I knew he was my mom's brother, but I couldn't take the smell, the pain, his yuckiness," she said.

Susan told Laura, the social worker, about the picture and suggested they all meet. Shirley, the mother, was a woman in her forties and looked like she worked hard. Her hair was straight, and her clothes were clean but simple. She wore no makeup. "I'm glad to be here and want to help," Hillary's mother said.

Laura asked, "When did you learn about what your brother, Becker, was doing?"

"Hillary came into my bedroom one morning, I was still under the covers, and she told me. Naturally, I was shocked."

"How long has your brother been living with you?" Laura asked.

"Oh, a couple of months. It's just temporary until he gets back on his feet."

"What happened when you learned about what Becker was doing?"

"I was horrified, of course. I went right into Becker's room and confronted him. I said, 'What the hell are you doing to my child?' "

"What did he say?" Laura asked.

"He said that he was just fooling around with her and he hadn't raped her, as if that meant it was no big deal."

"And what did you tell him?" Laura inquired.

"I said he wasn't to touch my daughter in any way. I told him to pack up his bags and leave because she was a minor and he was a grown man."

"How did he respond?"

"He begged me to change my mind since he liked staying with me. Why wouldn't he? I feed him, clean his room, don't charge him a penny."

"Where is he now?"

"He's still there, but I am trying to get him out. He's dragging his feet."

"You could call the police."

"I don't want to. He's my brother," she explained.

"Would you please ask him to attend our next family meeting?"

"Why?"

"I would like to ask him a few questions," Laura scribbled in her notebook; her eyes never leaving her written words. Susan realized that Laura was distraught with this family's situation.

The next family meeting was a few days later; Shirley returned with her brother to meet with Laura. Hillary joined the conversation.

Becker, a robust man with a ruddy complexion, came

in and said, "Here I am," as if he was doing everything they wanted.

"Hello, I'm glad you could make it, Becker," Laura replied. Susan, Hillary, and Shirley were all in the room too.

"May I ask you a few questions, Becker?" Laura said.

"Shoot."

"Have you abused a lot of children in your life?"

"A few," Becker spoke with a bit of a chip on his shoulder, a cockiness that covered his shame.

"When was the first time?"

"I think it was when I was a teenager. There was a kid next door I took a shine to. She was about five. I played around with her."

"What does that mean?" Laura asked, looking upset.

"I put my finger inside her, stuff like that."

"Did she complain?"

"A little, but I bought her ice cream and gave her little things to make her happy."

"When was the next time?"

"Probably when I got married. I touched my daughter, and my wife threw me out," he said.

"I didn't know that," Shirley yelped, scowling.

"So, you came and lived with your sister, and then you touched her daughter?"

"Bad habit," Becker said. He looked a bit sheepish.

"Do you know why you do this?" Laura stared into Becker's eyes, she wanted him to be honest.

"Well, I'm not sure."

"Had you been abused as a boy?" Laura inquired.

"Yeah, my father used to take baths, and he made me wash him. I didn't like it, but he insisted. He told me to wash his privates. He'd get a hard-on. Scared the shit out of me the first time it happened." Becker looked at Laura and just stared at her. Laura stared right back.

"Where was your mother?"

"Oh, doing housework, cooking, hanging clothes on the line."

"I think you ought to find another place to live. It's not fair to Hillary. You have a problem, and until you fix it, she's not safe with you in the house," Susan said.

"Am I too old to come into your program?" he asked.

"Why don't you speak to the registration and admittance people? You need to learn all the details and rules. That would be the first step," Susan answered.

Becker agreed and left. Shirley and her daughter sat in front of Susan and looked at her.

"Hillary needs to remain here for a while and work on her trauma. I think you and Hillary should have some family therapy. It was wonderful, Hillary, that you spoke up. That's a big deal." Susan complimented.

Becker made Susan nervous. He was older than a lot of the other men. His habits were ingrained. He seemed different in a way she couldn't put her finger on.

Doing some research and background checking, Susan discovered that Uncle Becker had a long history of psychiatric problems. He had been a difficult boy at school and had gotten into many fights. After high school, he drove a delivery truck for a pizza place. He became a long-haul trucker and was on the road for months at a time. He had been arrested when a woman from a convenience store accused him of rape.

Becker married a woman who had an affair with a priest. When she became pregnant, she had an abortion. After marrying Becker, they had a daughter together. Becker was discovered molesting the child when she was seven years old. The couple divorced.

Susan wasn't surprised when she read his biography. He lived with his sister because it was free. He took advantage of people and was a loser. He got away with minimizing his sexual abuse.

"Tell me how you dared to speak up, Hillary," Laura asked her the next time they met.

The child rolled her eyes and looked up at the ceiling. "Once, I saw a girl shout at this boy in the playground. 'Who let you touch me? Who made you the boss of me?' When I heard her say that, I thought it was very cool, and I liked how she spoke up for herself. So, later, when Becker did that stuff to me, I decided to speak up like that girl I had seen on the playground. I wanted to be strong and brave like her."

"I want you to tell that to a group of girls in the clinic. We're going to have group therapy, and I was hoping you could explain this to the other girls who are afraid to speak up. Can you do that?" Laura asked.

"Sure."

"Tell me, who do you think is brave? Is there a courageous person you know or read about?"

"I like Joan of Arc. I like Frances Perkins, the Secretary of Labor. I adore Eleanor Roosevelt."

"That's a great list. Anyone in your life besides that girl in the playground?"

"I have a teacher, Mrs. Robinson, who seems like a brave woman. She tells the kids to speak up and be confident. She pushes us to express ourselves. I try to speak up in class. But sometimes I get scared I'll give the wrong answer."

"You're a bold and honest young lady, and I am very proud of you," Laura said.

The following day, a twenty-six-year-old man entered the clinic. He claimed that he had gone to see a doctor for problems with male fertility. He had an on-and-off relationship with the doctor until he finally decided he was being assaulted.

210

He and Laura sat in the room where they made the first intake appointment so she could record all the pertinent information. Susan watched and listened from a one-way mirror.

"My name is Chuck Biddestone, and I've been married for less than two years. A year ago, I went to see Dr. Albert March, who specializes in male fertility. We couldn't get pregnant, and I figured it was my problem because my wife's doctor said she was fine. Dr. March took advantage of me, and I'm pretty messed up now."

"How so?" Laura asked.

He visibly tensed up and said, "I'm not eating, sleeping, can't have sex with my wife, and am self-conscious now," Chuck said, hanging his head.

"What kind of things did this doctor do?" Laura asked.

"First, he had me masturbate in front of him. He played pornographic stuff on the television and watched me. I was very embarrassed."

"Did you ask him to leave the room?"

"He said he had to observe."

"What else?" as Laura put her hair behind her ears.

"He groped me, pressed up against me for no medical reasons."

"Anything else?"

"He wrote me notes with sex jokes and sexual comments," Chuck answered.

"So, what happened?"

"My wife didn't like it and urged me to call the police, which I did."

"Good for you," Laura responded, recording this information.

"Yeah, the police said the doctor was just taking advantage of me for his deviant satisfaction."

"Okay. What can I do for you now, Chuck?"

"There were a few other of his patients that came forward. I need to get my head back in the right place. Sometimes I dream about the guy, the doctor. I'm messed up."

"It would be helpful if you stayed with us for a couple of months and had individual and group therapy. This way, we can work with you so you can hear how other men cope. It will be very illuminating," Laura explained.

During the two months that Chuck was there, he and his wife also had couples therapy. The whole experience was helpful.

Doctors who abused their powerful position to prey on patients were often trusted by their patients, who listened and took their advice. Sometimes, these abusive relationships went on for years and even decades before they stopped. The doctors in the 1950s through the '60s had great authority over women. One patient was abused for almost forty years! Susan discovered in her research that this doctor in England was charged with sexually abusing three unconscious patients. One was nineteen years old, one was fifteen, and one was fifty. The doctor lost his license. They called him a serial rapist and said he had no regard for human decency.

Then she discovered a popular male singer who raped twenty women by drugging them, as well as a victimized man who was studying singing at a school of music. After several years, the famous singer admitted his guilt and was sentenced to eight years on probation for committing a second-degree felony, and required to register as a sexual offender. After discovering the news about the singer, Susan read about a financier who exploited and abused minor girls at his home. He had pictures of underage girls, some as young as fourteen years old. He hobnobbed with politicians and royal family members in countries like Iran

212

and Egypt. Susan was shocked when she saw a past American President's name was on the list.

When Susan strolled home that night, she walked up the hill, past a dairy farm, and turned to her street, Robin Hollow Road. When she saw Chile, the family cat, stretched out on the street, her red hair matted and covered with blood, Susan turned and ran past the dairy farm, down the hill, then she picked up speed and ran until she sank to her knees and threw up. When she got to the house and told her family what had happened, it took several hours to take the poor cat to the vet and have his body taken away. The children asked if Chile was in cat heaven and things of that nature.

"He's up in heaven and sleeping. Chile will be better up there," Barry said. When the whole family sat down for dinner, the baby twins were in high chairs as the family tried to relax. The parents attempted to steer the conversation to other subjects. Chile had been the victim of a hit-and-run. Susan felt like the cat had been run over the way molestation knocked down people's lives and belittled them. Susan and Barry promised the older twins they would get a new cat that weekend if they wanted.

Barry shared some of the new cases with Susan. There was a teacher who was paying to have Hispanic girls flown into Boston, and when they arrived, he molested them. He had been arrested after the third girl was discovered. Barry shook his head.

The two sets of twins, the little ones, two girls, and the older ones, boy and girl, were growing and full of energy. As they sat around the dinner table and talked, as Susan had done at Poppins Lane, she liked recreating her family home life. Sharing and discussing were part of her mosaic; she also wanted her children to have that. There were no kicks under the table, no dirty looks, and no making anyone feel bad about what they expressed. There were always open discussions about your body, your boundaries, and speaking up.

"What happened today that you didn't like?" Susan asked her four children.

"I didn't like that our teacher gave us a surprise test," said Michelle.

"I always hated that too," Barry said.

Michael, the eldest, revealed, "I didn't like that some girl gave me a note that said she had a crush on me." He blushed.

"Now, why wouldn't you like that?" asked Barry. "Gosh, I always enjoyed it when girls liked me," he said. He and Susan smiled at each other.

"Frankly, I was embarrassed. She's nice and all, but I don't know. It was a little fast," Michael said.

Susan said, "Here we go. Now the fun begins."

Chapter Twenty-Four

Susan had been so impressed with Hillary's courage in going to her mother and speaking up about Uncle Becker that she wanted her in a group of less courageous girls. Remembering how difficult it had been for Susan and Ellen to tell their parents, Hillary's courage gave her a reason to explore this subject. Laura agreed.

Susan arranged the chairs in a circle and got the rest of the room ready for the group. One of the attendees was Anita, the child whose brother, Mitchell, came into her room, raped and impregnated her. Then there was Phoebe, who lived with Anita. Phoebe had been molested by her grandfather, who had a history of abuse. He would go right up to Phoebe and put his hands on her breasts. The family stopped inviting Grandpa to family functions because of his lewd behavior.

A twelve-year-old girl named Vickie joined the group. She had large breasts and the males she encountered often made snide remarks. She begged her parents to get her a breast reduction, but they refused. Susan and Ellen decided to join the group and share their common experiences. Today, she wore a navy blue suit and white blouse, her hair styled in a pageboy cut.

"How are we doing today, girls?" Laura asked.

Everyone nodded okay.

"Please go around the room and introduce yourselves. Add a little about why you're here," Laura said.

The first person was Hillary. "I'm here because my Uncle was coming into my room when he was living with us, and he would molest me. We didn't fuck, but he put his grubby fat finger inside me, and I hated the way he smelled. I finally told my mother."

"Very good," Laura said.

The next person was Anita. "I'm here because my

brother was coming into my room and messing with me. He came in and raped me, and I didn't say anything at first. I was too petrified. Then I got pregnant," she stopped talking as everybody gasped. "I know, it was terrible. I had to go to Washington D.C. and get an abortion."

Laura nodded.

Next was Phoebe. "I'm here because my grandfather has a bad habit of touching me. He did it to my mother too. Now, no one invites him to anything. It's pretty bad," she said, dropping her head.

Susan spoke next. "I know I'm older than you, but when I was ten years old, my cousin, who was living with us, came into my room and screwed with me. He called me his 'special one.' I was very confused and upset."

Ellen, who was in her nurse's uniform, spoke last. "I'm Ellen, Susan's sister. Our cousin Larry would enter my room, too; just ruining Susan was not enough for him. He also called me 'his special girl'. You can imagine how we felt when we figured all this out."

Laura said, "Well, what do you think of this group? It's pretty interesting isn't it? Does anyone want to comment?"

"I just want to ask if I'm the only one who spoke up?" Hillary asked.

Everyone looked around. Laura asked, "Why do you think everyone kept quiet except for Hillary?"

Phoebe said, "I complained."

"Okay, that was good," Laura said.

The following person was Anita. She looked around and said," I didn't say anything at first. I was too petrified. Then I got pregnant."

Susan said, "I couldn't tell, so I ate and ate until I got fat. Then I ran. Then I wrote. Then I had nightmares. Finally, I told my friend and teacher. My cousin, Larry, had no remorse. He was a prick."

"Let's talk about why so many girls can't say one word," Laura said.

Hillary said, "I spoke up because I wanted to be brave and end it. I hated it."

"I hated it too," Susan said, "but I couldn't get the words out of my mouth."

Laura asked, "Are any of you girls encouraged to speak up if you don't like something?"

Ellen said, "I tell my kids to have boundaries and not to let anyone go beyond their boundaries. I don't think anyone said that to me when I was younger, but I somehow knew it."

Anita said, "I wanted to say something, but I was scared, too."

"Hillary, please tell the girls about the kid in the playground," Laura said.

"There was this girl in the playground who yelled at this boy and said, "Who made you the boss of me? You're not my boss. I'm my boss."

"I like that, Laura said. "How do you learn to speak up? Do any of your mothers speak like that?" Laura asked.

"My mother is a scaredy cat," Phoebe said.

"My mother was compliant," Susan said. "Now I tell my kids all the time to speak up if someone does something to them they don't like."

Ellen said, "Yes, our mother was compliant until she wasn't."

Susan smiled. Change was happening everywhere.

Anita said, "I went to consciousness-raising here and learned about speaking up. I don't think I understood it before."

"Let's all get up in a circle, and each one of you challenges someone, and then the other person speaks up," Laura said. "Susan, could you begin."

"Okay. I'm speaking to my sister, Ellen. 'Why didn't you tell me Larry was coming into your room sooner?' "

Ellen revealed, "I was humiliated."

"So, you couldn't tell me?" Susan said. "What made you change your mind?"

"I think I figured out he was going into your room also, and then I became jealous."

"Interesting. Jealousy motivated you," Laura said.

"How can a person get brave?" Anita asked Laura.

"She can get furious," Laura replied.

"Who made the rules in your house, Hillary?" Phoebe asked.

"My mother always said that she and I had to stick together because my father left."

"No father around," Laura said. "Do fathers keep you from talking about sex?"

Susan said, "I didn't bring my father to Mrs. Norby, but I brought my mother."

"So, fathers can sometimes inhibit us," Laura concluded.

"I liked it when that kid spoke up in the playground. I wanted to be like her," Hillary said.

"Who can think of someone they admire who speaks up?" Laura asked. Her hand was raised with a pen, and she was ready to write.

"My Aunt Sally speaks up, and I think it's very cool," Anita said, "and I love Golda Meir."

"All of you go back to your rooms and think of very cool people who speak up. Bring me the names next time we meet," Laura said.

Later in the week, Susan and Barry went to Poppins Lane. Ellen and Zev came with their two children, Gail and her two youngsters joined them, and Ronnie and Chad joined them with their three children. Jeff was out of town. The weather had turned cold, and the wind was blowing, so

Dad made a blazing fire in the living room. The dining room looked beautiful, and Trudy had set the table with fancy china, a gravy boat, and everything else.

"Dinner's all set," Trudy said, pointing to a fancy cake with mocha icing and chocolate bits on the sideboard. Odell had taught her to make sweet potato and glazed pastrami, candied carrots, coleslaw, and warm challah.

Once the food was served, the family discussed Mama's forthcoming visit again and the possibility of Susan and Ellen going to Paris with her. Another trip to see Larry also came up. Rumor had it that Dad wanted to go see his nephew.

"I'm so psyched that Mama's coming again," Susan said, sitting down at the table.

"Me too," Ellen said.

"How'd you finagle a trip to Paris?" Ronnie asked.

"We have our ways." Susan giggled.

"Well, I'm next," Ronnie said.

Changing the subject Dad said, "How's that group therapy you're doing at the clinic, Sue?"

"It has potential. We are seeing a few things like dads are inhibitors, moms can be instrumental, and role models inspire girls to speak up," Susan said.

"Okay," Dad added. "I think that's an important subject."

"Are you going to see Larry?" Susan asked her father as she took a slice of pastrami and put it on her plate.

"I'd like to have a long talk with him." Dad forked some pastrami too.

"How about going to California and visiting Larry and then going through Carmel and Monterey?" Gail said.

"Dad, that would be awesome. I could take some really neat pictures," Max Jr. said.

The phone rang, and Trudy got it. She said to Ellen, "There's a phone call for you."

219

After a few minutes, she returned and said, "They need me at the ER. I'll have to go because they're short-handed."

"Tell me what happened, short version," Dad said.

"A girl got raped in the girl's bathroom at school this afternoon. Her father came in and asked where the boy was who raped his daughter. He beat up the kid. Now we have the police, more people hurt, a hot mess." Ellen went to get her coat.

Zev got up and said, "Let me drive you. It's too cold."

"I wish you could stay and tell us more," Dad said.

"Gotta go, you know," Ellen said.

Dinner proceeded, but the conversation was now about the phone call.

"The boy had a problem keeping his hands to himself. Ellen told me she'd heard about him. He went around sitting on girls' laps. They were just waiting for something bad to happen," Susan said.

"How old a boy?" Ronnie asked.

"Fourteen," Susan said. "Two other girls in an art class complained of him following them around."

After Ellen put on her coat and left, while the rest of them sat silently, Dad said, "Not to change the subject, but I think we will go out and see Larry and take Max Jr. to Monterey, Gail."

Max Jr. cheered.

Gail nodded. "I have to confirm the dates with the school calendar."

"When's your mother coming, Susan?" Dad asked, helping himself to some more pastrami and carrots.

"In a week," she said, taking a piece of challah and spreading butter on it.

"This glazed pastrami is delicious, Trudy," Barry said.

"Yes, it is," Chad added.

"And the vegetables, too," Ronnie said.

Dad said, "Don't tell Odell, but you're as good a cook as she is, Trudy."

Everyone at the table laughed.

The next day at the clinic, the buzz was about the rape and fight at the school. After speaking to Ellen, the night before, Susan reported that the boy raped the girl at 1:30 p.m. He laid her down in the girls' room and penetrated her from behind. Then he made her perform oral sex on him. The girl was thirteen. The father was wild with rage when he learned about it. The boy was still in the school, and the father took him outside by the scruff of the neck and pounded the kid. The boy was in the hospital with a concussion and had to have seventeen stitches. The parents pressed charges against the father. It quickly became nasty. All the staff at the clinic expected to see the girl inside the clinic when things cooled down, but they didn't know about the boy.

"I don't think we should have our group therapy today," Laura said to Susan. "There's too much talking about the boy who raped that girl at school. Let's allow things to calm down."

"I agree. But I think I'll make a chart about what we said. It was informative," Susan replied.

"Great idea."

"I'm also going to Xerox color flyers to pass out. The girls can keep it in a notebook.

"Speaking up is so important and relevant. I want to see what they come in with. Who are their role models?" Laura said.

"I have a few of my role models I'll throw in!" Susan laughed.

"It all depends on your age, right?"

"You got that right."

The family of the girl that was raped was interviewed by the local paper and said all the negative publicity was causing them ill health.

The mother revealed, "I have shingles, and I want to see a shrink."

The sister said, "I have nightmares."

The girl's father announced, "I can't sleep, and I'm afraid I'll land up in the hospital."

The girl's brother said, "I'm isolating."

The *Georgeport Daily News* ran an article on the front page, under the article on Nixon resigning, that said, "The boy who raped the girl at school was accused of sexual battery and rape. He trapped the girl in the stall for fifteen minutes. The girl said "no" several times. A warrant was issued for both the boy and the father, and the boy will probably be sent to a detention center for juveniles. Everyone is cooperating with the police, and more details will be provided soon. It was a heinous crime. The father who beat him up is going to anger management. The girl who was raped will be starting a three-month stint at the Penny Long Children's Treatment Center.

Ellen, who read the paper daily, reported everything to her sister.

"I heard about a principal in Europe who lured a dyslexic girl to his home and raped her,"

Ellen said.

"It's getting worse and worse," Susan said.

Sisi, the girl who was raped, came into the clinic with her mother. She was well-groomed but anxious. She glanced around the farmhouse where they check new patients in and looked nervous and distracted. Her mother, a pleasant-looking woman, was tall and erect and gave the information to the woman at the desk. "My name is Grace Claymor, and this is my daughter, Sisi, who was violated; it was in the newspapers. A boy at the junior high school did this in the girls' room. She is very traumatized."

Laura spent forty-five minutes with the mother and girl in the interview room, gathering the information and writing the intake. Susan read the entire report later.

"Where's your father?" Laura asked.

"He was arrested for beating up the boy."

"Did that upset you a lot?"

"Yes, I'm upset that my father beat the boy up and that he got arrested."

"Well, this is understandable. Did you and the boy have a relationship?" Laura asked.

"He kept following me. I told him to leave me alone, but he wouldn't listen."

"What's the boy's name?"

"Freddie Gold," she whispered.

"Fred has a bad reputation for bothering girls, doesn't he?" Laura said.

"He's annoying all the time. Now he's dangerous," Sisi said.

"I am so sorry you were put through this. Are you sleeping?"

"I have nightmares and flashbacks. It's pretty awful." She squirmed as she spoke.

"What else do you want to tell me?" Laura asked. She offered the girl a glass of water.

"He penetrated me from behind, and I'm very sore. The pain was awful." Tears fell down her cheeks as she sipped the water.

"Did the doctors at the hospital give you a full examination?"

"Yes, they did. I pray to God that I'm not pregnant. It's too soon to tell."

"Sisi should stay here for three months, and you should come for family sessions. I would like it if your husband joined us. This is a two-pronged problem. One, there was the

223

rape. Two, there was the attack on the boy. Sisi has a lot of scarring and tearing," Laura said.

"I would like to talk to someone in the clinic privately," Grace said. "I'm severely upset."

"I'll arrange a therapist to meet with you privately," Laura said. "How is the rest of the family?"

"Her brother is very angry, as you might expect. He'll come for family therapy."

Chapter Twenty-Five

Paris in the spring was everything it was supposed to be. Susan, Ellen, and Mom checked into the Ritz in the 1st arrondissement because it was in the center of Paris. Susan couldn't get over how everything in Paris was so old. They wanted to see the Louvre and the gardens, but first, decided to see the Eiffel Tower up close and go to the top at sunset.

Loving the feel of romance and enjoying the Musée d'Orsay with the paintings, they took a tour. They indulged in the finest cuisine and delighted in having chocolate croissants for breakfast. They walked down the Champs-Elysees in the 8th arrondissement and bought a green hat in one of the millenary shops like Mom's brother, Foxy, had done after World War II. Then they strolled down the Seine and watched the artists. The three women laughed, wrote postcards, and bought more clothes for themselves and little outfits for the children. Mama was a terrific guide, having been to Paris with Penny before. Finding treasures for her business, like ceramic mugs in multicolor and yellow Quimper ware, gave her a thrill. She shipped them to Bedford and wrote Penny about all her new ideas. After finding a black and white print showing a tailor working in his shop and another black and white print of a chef creating a wonderful soufflé, Mama mailed them to *Penlily*.

Susan laughed when Ellen said she wanted to make her kitchen entirely French by the end of their trip. The three women got along superbly and talked until the small hours of the night. They visited a hair salon, and each got a new hairdo, so they had a fresh look by the time they returned home. Susan bought a new French-American cookbook, Ellen purchased leather gloves for Zev, and Mom bought a pair for Barry.

"You both have wonderful husbands," Mom said at

their last dinner in Paris." I toast to you both. I hope your marriages continue to be happy ones."

"Mama, what happened to make Dad stray?" Susan asked.

"I think he just worked too closely with Gail every day, building and planning the clinic, and then she, being single, got her fingers into him and he was a cooked goose. I couldn't compete with a woman twenty years younger than me, and I guess I was too busy with whatever I was doing, planning the dinner parties and the gala, and we grew apart. I can't think of anything else. I have been over it a hundred times in my head." She looked at her two daughters and just nodded her head. "It still hurts, but I keep very busy with the new business, and Penny and I have a great relationship. We meet rich, good-looking men who want to wine and dine us and probably bed us down, but we are wary."

"It still makes me mad," Susan said.

"Me too," Ellen said.

"Listen, we're not the perfect family. After Larry did what he did to you both, I accepted that we were blemished. It was an awful time, especially when he raped that girl on Sagamore Way and had to go back to jail. The whole thing makes me ill," Mom said.

"But building the clinic was a wonderful idea." Susan smiled.

"Yes, the clinic is fabulous, but look at what happened between Gail and Dad. It changed our family," Ellen said.

"There's no doubt about that," Mom agreed.

"But you love your new life, don't you, Mom?" Susan said.

"I'm a new woman now, so much stronger and smarter. It boosted my self-esteem," Mom said. "Women are changing... look at the first class of women at the Naval Academy."

"Yes, it's pretty fabulous. When you get the time, you should write a book," Ellen said.

"When I get too old to run around Paris, then I'll write it," she agreed, laughing.

Christmas and Chanukah came at the same time that year. The Stern family celebrated both holidays. At the clinic, Susan, Laura, and a few male helpers from the kitchen decorated a tree and lit the menorah. The tree had gifts underneath, and stockings were hung by the fireplace at Poppins Lane with names attached. The staff at the clinic planned a holiday party with food, entertainment, and songs. Trudy was proud of her recipe for eggnog with freshly grated nutmeg, which she served at the Stern home. She made it with Wild Turkey Bourbon and separated the eggs, folding them in at the end so the bowl filled up with white waves of delicious softness.

Susan loved the holiday wrapping, shopping, baking, and decorating. Mom always said that the stores had the best selection of merchandise at the holidays. The shops stayed open late downtown, the tree in Georgeport Square was lit up at night, and the citizens sang carols. *Monique's* was open until ten p.m., and Lydia, in her fluffy hairdo, sipped her Wild Turkey behind the counter. When Ronnie dropped in for a party dress, Lydia greeted her loudly. "How are you, sweetie," she said. "How are the kids and Chad?"

"Oh, they're fine. The children are full of sass. Amy still loves hats like her mom."

"Ronnie, pick a dress and I will give you the holiday discount," Lydia said.

After choosing a silver lame frock, Ronnie accessorized it with dangling silver and rhinestone earrings, and left with a large shopping bag.

"Bye, bye, and thank you," Ronnie cooed.

"Won't you stay for a drinky-poo?" Lydia said.

"You know I don't do that anymore."

"You're no fun."

"I guess not," Ronnie laughed.

Back at the clinic, the staff prepared for the party. Clients continued to check in. The holiday season brought out sexual abuse because families spent so much time together, people drank too much, and uncles with dirty minds came to visit.

A father and daughter checked into the farmhouse admittance office. "Hello, I'm Charlie Cooper, and this is my daughter, Polly. She wants to check in."

"Please fill out this paperwork," the receptionist said with a smile, giving him the clipboard. Then Laura took them into the interview room, so she could collect the intake information.

"Tell me what brings you here," Laura said.

As Susan observed from the one-way mirror, Polly sat in a chair in a black silk dress and was wearing full makeup, dark eyeliner, heavy mascara, and red lips. Polly's feet were clad in stilettos and slim and almost delicate-looking. "My daughter needs some help. She goes out and works as a call girl and I disapprove. She drinks, stays out too late, and goes to bed with strange men for money. I don't approve and she is tired, too thin, and isn't doing her school work. I want her to stop. She has anxiety and nightmares, and I know because I hear her at night," Charlie Cooper said.

"Why are you doing this?" Laura asked, looking at Polly.

"I like the money. I can't make this much anywhere else."

"Is this what sixteen-year-old girls do now?"

"My girlfriends are doing it. They're strippers, dancers, hookers, and party girls. They make a lot of money."

"How long have you been doing this kind of work?"

"A few months."

"Your father doesn't approve," Laura reminded her.

"Daddy, I like the money," Polly said, looking at her dad.

"'What do you do for a living, sir?" Laura asked.

"I collect the trash for the city of Georgeport."

"Does it pay well?"

"I put the food on the table and pay the bills."

"Are you having bad dreams, Polly?"

"Yes," she said, looking nervous.

"Have you been abused in your job?" Laura asked, bending her head.

"It can get rough. Some of the men are demanding."

"Do you report this to your boss?"

"Yes, but he handwaves it away."

"'Don't you think you're underage for this work?"

"I tell them I'm eighteen."

"Tell me, Polly, have you been sexually molested in the past?" Susan listened attentively.

"Yes."

Her father looked at her and said, "When?"

"Your friend, Rick." She stares at her father for a bit longer.

"You never told me," he said.

"When did this happen?" Laura asked.

"When I was little, five, six years old; he would come over at the holidays and fool around with me."

"Why didn't you tell me?" Charlie said, looking visibly upset.

"I tried, but I couldn't get it out. I tried, Daddy."

"Where is your mother?" Laura asked.

"She left when Polly was a toddler. She said she didn't

like being married to a garbage collector and left." Charlie stared at Laura and just kept staring at her.

"Where is this Rick person now?" Laura asked.

"He still comes around, but he leaves me alone. I burnt him with a lit cigarette once." Polly said.

"Any other men bother you like that?" Laura asked.

"I usually can take care of myself," Polly said.

"How about you stay here for a few months working on some things that have happened to you? I believe there are things we need to uncover, and family therapy can help. What do you say, Polly?" Laura said.

"If you say so. I should talk about it. I'm getting too many stomach aches too."

"Then it's settled. You stay here, and we'll talk. Charlie is coming tomorrow for family therapy. I think it will be helpful," Laura said, closing her notebook.

"Fine," he said.

"One more thing; did this Rick guy ever rape you, Polly?" Laura asked.

"He tried, but because I was so young, I was too small, and it hurt."

"I'd like to kill that guy. Next time I see him, I may beat the crap out of him," Charlie announced, standing up.

"Daddy, stop. It's old news. He doesn't touch me now."

"You burnt him with a cigarette?" Laura asked, reopening her notebook. Susan thought that would make a good drawing.

"Yeah, I got him good," Polly laughed. Susan nodded behind the two-way mirror.

"I have a feeling your daughter knows how to take care of herself, Mr. Cooper," Laura said.

"I bet you're right," he said.

"Okay, let's stop for today, and you can finish getting settled," Laura said.

230

The following day, Susan met with Polly, and they discovered Polly liked art. "Could you draw me a picture of this guy, Rick, who fooled around with you when you were five years old?" Susan said. "Can you remember that?"

"I'll never forget it," she said.

She drew a picture of a girl in a closet. The door was closed, and it was dark. There were clothes on the floor, shoes, and a little bit of light coming through under the door. The child looked scared, hugged herself, and had big eyes.

"Tell me about this picture, Polly?" Susan asked.

"Well, my father's friend Rick came over at Christmas and tried to get me to undress. He said that he wanted to see my nipples. I told him that I didn't want to do that, so he locked me in my bedroom closet and said that he'd let me out if I agreed. I kind of didn't have a choice."

"What happened when he let you out?" Susan asked.

"He tried to rape me, but as I said, I was too small and yelled, so he had to stop. Then, when he tried again, another time, I burnt him with a lit cigarette."

"Where was your father all this time?"

"I guess he was watching a football game, sitting in his favorite chair, drinking a beer."

"Did you try to tell him?"

"Oh, I did, but I couldn't."

"Do you want to draw another picture?"

Polly worked on her drawing, which was very revealing. She drew a little girl with her face on her father's jacket arm. Susan asked her to explain it to her.

"That's me. I tried to tell him, but I got embarrassed and put my face on the arm of his jacket because I was shy. Daddy didn't understand, so he just stroked my head. That's when I decided to burn Rick with a lit cigarette. That did it!" Polly said as her face lit up.

231

"You're a very resourceful girl," Susan said.

They had a family meeting later in the day, and Susan told Charlie Cooper, "I have a few pictures Polly drew for me this morning. Would you like to see them?"

"Absolutely."

Susan spread the two pictures on the table and explained. "This first picture of Polly being locked in the bedroom closet by your friend, Rick. Tell your father about this one, Polly."

"Daddy, Rick came over on Christmas and wanted me to undress. He said he wanted to see my nipples. I was five years old and didn't want to do that. So, he locked me in my bedroom closet until I changed my mind. Then he let me out."

"I can't believe he did that. Where was I?" Charlie asked.

"You were watching football."

He shook his head back and forth. "I can't believe how unaware I was. I'm so sorry, kiddo." He hugged his daughter.

"The next picture is of Polly trying to tell you, but she got too nervous and just put her face on the sleeve of your jacket," Susan said as she showed the second drawing to Charlie.

"My, God, that's a good drawing, Polly. Look how you buried your little head on my arm. I didn't know. I could kill that guy," Charlie said.

"I tried to tell you, but I was embarrassed." Polly looked at her father and hugged him. "Daddy, it's a really good thing that you brought me here to this clinic. This is the best Christmas present you could have given me. Thanks, Pop."

"I waited too long, but we're here. Merry Christmas, baby," Charlie said.

"Do you have any idea where this Rick fellow is now?" Laura asked.

"Oh, I see him around; he's a handyman and works in town," Charlie said.

"I know this is a big stretch, but do you think he would agree to come in and chat with us, like join the family session? If he's someone you've known for a long time, maybe he would. Ask him if he'd like to help Polly and tell him what she's been doing and how that doesn't go down with you very well. Tell him how we've been talking about things. He could be doing us and himself a big favor if he could come in, private, no one needs to know; just us, and discuss it. What do you think, Mr. Cooper?" Laura looked at Charlie and waited.

"I'll give it a try," Charlie said. "I'll try."

Rick looked like a handyman in his sloppy old clothes and work boots. He had calluses on his hands a weather-beaten face. A few days later, he joined the family group.

"Rick, this was very good of you to come in. Polly has been working on some issues, and your name came up. She mentioned that you once or twice fooled around with her in an inappropriate way when she was little, maybe five years old. Does that ring a bell?" Laura asked as she peered into Rick's eyes and slightly smiled.

Rick turned red, his ears particularly. He moved around in his chair, and then he said, "I was probably drunk. Christmas time. Had a few too many," he said.

"Well, she said you put her in the closet until she agreed to take her shirt off," Laura said. "Does that sound right?"

"It was a long time ago," he said, looking embarrassed.

"She drew this picture of herself in the closet. Does that help you remember?" Susan said.

"Oh, yeah, yeah. I must have been drunk," he said.

"Why did you do that to my kid?" Charlie asked.

"I said I drank too much. I don't know," Rick said, looking awkward.

"It was a bad day for me," Polly said. "I was just a little girl."

233

"I did a terrible thing. I wasn't thinking right. Hey, man, Charlie, please forgive me. It was wrong. I never should have touched her. Please, I'm so embarrassed."

"Perhaps you should apologize to Polly, too," Laura suggested, looking at Rick.

"Aw sweetheart, I never should have done that... I am sorry. I was so wrong," Rick said, looking at Polly with downcast eyes.

Polly shook her head up and down and whispered, "Thanks."

"Can I ask you something?" Laura inquired.

"Yeah, I guess."

"Have you molested a lot of young girls?" Laura asked.

"A few."

"See, I'm having bad dreams and working as a call girl. They think it's all connected," Polly said.

"I can see how that can happen," Rick said.

Laura said, "See, we're trying to stop that kind of thing from happening. It's what we do here."

"Yeah, I get it. You're doing a lot of good work in this place. I get it," Rick said.

"I'm glad you came today," Charlie said.

"I get it."

"When did you start to fool around with young girls?" Laura asked.

"Oh, I don't know. The boys in my neighborhood did it," Rick said.

"Did you grow up on Little Street?" Charlie asked.

"Yeah."

Susan decided she'd ask Barry about that neighborhood tonight. She bet he had a few stories.

234

Chapter Twenty-Six

"Susan, I'm going to take you to a club where many of the guys down on Little Street hang out. The bar is not a very nice place." Barry paused as he watched Susan. "It's rough around the edges, down and out, but this is where they go, and I want you to experience it firsthand."

"Do these guys molest children?"

"Some of them have been known to. Some fool around with their sisters, cousins, you name it. They don't have a lot of respect for the female gender."

"Why didn't you take me sooner?"

"I didn't want you to get the wrong impression of me."

They looked at one another and smiled.

"I'm ready when you are," Susan said, slipping her jacket on. The twins were at after-school projects, and the housekeeper was busy, so off they went.

The Shipping Club looked like a low-slung rectangular box of bleached yellow brick, with no landscaping and just one neon sign announcing the place. On the street, a small parking lot was full of pickup trucks and a few beat-up compacts. A local cop car was always present as if the establishment needed daily protection. Inside was a neglected and worn bar surrounded by several middle-aged, overweight guys smoking, drinking beer, and hanging out. As they slipped into a seat, Barry whispered into Susan's ear, "Some of the men work as carpenters, masons, woodcutters, garbage collectors, and salesmen. Most haven't gone past high school. I'm sure a few of these guys have been in prison."

Susan nodded.

There was a pool table in the corner where a couple of men were playing; a gal with bleached hair was sitting in a chair nearby smoking a cigarette. A dart board was hanging across the room from the pool table, and next to it was a poster of Farrah Fawcett-Majors. As Susan and Barry sat on their bar stools, the bartender took their order for two beers.

"Well, well, Barry, we haven't seen you in a while. How are you doing?" the bartender asked.

"I'm doing okay, and you?" Barry replied.

"No point in complaining," the bartender gave them their beers and put some glasses on the shelf.

An older man sat at the end of the bar. He spent his days there talking to customers, having a bite to eat, laughing, and drinking. When he had a lot to drink, he sang songs. The bartender dried the glasses, mopped the counter, and moved on. One guy sat with a very attractive woman with long dark hair. He stroked her hand and lit her cigarettes.

"Ray, Raymond Burns, how have you been? Long time." Barry said, "Ray, this is my wife, Susan Stern."

"How are you, buddy? Good to see you. Susan, is your family running the new clinic here in town?" Ray asked.

"Yes, it is," she said.

The brunette said, "I'm Anne. I think that clinic is a godsend. So many girls get taken advantage of."

Susan looked at Anne and thought that she was pretty, but she had sad eyes. "Have you known anyone who went to the clinic?" Susan asked.

Anne looked down at her drink. "I did."

"No kidding?"

"Yes,"

"Do you mind my asking when you were there?"

"A few years ago. Some creep jumped me in an alley; I had to go to the ER; then they sent me to the clinic."

"How was it?"

"Helpful."

"Who was the asshole who raped you?" Barry asked.

"Some guy named Tim from around town," replied Anne.

"Tim Scott?" Barry said. "I know him. He lived next door to me growing up. A real jerk."

"Little Street?" Ray asked.

"Yes, I told Susan there were a few bad guys over there. They don't give a hoot about girls," Barry said.

"Did he get arrested?" Susan asked.

"Oh, yeah, I got him, picked him right out of a lineup, "Anne said, taking a drag of her cigarette.

"How long is he in for?" Barry asked.

"Ten years," Anne said. "He'd been stalking me for a while." She flicked her ashes in an ashtray. The four of them spent the next hour talking. They shared stories of Little Street and the neighborhood, the boys' poor attitude, and the dysfunctional families.

"I learned a lot about Little Street by playing with my friends who lived there," Anne said.

"I grew up there, so I learned firsthand," Barry said.

"You got out!" Ray commented.

"Yeah, I wanted better. Made up my mind and went for it. Then I met Susan, and the dye was cast. Haven't looked back." He kissed Susan on the cheek as she smiled sheepishly.

"I married a nice gal, but unfortunately, she died of cervical cancer. We had two beautiful kids," Ray said proudly.

"I was married too, but my husband was a disappointment. Sometimes, you never know until it's too late," Anne said. "No kids, though. How about you guys," she said as she looked at Barry and Susan.

Susan grinned and said, "We have two sets of twins."

"No, you don't? Two sets of twins!"

"Crazy," Ray said.

"One fraternal set and one identical," Barry added.

"That's terrific. Please invite me over so I can see them," Anne said. "Would you mind?"

"We'd love to have you over. I'll make dinner. Come

next Wednesday at 6 p.m., how does that sound?" Susan said.

"We don't want to put you out, really," Ray said.

"It is our pleasure," Barry said, and added, "We'd love to continue our discussion."

"Absolutely," Susan responded.

"You realize that Ray is a very smart man. He knows so much about so many things," Anne said, squeezing his arm affectionately.

"From reading a lot. I'm a big reader," he said.

"You work?" Barry asked.

"I work in a law firm as a paralegal. Never went to law school, but I know a lot of interesting stuff," Ray replied.

"You know I have a law firm; we specialize in sexual abuse," said Barry.

"Wow. That's terrific. Must be very interesting," Ray said.

The four of them smiled at one another and nodded their heads. It was the beginning of a meaningful friendship.

Wednesday night came. Anne and Ray arrived on Robin Hollow Road. Anne stood erect with a box of candy from the local store, *Something Very Sweet*.

"Hi there," Barry said as he opened the door. "Come on in."

Washed, shaved, and wearing a clean shirt, Ray held a bottle of red wine. The visitors entered the spacious home, looked around, and complimented everything in sight.

"Oh, I love your paintings," Anne said. She stared at them as she walked around the living room.

"Hey, look at all these terrific books you own. What a collection," Ray said as he examined the novels and biographies on the shelves in Barry's library.

"Oh my, what a pretty kitchen," Anne exclaimed as she saw the copper pots Susan's mother had sent her from *Penlily* in Bedford.

"Mama is in the housewares party business, so she gave me those wonderful pots hanging over the stove," Susan explained.

"Oh, they're lovely. Do you cook in them?" Anne asked, rolling her eyes.

"Sure."

The twins came downstairs and welcomed the guests.

"Now who are you?" Anne asked as she spoke to the older fraternal twins.

"I'm Michelle," the girl said, swishing back the dark hair she inherited from her mother. It was as straight as a stick, but the hair-do on Michelle made her look like a little Dutch girl.

"How old are you?" Ray asked.

"We're ten years old," Michael answered. He resembled Barry with a small, muscular stature and shining eyes.

"Do you fight a lot?" Ray asked.

They laughed, and Michelle said, "Sometimes. Don't all brothers and sisters?"

Then the identical twin girls peeked their heads into the kitchen – two adorable girls with straight brown hair and freckles.

"Well, can you please tell me about you?" Anne said.

One said, "I'm Kimberly."

The other said, "I'm Kate."

"I love your names," Anne bent down, and hugged them each. "How old are you?"

"I can guess," Ray said. "You guys are five years old."

"How'd you guess?" Kate asked.

"'Cause I'm a smart guy," Ray laughed, his eyes squinting from his smile.

Barry waved his hands and said, "Let's go in here and have a glass of wine. You kids can help Mom bring in some goodies."

The twins brought cheese, crackers, and cashew nuts, and Susan brought a dip with fresh vegetables. Everyone sat around in the living room and talked. It was an animated conversation, and the children sat on the floor, colored, and listened at the same time.

Susan served the food, and the kids helped. They enjoyed a delicious dinner of roast beef and baked potatoes. Odell's famous coleslaw was a hit. Barry and Ray discussed the law and the rising rate of sexual abuse, and Anne and Susan spoke about how difficult it was to get girls to be more assertive.

"We have to teach our girls to secure their boundaries and not let anyone invade them. It is their God-given right, and they must grow up learning and protesting," Susan said.

"I hear you," Anne said, "but you know the way men are. They act like you lured them on."

"It's a lie, and they know it. No is no," Susan emphasized. Anne said, "I agree."

"Do you work, Anne?"

"I work at the domestic abuse center. I handle the phones, take women to court, and help them get babysitters. There was a long training to get to be a volunteer, but I did it. I get a check from my ex-husband every month to keep me going." Anne shrugged. "I also clean houses on the side and pick up some nice money. I do what I can do."

"That domestic abuse work is so necessary," Susan said.

"And you?" Anne asked.

"I'm an expressive therapist three days a week down at the clinic. It's wonderful work, always something new," she said.

"My Mom is always coming home with stories. I could write a book," Michelle said.

"I've got a few stories to add to your book," Anne said.

240

"Sometimes, it's not pretty. What do you want to become when you're older?"

"I think I want to be a lawyer like my Dad and help women get more equal pay, better treatment, and generally more respect."

"Oh, you've got her trained right already." Anne clapped her hands.

It was a friendly evening, and the dessert was homemade apple pie and ice cream, which everyone enjoyed.

"Your mother is a great cook," Ray said, patting his belly.

"Ray may start coming to my office a few days a week and see what he can do to help me out," Barry said as they all finished eating.

"What a fine idea," Susan said.

The children said good night and went upstairs, and the grown-ups had coffee in the living room. They stayed late talking and getting to know each other. Susan couldn't get over how they met this couple at the Shipping Club. Wasn't life strange?

Chapter Twenty Seven

TWO YEARS LATER

When the mother and daughter entered the farmhouse to register the girl with the pigtails, she looked up and said, "I don't want to be here."

"Stop that nonsense. We discussed this already," the mom said through gritted teeth.

They filled out the paperwork, went into the room with Laura, and had the first interview and intake.

"Linda Slat," the girl answered when Laura asked her name.

"Tell me about what brings you in?" Laura said. Susan sat next to Laura as her assistant, explaining her interest in mother-daughter relationships.

"My mother has this idea that I've been abused by my neighbor. I told her nothing happened, but she won't believe me. I think she's jealous that he didn't fool around with her." Tthe girl sat with her hands folded in her lap, looking indignant.

"That's a mouthful," Laura said. "You believe that?"

"Yes, yes, yes!" the girl repeated.

The mother tapped her foot. She didn't say one word, however.

Laura looked at Chloe, the mom, and said, "Please share your side of this story."

Susan opened her notebook and waited.

"I think this boy Andrew, who lives next door, has been fooling around with Linda, and the notion that I'm jealous is the most absurd accusation." The mother and daughter stared at one another while Laura and Susan watched them.

"Did this boy and you have sex?" Laura asked the girl.

"Yes, we did because he wanted to, and I let him," Linda said.

"When did this take place?"

"Last week in my bedroom"

"Mom, tell me what happened from your point of view?" Laura asked.

"Andrew, who is sixteen years old, came to my house when I was out and had sex with Linda. When I returned, I heard them upstairs. The bed was unmade, Linda was half undressed, and then Andrew came walking down the stairs like he had no care in the world," the mother said.

"Well, Linda, it does look suspicious. Is this the way things happened?" Laura asked.

"Yes, pretty much, and I won't deny it."

Later, in the art therapy room, which was busy with people drawing and creating, Linda was painting a portrait of her mother in acrylics; a large portrait of her anorexic mother who had bleached blonde hair. Linda, a young-looking twelve-year-old, said, "My mother wears my clothes and then tells me to dress up in hers. I don't get it."

Susan asked, "Has she done that for a long time?"

"No, just since I got my period."

"Interesting." Susan wondered about this but stayed silent.

"I don't want to wear her clothes," Linda said. Susan had met the mother and thought the overexcited mom was trying to exchange identities with her daughter.

"Just say you'd rather wear your clothes and leave it at that," Susan said.

"I will, but I just hope she won't get mad,"

Susan knew the mother counted her calories and forced Linda to watch what she ate.

"I don't think I overeat, but she stares at me and watches me put food into my mouth. It makes me very uncomfortable," Linda said.

"Anne is coming in later, and we should do a drama

therapy scene between you and your mother, who is eating at the dinner table. What do you think? Susan asked.

Linda smiled. "I'd like to do that. It won't be pretty, though. She gets very annoyed."

Anne, Susan's new friend from the Shipping Club and now the drama therapist at the sex clinic, came into work an hour later. She was dressed in a long skirt and peasant blouse with her dark hair pulled back in a long braid. She had worked at The Penny Long Children's Treatment Clinic for six months and worked three days a week. This new position strengthened the friendship between Susan and Anne. Usually, they had a light lunch together, salad, and a piece of sourdough bread and butter. They loved to exchange stories about their cases, and Anne developed into a talented drama therapist in her interactions with the clients. Susan told her she was gifted, and Anne blushed because she was not used to getting many compliments.

Raymond now worked three days a week for Barry in his law firm. Barry benefited from Ray's competence and diligence. He was smart and thorough, which helped Barry access his cases and determine the best approach. In addition, Ray went over to their home on Robin Road and did a few house repairs.

"You could have been an actress, you're so pretty and talented," Susan said at lunch one day. "Tell me about your family."

"My family was complicated," Anne replied, "and we lived with relatives."

"That must have been hard," Susan said, remembering Flo and Larry.

"Oh yes, but I acted in plays, which gave me an escape," Anne said.

"You were making your mosaic," Susan said.

244

"We didn't talk about things," Anne said. "We avoided them."

Susan said, "I know how that works."

"We didn't discuss sex or what people did that we didn't like."

Susan observed when Anne and Linda got together that day to perform a scene of Linda and her mother eating together. Anne knew how critical Chloe, the mom, had been.

"Let's pretend we're sitting at this table, and here are plates, and we're eating dinner together." Anne sat down and picked up a fork. Linda sat across from her and did the same. "We are going to reverse roles," Anne told Linda. "You pretend to be your mom, and I will be you."

Anne pretended to eat. "This is tasty."

"Now, don't eat too much because you don't want to get fat." Linda was pretending to be her mom.

"I just sat down, for goodness's sake; quit hounding me."

"Now, don't criticize me; I'm your mother, and I know best." Linda continued as the mother.

Anne took another pretend bite of food. "I see you gobbling your food. Don't eat so fast," Linda as the mom said.

"Quit it. You're driving me crazy."

"You don't want to look like a big fat pig? Do you?"

"You're making me sick, Mother, and I can't even enjoy my meal." Linda threw her napkin down on the plate and pushed her chair away from the table.

Susan started to clap." That was excellent."

"Now I want us to switch roles. I'll play your mother, and you be yourself." Anne's eyes brimming with expectation. Anne picked up her fork on the other side of the table. "You better not stuff your face. I think you're getting chubby."

245

Linda looked at her. "Why do you have to ruin my meal? I was looking forward to this dish." Linda stared at Anne and gave her a dirty look. "See, you're giving me that look. It makes me feel self-conscious."

Anne said, "I'm your mother, and I think you need to watch your weight. I want a daughter who is slim and beautiful, not a fat blob."

"That's what I am to you, a fat blob?" Linda yelled. "Do you know how that makes me feel, you witch?"

Anne said, "I don't care how you feel. I want what I want, and you'll listen."

Susan started to applaud. "You gals have nailed this scene."

Anne said, "I suggest we have your mother join our group, and we should do those scenes in front of her. Let your mom see how you feel. Then, maybe she'll see what she is doing to you. What do you think?"

Linda nodded. Susan agreed. They set a time and invited Chloe into the room.

Chloe watched the drama unfold, squirming in her chair, folding and unfolding her legs, and rubbing her hands together. "I'm so embarrassed, but I can't help myself. I watch every calorie I eat, and I can't help myself," Chloe admitted.

"But your daughter is a fine weight; she's still growing, and you're giving her stomach aches and a complex," Anne said at the end of the session.

"I'll try to do better, but it'll be hard."

"At least you know how I feel, Mom," Linda tossed one of her pigtails behind her back.

"Yes, I do," Chloe said.

Susan said, "We'll be discussing your neighbor's violation of you at our next session."

"I think that went very well, Anne," Susan said the next day at lunch.

"That mother needed to hear and see it. She is so self-consumed with her sick eating. It's a shame."

"At least Linda stuck up for herself even more forcefully."

"I'd call it a good first session." Susan buttered her bread.

Anne smiled. "Thanks, Susan. You're a great teacher." She ate some salad. "This is much more interesting than cleaning houses. Between volunteering at the Women's Place for Domestic Violence and working here at the clinic, my life feels much more interesting and fulfilling. I love you, my new best friend." Anne squeezed Susan's hand across the dining table.

That evening, Susan shared the day with Barry. He was sitting in his library among his favorite books. "Anne was so effective with a new client today. Her drama is spot on," Susan said.

"No kidding."

"I'm telling you, she became the evil mother without a minute to prepare right into the scene. I loved the way she switched roles and showed the girl how to do the role-play. Barry, Anne is a natural drama teacher.

"Well, Ray is a whiz. Smart as a Harvard grad. He's helping me whip my cases into better order and adding a lot of pertinent information from places he finds. What a researcher."

Barry and Susan grinned at one another and Susan said, "I think we've done a positive thing on many fronts for the clients, the clinic, and ourselves. We had a hunch, and we followed it. I love you so much, Barry." Susan bent over and gave her husband of thirteen years a loving kiss, lingering on his lips and enjoying the warmth of this feeling. They were a match, the two of them, and Susan knew she had found this diamond in the rough from Little Street in Georgeport, Massachusetts. What a treasure he was; what a lucky girl she was. All part of her family mosaic. The colors of the mosaics

247

were glistening, the hues were multiple and varied like people, the shimmer of light gleamed through the darkness, and her family was a true work of art.

When she was a little girl, Susan had no idea what her life had in store for her. She didn't know how to make the bad better. She didn't know how to turn the corner and see herself out of the darkness. Now, she stood up tall and felt a lilt in her step. Dear Lord, she thought, give me another day. Keep it coming. I'm not done yet; no, I'm not; I'm still cooking away and creating my mosaic, threading in the pain and the beauty. Let me continue a little longer, Lord. It is not my time to stop yet. I have so much more weaving to do.

No longer a silent prayer and realizing how full her heart was, how creative and fertile her mind was, she smiled quietly to herself. No more stuffing herself with food, no more nightmares, no more sexual temptations with young children, no more poor choices with abusive men; she was growing and developing into one interesting woman. Thank you, Mrs. Norby. Thank you, Lord. Thank you wherever you are, God, for this chance and this gift of life.

EPILOGUE - 1982

One spring afternoon in April, with daffodils in bloom, Ray released the clutch in his old truck and drove to Susan's house. He arrived as the housekeeper was preparing to leave. Katie and Kim were in the yard talking about their day. The older twins were still at school, playing sports.

"How're you girls doing today?" Ray asked as he stood on the gravel driveway.

"Fine, Uncle Ray," they said in unison. The twins, who were ten years old, went into the kitchen and threw their book bags on the floor. After deciding on a snack of cookies and fruit, Kim went downstairs to paint while Katie walked upstairs to her bedroom. Ray followed with his carpenter tools.

Ray started by hand-planing the side of the bedroom door to the younger twins' room so it would close more easily. Then he began to sand it smooth.

Katie settled herself at the white French provincial desk to write her book report.

"I won't be too long, kiddo," he said.

"No problem."

"That's my girl."

He sanded quietly, and then he tested the door.

"It works now!" he exclaimed.

Katie said, "You're so smart, Uncle Ray."

He smiled his toothy grin and said, "Let me see how big you've grown."

Katie rose and pirouetted in a circle, showing him how tall and graceful she'd become.

"Come here, you little kitten," he said, scooping her in his arms.

Katie squealed with delight as he twirled her around and placed her gingerly on her bed.

Then he tickled her, which brought more giggles.

Bending down, Ray kissed her on her neck and said, "That's the sweetest spot; duck meat, the sweetest spot."

Katie smiled at him.

"Let's play," he said, rubbing her thigh up and down.

As this was happening, Susan arrived home and entered the kitchen, where her audio monitor was plugged in on the counter.

"I want to touch you, Katie," Susan heard as she stepped closer to the monitor. She clenched her fists and kept listening.

"My Mommy told me not to let anyone do that."

"But I like it, and it will feel nice."

Susan stood stone still as shock waves coursed through her body. She picked up the phone and dialed 911.

"No!" Katie yelled.

"Emergency. I can hear my 10-year-old daughter screaming. A man is in my daughter's bedroom molesting her," then, "45 Robin Ridge Road, Georgeport." She began to experience a flashback of her childhood nightmare when she dreamed of flying at her cousin, Larry, punching, kicking, pulling his hair, scratching his face, and plunging a large, shiny butcher blade into his doughy side. Grabbing the baseball bat from the coat closet, Susan ran up the stairs to the bedroom.

Smelling of wood and sweat, Ray slid his finger inside Katie. She kicked, and the bed moved; her stuffed animals fell over. Susan plunged the head of the bat into Ray's midsection, resulting in a loud yelp. Katie pulled away as Susan raised the bat, ready to strike again. Mother and daughter watched Ray fall to the floor on top of the woodworking plane, he'd left blade-side up. Suddenly, red, sticky blood began to stain his shirt, clashing with the pale pink rug.

Susan peered over Ray, spit on his face, and said, "You won't take away my child's life."

The bell rang, and the police rushed upstairs.

Acknowledgements

As a licensed clinical social worker, I counseled numerous clients and listened to stories from men and women who had been sexually abused as children by people they knew. Their lives were damaged because, as youngsters, they carried their secrets and coped in unhealthy ways. Some engage in binge eating, are promiscuous, have angry outbursts, or lose interest in both school and their social lives. Many children keep their secrets forever due to shame, embarrassment, or fear.

2 Poppins Lane explores the individuals who keep these secrets and examines the perpetrators in detail. I encourage parents to teach their children to speak out and protect their bodies and minds. This is essential, and I wrote this book because I am passionate about this issue.

I have many people to thank. My first editor, B. Lynn Goodwin, helped me express my thoughts and pushed me to make the story resonate. I also want to thank Sonia Ravech, my writing mentor, who generously edited and advised me. She saw what my book needed and showed me how to get there. I also want to thank all the gals in my writers' group in Boca Raton, who cheered me on and advised me to write precisely and tell my story.

I want to thank my daughter, Danielle, and her husband, David Jacobs. They are my first readers and offer creative insights. My son, Jonathan, wasn't afraid to share what he liked and didn't like, which was courageous and essential! And my incredible partner, Manny, never overlooked a detail or an opportunity to help me improve my book.

I want to give a big shout out to Chris Burlini, who encouraged me to paint the picture of *2 Poppins Lane* that is the front cover of this novel.

Thank you to Gill, my publisher at Bridge House

Publishing in England. Her enthusiasm and editing improved this book in many ways.

To all my friends on Facebook, your enthusiasm knows no bounds. God bless you all!

About The Author

Patricia Striar Rohner was born in New York, New York, where her mother spent New Year's Eve in the Doctors Hospital. She spent her childhood in South Orange, NJ, and attended Kimberley Academy, an all-girls high school in Montclair, New Jersey. She loved to paint and write and continues those endeavors today. Rohner graduated from Brandeis University, where she majored in theater arts. She later received a Masters' in Social Work from Simmons College and a master's in Creative Writing from Lesley College in Boston.

She worked as a clinical social worker and owned and ran a gourmet kitchen shop in Newburyport, Massachusetts. Rohner has published ten short stories in literary journals, two novels, and a children's book, which she also illustrated.

Rohner has four wonderful children, a daughter and three sons, and twelve grandchildren, all of whom bring her great pleasure. She also plays golf, paints in oil, and loves the Boston Red Sox. She lives half the year in Ipswich, Massachusetts, and the other half in Boca Raton, Florida.

Like To Read More Work Like This?

Then sign up to our mailing list and download our free collection of short stories, *Magnetism*. Sign up now to receive this free e-book and also to find out about all of our new publications and offers.

Sign up here:
   http://eepurl.com/gbpdVz

Please Leave A Review

Reviews are so important to writers. Please take the time to review this book. A couple of lines is fine.

Reviews help the book to become more visible to buyers. Retailers will promote books with multiple reviews.

This in turn helps us to sell more books… And then we can afford to publish more books like this one.

Leaving a review is very easy.

Go to https://amzn.to/45s3hz2, scroll down the left-hand side of the Amazon page and click on the "Write a customer review" button.

Other Publications By Bridge House

Kathleen
by Amanda Jones

Living with disability is not easy.

Staying alive with hope and joy as well as the pain is possible. A harsh life is yet beautiful as the prose, poems and pictures show in this little volume.

Amanda Jones shows us a truly feisty woman in *Kathleen*.

Order from Amazon:

Paperback: ISBN 978-1-914199-60-8
eBook: ISBN 978-1-914199-61-5

Dry River

by Alicia J Rouverol

Sara Greystone's career as a public defender is spiralling after a disastrous court case, and now her husband's IT career is also in jeopardy. A move to California is supposed to get them both back on their feet, but the state is in the midst of a crippling economic downturn-and then Sara's mother falls seriously ill. In the face of migration, illness, unemployment, and the tantalising possibility of infidelity, Sara has to work out who she is and what she really wants.

Spanning 1997 to 2012, *Dry River* echoes Wallace Stegner's classic Angle of Repose, moving across place and time to chart the slow collapse of a marriage alongside a declining US economy.

"Beautifully written story of life's crossroads," (*Amazon*)

Order from Amazon:

ISBN: 978-1-914199-44-8 (paperback)
978-1-914199-45-5 (ebook)

Invisible on Thursdays

by Peppy Barlow

Peppy Barlow is a playwright and screen writer who lives her life looking for meaning and material in all her experiences. In this book she and her friend Persephone/Lucia explore childhood memories – both good and bad – and travel with their children to Crete where ancient myths emerge to haunt them.

A very personal account of a friendship which takes Peppy back to England and ends with Persephone returning to the Underworld. Authentic, brave, honest, funny and touching – the author's voice shines out from these pages.

Author Peppy Barlow guides us through her turbulent and rich life adventures. Truly a life well-lived.

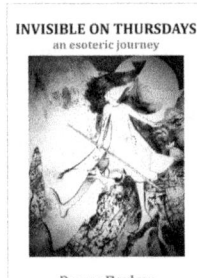

INVISIBLE ON THURSDAYS
an esoteric journey

Peppy Barlow

"I loved it… what a roller coaster ride. Living life as it occurred. For me there were laughter and tears in equal measure." (*Amazon*)

Order from Amazon:

ISBN: 978-1-914199-17-2 (paperback)
978-1-914199-18-9 (ebook)

www.ingramcontent.com/pod-product-compliance
Lightning Source LLC
Chambersburg PA
CBHW072215170626
46813CB00003B/949